Uroboros Saga

BOOK SEVEN

By Arthur Walker

For Pickle Pig

"Is the truth depressing? Some may find it so.
But I find it liberating, and consoling."

~Derek Parfit

CHAPTER 1

MARS COLONY, WRECKER LINE 099, INDUSTRIAL DISTRICT

June, 2187

On Mars, being dead was almost better than being poor.

The wrecker line was quiet, having been silent through weeks of contract negotiations. Miners and line workers were preparing for an ever rarer day of paying work, checking their equipment, and swapping small commodities. Shipments of parts had been delayed for months and the wrecker line was sparse. Many miners had lost their union leases with all the delays. The prison was always hungry for debtors, and if you couldn't pay to work in Mars Company orange, you'd work in prison teal until you could.

Shane Vedter had brought his nephew, Simon, to work with him the last few days. His brother returned to Earth with his wife in hopes of finding work. That was a few weeks ago now. Mars was no place for children and conditions made it a hazardous place to raise a family. There was no affordable childcare for working class people. Klaxons sounded, letting the workers know the wrecker line would begin moving soon. Workers typically had five minutes to climb up onto the line and get their crushers running.

"Simon, stay near the utility shed while I work the line. The company can only afford to move the line for about three hours, so we won't be long," Shane said, unlocking the shed.

"Will we get Auntie's medicine after?" Simon asked.

"Yes, we'll try."

Shane usually worked as the foreman, but the number of workers on the line was already sparse. Everyone would work a crusher today. The crusher line was essentially a huge conveyor, delivering raw ore. The miners used pneumatic hammers to break up the larger pieces before they went to refining. They had to be under a certain size to make it through to the sifting process. It was dangerous work.

Workers were supposed to wear safety cables, but it hindered a worker's reach, and everyone was paid by the pound, everyone splitting the proceeds from the load. The tethers weren't worth the difference in pay. Still, enough workers were lost annually on the crusher lines that politicos avoided the word 'bloodline' or 'lifeline' when referring to the central industries on Mars.

Simon watched from below for awhile before moving into the utility shed. It was full of pneumatic hammers and pressure suits, mining helmets, and rig radio equipment. He turned the radio on so he could hear the miners along the line talking to one another.

"Big accident on the red line, four Union 031 guys got dead."

"I'm hoping the conglomerate wars end and profits get shared before any more accidents happen."

"Not likely. You can't even trade for currency right now."

"I heard you can get bearer bonds, U-trade grade securities in the teal if you have narcotics."

"Bah, no one has narco right now."

"Yeah, the O-Z derby teams pretty much soak up everything from the street for competition."

"I hear the fish make a fungus that delivers a quick high."

"You hearing this guy? The fish, he says."

The wrecking line shook, the one hour interval chime sounding as the conveyor slowed to a halt. Angry miners growled over the radio at the delay before a woman's voice spoke over the frequency. Simon had never heard her on the rig radio before, but she had an Earthen accent, and spoke like she wore administrative white.

"I warned you to not run the wrecker today, Shane," she said, apologetically.

"People have to eat," Shane replied, sounding angry.

"I hope you all opted for the company life insurance during orientation," she said, sending the miners into a panic.

Simon scrambled out of the shed to find his Uncle Shane watching as miners began sliding down pipes and girders to the ground below. Some didn't wait for the freight elevator, leaping from almost thirty feet above. Shane was still above on the conveyor directing miners to the emergency drop ropes when explosions tore through the wrecker. Orange company steel, gantries, girders, and raw ore slid to the side as the conveyer buckled and fell.

Miners above tried to leap to nearby catwalks and precipices, while those already below ran for their lives. The conveyer pulled down the supports for the biological shielding over the wrecker, badly damaging the containment layer. The thick polycarbonate sheeting held, turning white as it bent under the pressure but it wouldn't hold for long. Simon ran through the clouds of dust toward where he'd watched Uncle Shane fall, but could not find him.

"Everyone out! We have to get to the next segment of the wrecker and seal this off!" one of the miners screamed over the clamor.

The lighting and other systems along the wrecker failed, swathing the area in darkness. It was chaos, as fifty bloody and battered men scrambled toward gantry controls in the next section so they could separate the wrecker from the damaged area and close the emergency containment doors. Simon fought his way the other direction, trying to find his uncle.

Simon found his uncle lying under several hundred pounds of rubble. Even if Shane had somehow survived the fall, his body had been crushed by heavy rocks rolling across him. There was nothing Simon could do for his uncle. He was gone and there was hardly a moment for grieving. Picking up his rig radio and keys, Simon ran toward where the others were furiously working to unlock the partition on the wrecker line. If they couldn't get it uncoupled and the containment failed, the emergency protocols would blow. It would seal the line from the biological dome forward, dooming them all.

"Kid! Get over here!" one of the miners yelled, beckoning for Simon to come over.

"Where's your uncle?" another miner asked, activating the enclosure doors.

The rig radio suddenly sprang to life, the woman's pristine voice coming across loud and clear. "Shane, please understand that the insurance paperwork will be simpler if there are no survivors."

A second battery of detonations filled the wrecker line with sound and fury. The line further up the incline bounced upward into the biological enclosure and then back down with a deafening crash. Thousands of tons of machinery and ore slid down toward where the miners were trying to sever the line. Some worked more quickly, trying to clear the gap so the doors could be closed. Others fled. Simon watched the tumbling debris coming toward him for as long as he dared, before closing his eyes.

The impact against the lower deck threw him and everyone else into the air before continuing to descend through the partially closed doors. The muffled alarms from the facility below sounded as emergency containment protocols were enacted, sealing the wrecker line from the rest of the colony. Simon had heard stories of similar things happening decades ago, during the last jailbreak incident. He gave it little thought as he fell helplessly amidst tons of debris, roughly coming to rest atop a condensation collection unit jutting from the side of the tunnel.

There was a loud bang as the containment failed and then deathly silence. He would have been whisked away but his tattered overalls were entangled in ruined mesh across the condensation collector. There was no air to breathe as the cold rushed in around him, his body fluttering like a leaf as the atmosphere slowly escaped containment out across the Martian mountain outside. Simon kept his eyes shut, hoping the pain would end, and that he'd be with his uncle soon.

Death did not come.

Simon awoke in a mining company infirmary, a concerned staff of doctors standing around him. The orange-painted walls were muddy with soot, covered with handbills and posters. The lighting flickered as what sounded like a cheer went up from outside somewhere. Beside the doctors was what Simon guessed was a Drone, his cement gray skin glistening, eyes covered with goggles. One of the doctors clapped the Drone on the back and smiled.

"The boy's going to be okay," the doctor said, his words doing little to liven the demeanor of the Drone.

"It's a miracle he got caught up next to the condensation unit. It was broken and allowed some breathable atmosphere to leak in. The other containment protocols actually worked. This in spite of the fact no one was meant to get out of there alive," the Drone replied, his words sharp with tunnel-speak accent.

"Watch your tone," the doctor hissed, gesturing to a well-dressed woman just entering the room.

"How is the boy?" she asked, her voice and accent familiar to Simon.

"He will need some assistive medical supports and a lot of rehabilitation. He won't ever be able to walk on his own. The damage to his spine was…"

"Yes, whatever he needs," the woman said, coming to stand beside Simon's bed.

The hospital staff stood around awkwardly for a moment before the woman waved them away. Everyone but the Drone left the infirmary, mining company adjusters in black rubber suits lingering near the entrance. The woman was dressed all in white, her business attire betraying her as one of the administrative staff. She worked for one of the various mining companies. Simon had only ever seen such folks from behind a chain link fence.

"What do you remember about the accident?" she asked, the Drone at her side pushing his goggles up to reveal his eerie reflective eyes.

"Nothing really, there were explosions and…"

"Tsk, don't lie. My associate here found your uncle's rig radio tucked in your overalls when he found you," she replied.

"Who are you?" Simon asked, trying to sit up.

"Cerise Laplace, but my name will mean little to you."

"You killed all those people. I am going to tell everyone what you did," Simon said, failing to sit up, the weight of the life support harness around his torso holding him down.

"The kid's brave, could be a problem," the Drone stated, shaking his head.

"Yes. Long ago, I knew a brave little boy, much like you. Smart, too. He faced off against a terrible monster, and got his whole family into a lot of trouble. Even to this day, they are all never going to be the same," Cerise said wistfully.

Simon winced.

"Who will get your aunt her medicine if you're dead, or languishing in the teal? Who will collect your uncle's pension and life insurance credits when she's too tired to go out? If she doesn't keep up on her rent, she might be the one that ends up dead or in the teal," Cerise whispered, gesturing to the men in black rubber suits at the door.

"What do you want from me?" Simon asked.

"That you survived was fortunate. Our demolitions experts weren't as capable as we thought. An external third-party review may report that the wrecker line was sabotaged. If I had a witness that could testify, stating that it was catastrophic mechanical failure, that would make my life simpler," Cerise said, sliding a clipboard with a statement composed of several pages typed up on it.

Tears began to roll down Simon's face. "And if I do this, you won't hurt my aunt?"

"If the external review gets involved, the case could get tied up for years. I'll need you alive for the duration, so I can fight the details of their report in front of judicial review. Depending on what our competitors try to do, you'll need our protection," Cerise explained.

Simon lowered his head, wondering what his father or uncle would do.

"We should move him to the Mechanical Zone, unlisted resident, stipend, the works," the Drone suggested, gesturing to the clipboard.

"That's awfully generous," Cerise said.

"It'll be cheaper than paying someone to protect a cripple and some old lady. And, don't even ask me to do it. I dislike babysitting," the Drone hissed.

Cerise smiled. "Sure, whatever. So, what do you say, Simon? Are we business associates?"

Simon reluctantly held out his hand for a pen, and then signed the statement, each letter of his name a heavy and shameful weight he knew he would bear for the rest of his life. Cerise stood up, smiled faintly, and blew on the ink.

"You did the right thing, trust me," Cerise said, walking out.

The Drone watched her leave, the two company adjusters going along with her.

"Do you really live underground?" Simon asked.

"Yeah, kid."

"Is it better than living up here?"

"It is when humans leave us to do our jobs and not threaten the secrecy of our home," the Drone replied.

Simon nodded. "Thanks for saving me."

"You want to thank me?" The Drone asked.

Simon blinked, not sure what the Drone meant.

"If you ever get a chance, you kill that bitch."

CHAPTER 2

MARS COLONY, VEDTER MACHINEWORKS –
MECHANICAL ZONE 062

August 4th, 2200 (13 years later)

Simon awoke, his Aunt Ruth's hand on his chest, the sound of her labored breathing reminding him they were a day overdo to get her medication. The small apartment they shared above his machine shop was sparsely decorated, not a single picture hanging on the wall. What little they had was meticulously clean, everything in its place. The living space his aunt kept was a stark contrast to the chaos that was his workshop.

"Aunt Ruth, we should have gone to the Facility Zone and tried to get your medication yesterday," Simon said, slipping his assistive leg braces over his trousers and locking them into place.

"Today will be a better day. Have you been watching the news?"

Simon sighed. "I never do. It's a bunch of Mars Company propaganda and nonsense. You shouldn't be watching it either."

"There are outages and work disruptions. It's like the Ares System is on strike or something," she said, rising weakly from her chair.

Simon was aware that something was going on, noticing that he had a long line of maintenance calls at the comm station in his workshop when he got home the night before. Many of the calls were due to "regulation

errors" where the Ares System hadn't performed the proper system maintenance. He was used to getting maybe two or three a year, but he'd seen
that many in the last few days.

"I'm sure it's nothing to worry about. It's not like the Ares System can
just quit," Simon said, helping his aunt find her cane.

His aunt squeezed his arm as they went to the exterior door. "Trust
me, something is wrong."

"Because of the shift in mining company leadership? Or something
else?" Simon said, humoring her.

"The colony even smells different. I hadn't thought about the leadership shift, but yes, the last time that happened there was a war on the Wardens in the teal," Aunt Ruth said, blinking her eyes as they stepped outside.

They exited Simon's red mechanical workshop, the exterior decorated
with only a single ornament, a sign that read "Vedter Mechanical." They
lingered in the light beneath the doorway, waiting for a dispute in the street
to resolve. The local pushers were arguing loudly with their company sup-
plier, armed company adjusters standing at the ready.

"Not like the company to miss narcotics shipments," Aunt Ruth
whispered.

"What would you know about it?" Simon asked.

"I wasn't always an old woman and, even in the worst of times, they
made sure all the street trade kept moving in a profitable direction."

Simon nodded. "But not today. Not when we're trying to get to the
tram."

The street dispute eventually cleared, all parties going their separate
ways. The Mechanical Zone's orange tint had faded somewhat recently,
the biological shielding overhead heavy with condensation. You could taste
it in the air, a humidity that wasn't good for mining operations. Simon
couldn't help but wonder if his Aunt Ruth was right, that something was
going on.

Usually if one looked up they could just see the darkness of the stars
or the Martian wind blowing violently outside. Now, it was just the heavy
mist of uncollected condensation, trying to form clouds. Simon took note
of the long lines by the scrap yards, a far greater than normal number of
people trying to find and sell parts.

Simon stopped to exchange spent power cells for new ones, getting fewer than he'd hoped for. The charging facility had intermittently lost power itself, requiring that portable power units be rationed. It was particularly inconvenient for him because his exoskeletal leg braces required power cells to function properly.

The twenty-minute journey to the tram at the far side of the zone took nearly forty-five minutes with the extra stop. Aunt Ruth was moving slower than usual and his own bad legs were not helping them navigate the unusually dense crowd. He winced as they approached the stairs leading down, a familiar woman wearing onna-zumo armor and carrying grav-boots appeared among the crowd. He prayed she wouldn't see him.

"Legs! Hey!" Camille Ishihara bellowed, knocking people aside with ease as she made her way toward him.

She was almost six feet tall and over two-hundred pounds, easily as big, if not bigger than Simon. He had defined arms from his work as a mechanic but nothing like Ishihara who, coupled with her natural athleticism, was muscular and bulky. While many on Mars descended from the original Sumitomo Mining Company employees, Ishihara looked like she was fresh off the transport from Japan.

"Ishihara, I don't know if I can look at your boots today. Aunt Ruth and I are just going to get her medicine," Simon said, pointing toward the tram.

"You want me to come along? We could do it when we get back," Ishihara said, smiling broadly.

Camille played professionally in the Onna-Zumo Derby league, racing high in a tournament loop in the Entertainment Zone. It was good promotion for his machine shop to fix her equipment but she would take the whole day hanging out in his shop, usually due to the tram schedule.

Simon sighed. "When is the next Derby match?"

"Tomorrow," Aunt Ruth said, nodding to Ishihara.

"Are there any mechanics in the E-Zone that can help you?" Simon asked.

"Don't be rude, Simon, she came all the way from E-Zone," Aunt Ruth scolded.

"Yeah, don't be rude, Legs. Yeah, yeah, there's mechanics, but they always mess up my shit and I don't have time for that sixty feet above the ground, fifty miles per hour, pressing meat for points," Ishihara said, worried she'd made the journey for nothing.

"Simon will help you, just go to the shop and wait for us to get back," Aunt Ruth said, handing Ishihara her house key.

"Thanks, Auntie. See you soon, Legs," Ishihara said, knocking a miner down as she made her way back toward the center of the Mechanical Zone.

Simon grumbled watching her plow through the crowd.

"With your disability, you can't be choosy, my boy," Aunt Ruth said, smiling.

"She's not coming to visit because she likes me," Simon said, a little scared his Aunt was right.

"Nonsense, no one burns up grav-boots that fast. Not after you've fixed them anyway," Aunt Ruth said, laughing at Simon's discomfort.

"How would you know?" Simon said, carefully negotiating the stairs to the tram platform below.

"I watch Derby every night. Camille is good. Although, she hasn't played the same since that girl on H-Zone Squad was killed. Tsk, what a shame that was," Aunt Ruth said, sliding her travel vouchers into the automated ticket counter.

"Killed? I thought they wore harnesses to make sure no one falls," Simon said, keeping a watchful eye on the other travelers on the platform.

"Ishihara hit this girl, and she somehow made it outside the safety lane and hit a camera drone. She was clocked at forty-two miles per hour and she was skating backward. She broke her back, lingered in medical for days, and then passed. Really sad."

Simon wrinkled his brow. "This was recently? There's all kinds of countermeasures that should have prevented an accident like that."

"It was a couple weeks ago. Didn't you see Ishihara's uniform?"

"What? No, I try not to look at her."

"WELL YOU SHOULD! There's probably a lovely girl under that armor she wears. Anyway, she calls herself 'The Roman' now, the same as the girl that was killed."

"You're the only woman I need in my life."

"Nonsense," Ruth scolded.

"She took that moniker, as a penance, or something?" Simon said, hoping the tram would come soon.

"It's rare one of the girls gets killed, but usually someone on the opposite team carries their name until they win a championship. The game has so many traditions. You really should watch it with me some time," Aunt Ruth said, brandishing her cane.

"Okay, okay, I'll watch it with you."

The tram ride was normal by Mars standards, harrowing by any other. Aunt Ruth was used to the way people acted on the tram, men exposing themselves, narcotics changings hands, fights between rival unions, and worse. Simon had to steel himself to the task every single time, letting the terrible things happen around him as they waited. Often, no one would move or allow his aunt to sit down. The swaying of the tram and constant stop and go between stations played havoc with his own crippled legs.

It would be a day like any other on the tram, with at least one man dangling his genitals in the direction of Simon's aunt. The prison culture meshed with the mining unions as people would come and go between the orange and the teal. Sexual assault was something the average citizen either endured or tolerated having in their presence, conduct laws being mostly ignored.

Mostly.

The tram car shuddered, the doors behind Simon opening as someone moved between cars. He could hear her before he could turn to see her, the Marshal of Mars. The man turned too late as the Marshal's armor hissed, propelling her forward. Passengers dove to the side trying to get out of the way but a few got a hard knock instead.

Before the flasher could compose himself, the Marshal grabbed him by the wrist and gave it a swift turn, fracturing his arm. "You are in violation of Mars Decorum Code 0145, the penalty is 1200 Mars Company Credit Vouchers," the Marshal said, her voice deafening over her Aegis Armor's loudspeaker.

"Okay, okay…" the man cried, producing his Mars Company work ID.

The optics on the suit scanned the card, a red indicator light on the card's swift chip turning from red to green. The man grumbled, struggling to free his ruined arm, but the Marshal held on. Simon couldn't see the

Marshal's face through the visor and voice modulation hid the gender of the occupant within the armor.

"I'll remember you. If I catch you doing this again, you won't end up in the teal. The SO unit is full, so they'll just jettison your corpse into one of the old shafts," Marshal Rider warned, gauntlets patting the sidearms at both hips.

Simon had never been this close to a Marshal, let alone gotten a glimpse of the armor they wore. There was something very familiar about the armor but he couldn't put his finger on it. The visor snapped back to reveal a young light-haired woman inside, her eyes narrow, lips curled angrily. The flasher had given up trying to escape and was one-handedly trying to remove his genitals from view.

"Mister Merrick, remember what I said," the Marshal said, her real voice every bit as terrifying as the modulated one that issued forth from her armor.

"Someone will get you, just like someone got your dad. Only good Marshal is a dead Marshal," Merrick said, spitting on the floor of the tram and rubbing his fractured forearm.

The tram car nearly emptied, as anyone with a reason to avoid the Marshal departed. Simon helped his Aunt Ruth to a nearby seat and took one up beside her.

"Thank you, young lady," Aunt Ruth said, leaning forward and grabbing the gauntlet-clad hand of the Marshal.

The Marshal turned a hard gaze downward, the optics on either side of the armored mantle across her shoulders clicking. Two green holographic citizen records popped up in front of her, causing her expression to soften slightly. "You are most welcome, Miss Vedter. I'm sorry you had to see that."

"Seen it plenty of times, but it's good to see them get their comeuppance once in awhile. This is my nephew, Simon," Aunt Ruthie said.

"Hello," Simon said, shyly.

"You riding the tram isn't a regular thing. Is everything okay?" Aunt Ruth asked.

The Marshal hesitated for a moment, as if to consider her words carefully. "No, everything isn't okay, but it will be. When we arrive at the station, you need to get clear as quickly as you can or just stay on the tram."

"Are we in some sort of danger?" Simon said.

The Marshal smiled. "Lived on Mars your whole life?"

"I was born on Earth but I came here young enough I don't remember," Simon replied.

"Me, too," Marshal Rider replied, checking the time on her flex monitor.

Facility Zone 061 came up minutes later, the tram creaking to a halt at the adjoining tram station. The Marshal let go of Aunt Ruth's hand and proceeded into the station, her visor dropping as she broke into a heavy run up the stairs opposite the platform. Simon and Aunt Ruth made their way through the crowd, people fighting to get both on and off the tram before it departed.

At the base of the stairs, Simon could hear the Marshal's modulated voice come across her loudspeakers. "Lay down, or die, I don't care which," followed by the sound of weapons being drawn.

Aunt Ruth grabbed Simon and pulled them both aside as the Marshal and a huge man with black hair and handlebar moustache came tumbling down the stairs. People went flying, careening off the walls and ceiling, as the two barreled through the crowd. Simon fell backwards, hitting the platform hard in the middle of his back. He could feel his assistive exoskeleton across his legs jump and then go limp.

Aunt Ruth fell over him as the sound of the Marshal's sidearm filled the tram station. Tortured screams and chaos obscured Simon's view as he fumbled with the damaged power cell on his leg braces with one hand and his satchel with the other. Aunt Ruth feebly tried to pull them both clear to keep from being trampled but it was a kindly bystander wearing a canvas mining uniform that grabbed them both and pulled them behind a pillar.

Simon managed to get the power cells switched in time to see the black-haired man haul the Marshal, armor and all, up into a passing tram. There was bright flash as metal ground into metal, the force of the impact sending the two of them clattering to the floor. Simon could smell the telltale fragrance of damaged circuitry, helplessly watching as the Marshal's armor went limp from the damage.

The big man limped, his shattered leg making a wide pool of blood on the tram station platform. He fell and resorted to crawling up on top of the Marshal's armor, breaking the protective cowl with his bare hands.

He grabbed the Marshal, a slender young woman in a flight suit out of the armor and rolled over on top of her, gripping her by the neck.

"Been a long time since I killed a cop," the man growled, beginning to strangle the Marshal.

"No…" Simon whispered, trying to get his footing.

The Marshal jabbed her thumbs into the man's eyes and then pushed her hand into an open wound on his neck and twisted the torn flesh as hard as she could. He rolled off of her, roaring in agony as she kicked away, still clutching a handful of his neck flesh. The Marshal rose quickly, grabbed the bent power plant cover from her armor and hit the man across the head, knocking him down.

In the opposite direction, a cyborg with a limb enhancement and some kind of military-grade Metasapient pushed through the crowd. They were shouting out for the Marshal. Simon hoped they were friends, having never felt so helpless since he was a boy at the wrecker. The Marshal grabbed up one of her fallen pistols and turned it on the black-haired man, dropping into a wide stance to soak up the recoil.

Simon looked on as she pumped the remainder of the magazine into the man, reloaded, and opened fire again. The big man finally fell, whatever was keeping him alive giving out at last. The cyborg and Metasapient woman ran up embracing the Marshal, obviously close friends. The trio stood there over the body, weapons ready, until it finally stopped moving.

The Marshal knelt down beside her ruined armor, her face displaying deep and intense sorrow. Simon had worn that same expression on his worst days, missing his family. She removed the star from the armor, and pinned it to her flight suit before salvaging the equipment and the gun belts. Lastly, she removed the NAVCOM and memory core from the armor and tucked it all into a satchel.

The trio gathered the fallen man up into a body bag salvaged from the supplies on the Aegis Armor, the Metasapient woman throwing him over her shoulder. Marshal Rider took one last moment to kneel down beside her wrecked armor, placing a hand on it before standing back up. Simon watched as the three dropped into the tram tunnel, disappearing into the dark.

"Aunt Ruth, are you all right?" Simon said, shaking his head and looking back.

"I'm fine, a little battered, but what a thing to see!" Aunt Ruth said, patting Simon's shoulder.

"That man, with the black hair. He looks kind of like the new Mining Company Conglomerate CEO, doesn't he?" Simon said as he limped over.

"I guess so, after a fashion. No one ever looks the same in real life as they do on the vid," Aunt Ruth said, recovering her cane from the floor.

The Facility Zone was abuzz with rumors of a battle in one of the high rises and that someone had jumped from the top floor. Simon could see the countermeasures had been deployed but there was no body. It seemed strange as they'd never saved anyone before, being badly designed for the purpose. Simon and Aunt Ruth didn't linger, heading to the hospital as quickly as they could.

The Medical Dispensary was a crowded mess, and several people had been waiting in a line that went out the door and around the corner, for hours. Simon hoped he had enough power cells for his leg braces to wait and still make the journey home. Mechanical services in the Facility Zones didn't usually carry commercial grade batteries.

He quietly calculated the cost of converting regular civilian grade power sources in case that would become necessary. "It'll be okay," Aunt Ruth said, seeing the vexed expression on his face.

"I feel bad about what happened to the Marshal's armor," Simon said, taking his place in line behind his Aunt.

"She is a lovely girl. She'd probably appreciate it if you fixed her armor for her," Aunt Ruth said, winking mischievously.

"Please, stop playing Cupid all the time. I've enough trouble without a girlfriend," Simon groaned.

She regarded him with a tight smile, trying not to laugh.

"I wouldn't know how to fix it anyway. It's probably very advanced military-grade tech. Aegis Armor is from Earth and finding parts for it might be impossible," Simon said, doing nothing to banish his Aunt's smile.

"I guess if it's too hard, maybe you shouldn't try it," Aunt Ruth teased, leaning up against the outside of the dispensary.

Simon grumbled, putting his hands in his pockets. "Why the interest?"

"I met her father once, and regret how I acted. It would be nice to speak to her again, maybe put some of those regrets to rest."

"Maybe we could just go by the Marshal's office, drop her a note?"

"No. I'd like it if she came to us," Aunt Ruth said, somewhat more insistently.

They would spend almost ten hours waiting to get Aunt Ruth's medication, trading a few bits and baubles from Simon's satchel for food and water. They slept in the street to hold their place in line, taking turns to make sure someone was keeping an eye on the mining crews as they went by, to and from work. The tram station had been closed, so they had to hike to the next Facility Zone. It was more than two miles away and the route had gone dark from some sort of outage.

The tram ride was blissfully uneventful as they were riding in what was the middle of the night for that part of the Mars Colony. Aunt Ruth slept for the entire hour, resting her head on Simon's leg as he kept a vigil over her. Back in their own Mechanical Zone, they took the last few agonizing steps to find that the lights were on in both the shop and the living area of their home.

"God, what now?" Simon grumbled, hoping they weren't getting robbed.

CHAPTER 3

MARS COLONY, VEDTER MACHINEWORKS – MECHANICAL ZONE 062

August 6th, 2200

Before Simon could reach for the handle on the shop access door, it flung open. Camille stepped out, a big smile on her face. She was standing there in pajama pants and a halter top, a plate of food in her off-hand. Simon just stood there for a moment, blinking at her.

"What are you doing here?" he growled.

"Your aunt gave me the key, remember? She said I could wait until you got back so we could look at my boots."

"We've been gone almost twelve hours, and…" Simon said, trying to push past her to make sure she didn't touch anything in his shop.

"And you're out of food," Ishihara said, stepping aside.

"Out of food?! There was enough for both my Aunt and me for a couple of weeks," Simon bellowed angrily.

"Hey, I waited as long as I could. I was starving," Ishihara said, licking her fingers.

Simon glared at her for a moment before limping about his workshop to make sure she hadn't messed with any of his projects or experiments.

"Chill, Legs. I didn't touch your stuff. Your bed sucks by the way," Ishihara said, helping Aunt Ruth through the door.

"You broke my bed?" Simon said, turning an accusatory finger in her direction.

"I broke your bed," Ishihara admitted with pride.

"Camille, this is why..."

"Oh, do shut up, Simon," Aunt Ruth scolded. "We can always get more food."

"And my bed?" Simon asked, eyes wide.

"Make sure you're in it with her next time she breaks it," Aunt Ruth said, winking.

Simon had wondered previously if death by embarrassment was possible and he wasn't pleased to discover you could survive even the most lethal dose. Ishihara chuckled at Aunt Ruth, then winked lasciviously at Simon. Simon turned beet red, fleeing the situation to instead look at Ishihara's boots.

Aunt Ruth looked on as he tinkered with them, taking some food from Ishihara's plate. "Camille, you be kind to my nephew," she said.

"How long do you think you have?" Ishihara asked, quietly.

"A couple months maybe. I only keep going to get my meds so he won't worry."

"Helluva trip, just for that," Ishihara said, nodding sadly.

"The worst, but it was worth it. We saw the Marshal fighting with the Conglomerate CEO on the tram platform. She killed him," Aunt Ruth said, quietly watching as Simon worked his magic on the gravity boots.

"The Mars Marshal? She's a she? She killed that huge mean guy from the teal?" Ishihara said, somewhat surprised.

"Yes."

"That can't be easy. Women aren't exactly a protected class on Mars," Ishihara said, massaging her knuckles.

"Her armor was damaged. Simon will need your help to recover it. It's important that he repair it," Aunt Ruth said, gesturing toward Simon.

Ishihara sighed, folding her arms.

"Is our delayed return going to make you miss your match?" Aunt Ruth asked.

"I wish. The whole league is shut down right now. A change in management is happening. I might have a new coach in a couple of days," Ishihara said, frowning.

Aunt Ruth nodded, knowing what that probably meant.

"Your boots are fixed, Camille. Quit burning them up to block. You can't draw down on the artificial gravity of the Colony efficiently the way you have these set. I know it makes you like a wall, but it's going to get expensive to have me fix these every other match," Simon said, walking slowly over to where Ishihara was talking to Aunt Ruth.

"Maybe I could work it off instead? You need anything done?" Ishihara said, reaching a hand out toward Simon.

He pushed her hand away. "No, and you can go now."

"Simon, she's nowhere to go. The team stables are closed and the league is in lockdown. There's a change of management," Aunt Ruth explained.

"Ah, and no paycheck to pay me for the repairs?" Simon said, glaring at Ishihara.

"Nope," Ishihara said, smiling warmly at him.

"This is not happening. I'm dreaming. In a moment I'll wake up," Simon muttered, covering his face with his hands.

"Legs, I'm sorry about all this. Can I please crash here with you guys? It'll be just for a couple of days," Ishihara said, looking over at Aunt Ruth who was already nodding her approval.

Simon sighed. "Are you really sorry, Camille?"

"Not really, but I do really need a place to stay. I'll do my best to pretend."

Simon wordlessly proclaimed his exasperation, throwing his arms into the air, before moving past them to the living space. He collapsed on the couch, pulling a blanket up over his face. Aunt Ruth patted Ishihara on the arm before retiring to her own room. Dropping her duffle on the floor next to the couch, Ishihara laid down on the floor, crossing her legs and commenced throwing crumbs up at the ceiling fan.

"Legs."

"What?"

"I spilled juice on the couch, it might still be wet."

"Argh, so that's what's in the middle of my back. Thanks for letting me know," Simon said, sarcastically.

"Don't mention it."

There was a long silence, only the sound of Simon grinding his teeth and the light tap of small projectiles bouncing off the ceiling fan broke the silence. Outside, there was commotion, anarchy had been building with each passing day as fewer people could get to work. It wasn't just the onna-zumo derby leagues that were shutting down, but many of the Mars Company Mining operations as well.

"I need your help, Camille" Simon said at last.

"No, everything you do is boring," Ishihara said, laughing quietly.

"We need to steal a Mining Company Personnel Transport and get it across a half dozen zones undetected. It'll be dangerous if we get caught," Simon explained, pulling the blanket down from his face.

"Ha! Never mind, I'm in."

"Just like that?" Simon said, incredulous.

"Sure, if it means I don't have to pay for the repairs to my boots this time…"

"Okay."

"And next time."

"Huhh… fine, it's a deal."

"Great, when do we start?" Ishihara said, clapping her hands together.

"Don't you want to know why we're stealing a transport?" Simon said, sitting up and looking at her.

"We're going to get the Marshal's damaged armor, yeah?"

Simon looked shocked. "How did you…?"

"Ruth told me."

"I didn't even know I was going to do it until just now," Simon said, baffled.

"The old lady knows you pretty well. No offense, Legs, but you are kinda predictable." Ishihara said, smiling at him.

"I doubt I'll be able to fix it."

"Probably true."

"We might not even be able to get it out of the tram station. It could all be for nothing."

"Uh-huh."

Simon paused and rolled over to better stare at the ceiling and scratch his chin.

"My aunt thinks you keep coming around because you like me," Simon said, hesitantly.

"That's messed up. You're a barely useful cripple. I doubt anyone likes you," Ishihara replied, tossing another crumb upward.

"And you're a flabby second-stringer that got another girl killed it sounds like. Imagine it, a Japanese girl calling herself 'The Roman'. That's what's messed up," Simon said, deadpan.

"Yeah, pretty messed up," Ishihara replied, drifting off to sleep.

Simon turned to look at her, watching her sleep peacefully, chest rising and falling slowly with each breath. On Mars, it was dangerous to let anyone know who your friends were, because someone might try to use them against you. If you saw someone being cruel to someone else, you'd have to guess whether they were rivals or lovers. Simon wasn't sure exactly what Ishihara was to him, but he was glad to have someone close to his own age to talk to.

Sleep wasn't a common luxury on Mars. You got it when you could, every zone operating on a separate schedule. Simon awoke to his Aunt gently shaking him. She looked a little concerned, at first, but smiled as he sat up.

"What? What is it?" Simon said looking around.

"Some men tried to break into the shop. Camille got rid of them."

"Crap, did they damage anything?"

"I'm not sure, you'll have to go look," Aunt Ruth said, returning to the stove where she was making the last of their food.

Simon hobbled stiffly, a symptom of sleeping with his leg braces on. The shop was undisturbed, but Ishihara was at the shop sink washing red from her hands. She looked up as he approached, looking a little frightened. She had a shiner and a bruised lip.

"You okay, Camille?"

"Legs, you see anything weird on your way to the Facility Zones? Besides the Marshal wasting some guy?"

Simon nodded.

"Is the colony falling apart? I can't remember the last time I saw people this desperate. I mean, looting in a Mechanical Zone? Who does that?"

"Something is wrong, I just don't know what it is. Maybe they are doing maintenance on the Ares System and don't want to alarm anyone," Simon said, stooping to wash his face and gaze into the mirror over the sink.

"We still going to do this heist? What if they come back?" Ishihara said, worriedly.

"Go, I'll be fine," Aunt Ruth said, setting a plate out for each of them on a work table.

They ate quietly, Ishihara "helping" Simon with his breakfast while he was distracted, riveting the overhead and entry doors to the shop closed. They gathered up the tools Simon thought they'd need, dressed in dark clothing, and headed out. They'd have to walk across the zone, roughly three miles to the transport depot.

Along the way they saw riots outside contract offices and sporadic looting. The vids that normally played the news and displayed colony events and information were mostly dark, issuing forth a steady hiss of static. Ishihara carried a length of pipe, walking ahead as heavy condensation dripped down like light rain from the biological enclosure far overhead.

Simon did his best to keep up, his legs still stiff. Closer to the residential end of the zone, there were heaps of trash that had gone uncollected, recycle trucks apparently having missed their last pickup date. Someone had been going through them, looking for something, much of the trash spread halfway across the street in between the large orange dormitories.

Rounding a corner, Ishihara tripped, stumbling to keep her footing. She stooped to look at the heap she'd caught her foot on to find a man wrapped in construction plastic. He'd been clubbed to death, all his worldly possession taken, his body dumped in the walkway.

"Gross," Ishihara said, checking her boots.

"What is going on?" Simon said, shaking his head as he stepped over the corpse.

"Someone knows something we don't. C'mon, let's get this done," Ishihara said, waving to Simon.

The last leg to the transport depot was uneventful, but dark, as most of the colony illumination was out in the area. It was unnerving but also fortunate. Even if station surveillance drones came by, there was less of a chance they'd pick up interlopers. The gate was guarded only with a padlock and a chain. Ishihara was able to easily bypass the lock with Simon's bolt-cutters and push the gate aside.

Inside were several Mining Company transports, but Simon was looking for a particular type. He didn't want one that carried men or raw ore, he needed the type that moved heavy EVA mining suits, a sort of powered armor that miners used to work outside of the colony in remote excavation zones across Mars. They'd almost given up when they found an older model, a TZ-100 Transport, languishing inside one of the machine shops.

It was about twenty-five feet in length, less than half as wide, and built to endure terrible punishment. The older engines were still in good shape, Simon nodding as he opened panels to gaze inside at power coils and other components. The key was in the machine shop foreman's office and it worked like a charm, opening up the vehicle for them.

"Now comes the hard part," Simon said, sitting in the pilot's seat and powering up the transport.

"What's that?" Ishihara said, plopping down in the seat beside him.

"I have to convince the Ares System that I'm supposed to be taking this transport, and then I have to fly it," Simon said, smiling slightly.

"What? You've never flown one of these things?" Ishihara asked nervously.

"I've got about three hundred hours on the simulator at home, but no, never actually taken one of these things up. Mining Company employees fly these. How hard can it be?" Simon said, plugging in an external storage device loaded with a program he hoped would override the Ares System control of the transport.

"Shiiiit… we are going to die," Ishihara said, buckling herself in and putting a mining helmet on.

"Odd," Simon said, looking quizzically at the display.

"Odd? What's odd?" Ishihara said, a little panicked.

"Camille? Are you afraid of flying?" Simon asked, a wide grin breaking across his face.

"No, not even a little bit. You said something was odd?" Ishihara replied, trying to change the subject.

"I can't hack past the Ares System," Simon said, furrowing his brow.

"So we're done, we can't take off?"

"No, I can't hack the Ares System because it isn't there," Simon said, blinking in astonishment.

"Legs, that's impossible. Right?"

"Maybe the network relays are down, like the lights? I've got a couple work requests to repair similar colony equipment elsewhere. I don't know. Either way, we've got control of the transport for now," Simon said, taking the controls.

The transport rose slightly, engines humming in the dark as Simon kept the exterior vehicle lighting off. Dust and a couple of tools fell from the top the transport as it slowly built up speed. It plowed through, making a path through the yard, shoving machinery and smaller transport vehicles aside. The orange towers that stretched up to meet with the biological enclosure rose in front of them through the viewing ports as Simon pulled up, gaining altitude.

"You're good at this," Ishihara said, astonished.

"Yeah, I'm good at taking off. I don't think I've ever landed one of these in the simulator without wrecking though," Simon said, deadpan.

Ishihara covered her eyes. "Eee... oh, God."

Simon smiled quietly to himself, taking the transport up into the vehicle flight lane and toward the illuminated passages between zones. He flew slowly, letting what little air traffic there was pass over him. Finding a pair of ore transports, he settled in between them, taking his time. Throughout the flight, there was no Ares System contact, but looking over he could see both of the ore transports were automated.

The street below was choked with pedestrian traffic, everyone in that part of the zone having to walk. The tram entrance was mostly obscured with just the wide stairs leading down being visible from that height.

Simon brought the transport about, carefully dodging power lines, and keeping the engines pointed either down or up the street.

People scattered from the street as Simon set the transport down at the top of the tram station, while Ishihara closed her eyes and rocked back and forth in her seat. He could see there were barricades now, and the steel shutters to the platform had been drawn down. It was sort of a relief, because this way there was a chance scavengers hadn't gone over the armor yet. Ishihara stepped out to a crowd of onlookers, baffled at the appearance of a mining company transport in a Facility Zone, and right next to the high rises.

"Subtle we are not," Ishihara teased, kicking a barricade to one side.

"Let's just get it done," Simon growled.

They used the winch on the front of the transport to pull the metal shutters off the entrance. Once inside, they found the armor intact, or as much as it was the last time Simon saw it. Using the fallen shutter as a sled, and the winch on the transport, they hauled it up to street level before using the mechanized EVA suit caddy inside the transport to pick the armor up at hard points, and place it inside beside an older mining exoskeleton.

"So far, so good," Simon said, patting the armor as Ishihara strapped it in.

"Legs, what if she finds out we took it?"

"She?"

"The Marshal, you dunce."

"I'm not sure how she would, and besides, my intent is to fix it up and return it to her."

"Say what? This thing has to be worth a few vouchers. I say we fix it up and sell it," Ishihara said, tightening the last strap.

"Let's worry about fixing it first, and what to do with it if I actually can," Simon said, heading for the cockpit.

The flight back to the Mechanical Zone was more eventful as flight lanes were disabled halfway through, requiring that Simon fly half-blind. Fortunately, all automated traffic was required to set down during these outages. They encountered only one other transport along the way, flying in a similarly cautious pattern to their own.

Simon's home seemed untouched as he landed the transport behind it, inside a fenced off area adjoining the machine shop. He powered the transport completely down, letting the engines cycle through all the necessary protocols. Ishihara began unstrapping the Aegis Armor and then waited patiently until they could disembark.

"Legs, do you even have enough tarps to cover this thing?" Ishihara asked, pointing back to the transport.

"I've got this," Simon said, opening a panel on the shop wall and hitting a button.

A large awning slowly extended out, accompanied by a mechanical whirring sound as it covered the whole yard. "I installed it for when I'm doing salvage. The condensation rusts everything it touches if I don't keep it covered up."

"Nice," Ishihara replied, smiling.

It was a chore getting the armor inside. They tried using the mining exoskeleton first, but it wasn't operable for some reason. Then they bent Simon's cherry-picker trying to move it before finally getting it on a dolly designed to move transport engine cores. Once inside, Simon seemed to disappear, completely ignoring his surroundings as he dove into every panel and damaged component of the armor.

"I'll be in here, talking to your aunt," Ishihara said.

Simon just nodded, waving dismissively.

"Get what you went out for? I heard a racket out in the yard," Aunt Ruth said, scrubbing a spot on the couch.

"Yeah…" Ishihara said, laying down on the floor.

"Ah, good. Hopefully, he'll be able to fix it," Aunt Ruth said, going to the kitchen for some water.

"He did well. Calm and kind of confident. It was a different side of Simon to see," Ishihara said, accepting a glass of water.

"My nephew is strong. He survived something fifty other hardened miners did not. He'll find his way in life, once he figures out what that is," Aunt Ruth said, sitting down and taking a sip from her own glass.

"You'd have to be tough to survive on Mars as a cripple," Ishihara said, lost in her own thoughts.

Simon suddenly appeared at the door, an odd look on his face. "I can fix it," he announced.

"I sense a 'but' is coming," Ishihara said, sitting up.

"The first thing I learned to take apart was my leg braces. They're ingeniously made, allowing me to walk with very little power consumption. I'm told the best cyber-armorer on Earth made them," Simon explained.

"So?" Ishihara said dismissively, taking another drink of water.

"The Aegis Armor was made by the same person, or at least the same facility. The craftsmanship built into the armor is identical to my leg braces," Simon said, heading to the kitchen.

"That's a lucky coincidence," Aunt Ruth said, pulling a blanket over her legs.

"Yes, and no. There isn't a single person with that expertise on Mars and there have only been two or three on Earth. The mining exoskeleton outside is similar but made by someone else. I think whoever made that Aegis Armor and my leg braces is the person everyone else copies, or tries to. They're the master armorer," Simon said, returning with a bourbon.

"You have booze? I looked all over for booze while you were gone," Ishihara said, pouting.

"Yeah, in a secret place so Aunt Ruth doesn't drink it all," Simon said, downing the drink in a single go.

"Working on the armor right away?" Aunt Ruth asked, paying careful attention to the part of the shop Simon had just returned from.

"Yeah, the Marshal will need it soon, if what we've seen lately is any indication," Simon said, walking back toward his workshop.

Hours went by as Simon worked on the Aegis Armor, repairing what he could with the parts he had on hand. Many of the seals and other cosmetics could be fixed by robbing the mining exoskeleton for different bits and bobs. The power plant was ruined. Nothing Simon had on hand would work. The suit needed enormous power in a very small package. While most of the suit was designed originally to be an assistive technology of sorts, the power source was definitely military-grade.

He emerged from the workshop, and headed to his room out of habit. Ishihara was laying in his broken bed, already fast asleep. He sat down on the edge of the bed and slipped out of his leg braces. She stirred looking over her shoulder at him. Simon regarded her wearily, searching for a blanket that wasn't already entangled in Ishihara.

"You want me to take the couch?" she asked, rubbing her eyes.

"No, it's fine, as long as you don't think it's weird that I'm lying beside you," Simon said, slipping off his shirt.

Ishihara slid over to give him a little more room, pushing a spare blanket in his direction. Simon laid down, pulling the blanket over himself, his hands sore from working with tools for hours. He checked his watch, then looked at the stack of work requests on his desk. He'd have to actually go to work tomorrow and he wasn't looking forward to it.

"Did you fix it?" Ishihara asked, sleepily.

"Not yet. There's a problem."

"Mmm," Ishihara replied.

"You back on the league payroll yet?" Simon asked.

"Tryouts are tomorrow. Hopefully, I can get back on the team."

"You flying as 'The Roman' still?"

"Until I win a championship, yeah. It's the only way to honor that girl's spirit."

"Spirit?"

"Spirit, memory, whatever."

It had seemed ridiculous before, but looking inside the Aegis Armor, it was clear from the inscriptions that it was more than just armor. It was a Rider family legacy, and getting the armor back to the Marshal was important. Mars only had a single police officer when it needed a hundred, and right now, she was out there without her protection, and the spirits of her father and grandfather. Simon could relate, given all his own family had lost to the corruption of Mars.

"Camille?" Simon whispered, but she was fast asleep.

Simon was tall, like her, so it was no mystery why she'd chosen his bed over Aunt Ruth's while they'd been away. What Simon could not understand was why she kept coming around, or anything about her real desires in life. His aunt was right, that Camille was lovely in her own way in spite of being built to destroy. She was over two-hundred pounds but carried it with confidence, her height eating up most of it.

He couldn't dream that someone like her would find him interesting, but she was the only woman that he regularly talked to. It wasn't for his own lack of charm but that men outnumbered women on Mars nearly four to one. Because the colony was half mining operation and half penal facility, it leant strongly to the presence of men. Worse, pleasure-rated Ichthyic Metasapients, that were illegal in most places, were legal on Mars.

When Simon awoke, it was to his aunt hovering by his bedside, a look of pure rapture on her face. Simon sighed, rubbing his eyes. Only a couple hours had passed, but the comm on his desk was flashing now, many of the work orders sent to him being overdo.

"Nothing happened, Auntie," Simon said, waving her aside so he could slip his leg braces on.

"I know, but I can dream," Aunt Ruth said, looking lovingly at Ishihara as she snored loudly, one broad arm up over her eyes.

"I have to get to some of these today or we'll lose some badly needed income," Simon said.

"Oh pish-posh, we're doing fine," Aunt Ruth said, dismissively.

"Not if she's going to keep staying with us. She eats in a day what we both eat in a week," Simon said, gesturing toward Ishihara.

"She's an athlete. She needs to maintain her fighting weight," Aunt Ruth said, holding up a single scolding finger.

"Yeah, she eats like a whole team," Simon said, grinning.

Aunt Ruth brandished her cane menacingly in an attempt to banish Simon from the room. He shoved a handful of work requests in his pants pocket and fled. Satisfied that he was gone, Aunt Ruth woke Ishihara, gently shaking her by the shoulder. She sat upright, almost knocking heads with the elderly woman.

"Oh, ah… sorry. I haven't slept so soundly in a long time," Ishihara said, pulling her legs around to dangle off the bed.

"He's gone to work, and you probably should too, Camille. Unless you want to be late," Aunt Ruth said, handing her some toast wrapped in a bit of waxed paper.

Camille washed herself in the shop sink and brushed her shoulder length hair out before tying it back in a bun. She was nervous about the tryouts being on the same day they would have a new coach. The other girls were her friends and fellow warriors, but everyone had to eat, and not everyone would get a top spot on the team. She knew the coach would ask about the girl formerly known as 'The Roman'. Getting denied a place on the team would be like a spiritual death for both her and 'The Roman'.

Neither of them would get to see a championship in the flesh or in name.

The tram ride was the usual obstacle course of groping hands, exposed genitalia, and someone trying to ejaculate on her. She'd gotten numb to it all previously, but getting to ride in a transport alone with Simon robbed her of some of that resolve. She wished she could just ride everywhere like that instead of with filthy miners and ex-convicts looking for contract work. Kicking a set of testicles pulled out for her benefit did little to quiet that desire.

She longed to fly again, both in the ring and in the mining transport.

CHAPTER 4

**MARS COLONY, UTOPIA LTD. LUXURY HIGH RISE –
PERSONNEL ZONE 002**

August 6th, 2200

Cerise stretched out on the leather sofa, pushing a throw pillow under head. Her hand wandered to the glass coffee table nearby, grasping blindly for olives in a glass dish. She was dressed in tight workout pants and a peach-colored flowing top that was cinched off at her slim waist.

Octavo sat nearby, wearing teal machinist's coveralls. They clung awkwardly to his skinny frame bunching up in the wrong places. His work boots were unlaced, which seemed a stark contrast to his careful grooming. He used nano-bleaching to whiten his skin, and had long undergone treatments to banish body hair, including eyebrows and facial hair.

In the corner, a Drone tugged at his long black rain slicker, his goggles obscuring his eyes. Both he and Octavo looked painfully out of place in Cerise's private residence. To describe the place as opulent or even decadent would be a gross understatement.

"He arrived yesterday with Taylor IA and Ezra One," Cerise said, lazily dropping olives into her mouth.

"You seem pretty calm about this, considering the judiciary is swamped with control disputes by everyone else connected to Archie," Octavo observed, reaching out for some olives.

Cerise swatted his hand away, and sat up. "I'm good at protecting what's mine. It's all part of the plan."

The Drone sighed. "Ezra One is going to be a problem. He's a war hero, a legend among my people. He's old, maybe even Factory unmitigated."

"You overcame your directives to join us in the light," Cerise said, straddling Octavo in his chair and dangling a handful of olives over his face.

"You didn't really leave me a choice. Trust me, my skin crawls every time there isn't a tunnel over my head," the Drone replied, disdainfully.

"You know, I'm not really into this," Octavo said, gently pushing Cerise off of his lap.

"I know, but watching you squirm is delicious," Cerise said.

"And Silverstein? Are we going to get to watch him and his friends squirm?" Octavo asked.

"We'll all get what we want, you just need to follow the plan," Cerise cooed, wrapping her arms around Octavo, pressing herself into his back.

The Drone turned to gaze out the window, hands in his pockets. "I wish we knew what that plan was."

"It's a matter of maintaining operational integrity. There's a good chance Silverstein has already identified you as players, and is watching the little bit of allowed colony footage of you that exists. He's very good at reading people, predicting what they'll do," Cerise said, picking up a chair and hurling it into a large mirror, startling both of her allies.

"What the hell is wrong with you?" Octavo said, looking down at the broken shards.

"Like Silverstein, I'm good at predicting what people will do as well. It isn't a coincidence that like him, I've got a Drone and a tele-mechanic assisting me. To make this work, he'll have to be distracted. The best way to do that is to break things," Cerise said, hurling a handful of olives at Octavo.

"That a fact?" Octavo said, looking at the blotches of olive juice on his previously pristine teal work suit.

"Yes," Cerise said, pressing the barrel of a suppressed handgun to Octavo's temple.

"Shit," he said, jumping back, much to Cerise's amusement.

"Men are so easily distracted. Archie wouldn't be dead, but he got off point, worrying more about his legacy than his future," Cerise said, tossing the gun onto the sofa.

"Quit playing around and tell us what you need done next," the Drone growled.

"Patience, not everyone has come to the party yet," Cerise said, walking over to a buffet table and helping herself to some melted cheese and sausage.

She grabbed up a handful of bound reading materials, each protected with a plastic cover. She threw one at the Drone's feet and handed one to Octavo. They both opened the binders and looked inside.

"You have a pool of investors, and you've decided to buy a roller derby team?" Octavo said, fanning himself with the thin binder of materials.

"I am all the investors, but yeah, I bought the Black Dragon Stable and intend to run an onna-zumo roller derby team," Cerise said, licking melted cheese from her fingers.

"This would have been a lot of money," Octavo said, eyes wide.

"The first thing Silverstein will do is look for my liquid assets, and try to associate those funds with property to find me. The last place he'll look is at a roller derby team. He'll search every public fund, mining company firm, refinery firm, and the various enterprises associated with the teal, in that order probably," Cerise said, giggling at her own genius.

"If he has an institution grade AI, he'll be able to make the search in hours. That doesn't give us much time," the Drone muttered, dropping the derby team prospectus to the floor.

"Oh, it'll go even faster if he rigs an airlock to allow Taylor IA to step into a vacuum while accessing the colony systems. Quantum capable intelligent agents need electromagnetic shielding, low temperatures, and a vacuum to work to capacity. We could have minutes, instead of hours," Cerise said, smiling broadly.

Octavo looked shocked, readying a comment, but there was a knock at the door. Cerise opened it, allowing several rubber suit-clad collectors entry. They dropped a squirming canvas sack on the floor, then departed hastily. Cerise took the drawstrings on the sack and untied them excitedly like they were a gift. Giving the sack a tug, it toppled over.

A large man sporting a short beard tumbled out. He wore prison teal and was bound at the wrists and feet, gagged with one of his own socks. His shoes were loose in the sack as well, tumbling out onto the fine carpet of the penthouse. He was sweaty and bleary-eyed, having just woken from a drug-induced slumber.

"That's Dell, a bookmaker. We served time in the same block," Octavo observed.

"Why do we need this guy?" the Drone asked.

"Every derby team needs a coach to compete," Cerise said, giving Dell a nudge with her foot.

Octavo let out a cruel chuckle. "This guy is a sex offender, a walking decorum statute violation. You're going to put him in charge of a bunch of shapely women and girls?"

Cerise knelt down beside Dell, looking into his wide eyes and plucking the sock from his mouth. "He's only going to handle one or two of them, isn't that right Dell?"

"You're the boss, Boss," Dell stammered, holding his hands up to have his restraints removed.

"No, I rather like you this way, at least for now."

Dell looked at Cerise fearfully, then to Octavo.

"We'll leave you to it," the Drone said, motioning for Octavo to follow him out.

CHAPTER 5

MARS COLONY, BLACK DRAGON STABLE – ENTERTAINMENT ZONE 113

August 7th, 2200

The new coach showed up in prison teal, never a good sign. As Ishihara came in, he was talking to the new owner, a woman dressed in administrative white. A second man in teal, his arm in a fresh cast, looked on. The whole scene gave her a feeling of disquiet.

The locker room was unchanged, Black Dragon logos still hanging about. It was also never a good sign that an owner didn't want to make the team 'theirs' by changing up the identifying characteristics of the stable. They were in a buy and dump situation most likely. The other girls whispered to each other as they donned their equipment and checked their boots and harnesses. The locker room was tense, more than even before a championship game.

The coach, a balding and slightly overweight convict walked into the locker room in spite of some of the girls being in a state of undress. His eyes wandered about, but he spoke without a hint of the accent usually associated with people from the teal.

"My name's Dell. I just came over from the teal to be your coach. Miss Laplace here bought the team with the intent for us to make a real championship run. That said, we're only taking eight on first string, four on second, and the rest of you will be on unpaid reserve. Any questions?"

The girls nodded somberly, doing their best to cover up. He looked around, smiling at his new stable before heading back out to continue his conversation with the woman in white.

"He's a pig. How much you wanna bet you have to sleep with him to be first-string?" Mars Mauler said, banging her wrist brace against a locker.

"We could do him, like we did Coach Trimbleton. I could make it look accidental," Crusher Line X muttered, pulling on her harness.

"He's got administration backing, a white suit out there right now. If they gamble high on a championship game, we could all cash out if we play it right," Midnight Hauler said, trying to find a silver lining.

"I don't really care, so long as we reach a championship, and 'The Roman' is allowed to rest in peace," Ishihara said, strapping on the rest of her derby armor.

The other girls nodded reverently, each acknowledging the burden Ishihara carried into the ring with her. They each hovered out to the ring in turn, watching each other warm up high over the grandstands below. After testing their gravity boots for stopping power, arm braces for thrust, and harnesses for safety, they dropped low over the repulsion ring beneath the track. It was important to make certain they couldn't get close to a red zone and fall.

The track was brand new, no expense spared in repairing and upgrading the arenas after the last accident. The girls were clocking in at close to fifty miles per hour on the straightaways, with about a foot of extra variance on the outside. It was difficult for some of the girls to adjust, used to the old quirks and personality of the older equipment.

It helped Ishihara that she was 'skating' on freshly repaired boots, but she sensed some of the other girls were holding back on their times, particularly those lighter than she was. They were pulling for her to make first string so that two of their sisters could know peace. She knew it would mean little facing off against other teams, but it was nice her own teammates were looking out for her.

When it came to stopping and setting up a wall to block someone from scoring points, Ishihara excelled without any assistance. She used her size and strength to her advantage, throwing her heavy frame toward anyone trying to get past her. During one particularly hard hit, she could almost see 'The Roman' tumble to the side and fall, her mind flashing back to that moment.

Once tryouts were complete, Ishihara returned to the locker room exhausted. The other girls quickly pushed their gear into their lockers, trying to not be the last one out. Ishihara had already resigned herself to that fate, her way of thanking the others for helping her place on the first string roster. She hoped it would all be worth it.

"Real-deal Japanese onna-zumo derby girl," Dell said, lingering in the doorway of the locker room.

"Sounds like you've finished the first-string roster already," Ishihara said, looking wearily at her coach.

Dell nodded, clumsily assaulted her, one hand down his pants, the other wandering across her body. She endured it, like she had with the first coach that had taken her onto a team. Having suffered it before didn't make it easier, Dell shredding some of her dignity in the process of gratifying himself at her expense. When he was done, he wiped his hand on a towel, grinning to himself.

"You can go," he said, waving his hand toward the door.

Ishihara bolted, running past the stable offices to the empty street outside. Certain no one was around, she covered her face. She felt like crying, but the tears wouldn't come. She could still feel Dell's hand on her, the sound of his heavy breathing still whistling through her ears. It took several minutes for her to calm herself before she was okay to head back to Simon's.

There was a little boy outside, or what Ishihara thought was a child. It was an odd sight in an Entertainment Zone, as they weren't really safe for anyone. Ishihara resigned herself to helping the boy find his way home.

"You okay, miss?" he asked, his voice deeper than what it should have been.

"Yeah, just some dust in my eye… and sheezzzuuss!" Ishihara blurted, realizing it wasn't a child standing there after all.

He was a small, well-built man, with slate gray skin, goggles with green lenses covering his eyes. Slung to his side, was a short rifle, built specifically for him. His clothes were tailored and expertly crafted of ballistic nylon. On the sleeve was a patch that read, "Slayer."

"Don't be alarmed, I'm just looking for someone," he said, holding out a gloved hand.

"You're a Drone, right?" Camille said, shaking his hand.

"That's right. I'm called Ezra One," he nodded.

"You said you were looking for someone?" Camille said, embarrassed.

"I am, but you look like you have enough problems. I don't want to get you involved," Ezra One said, sniffing the air.

"What's in it for me if I help?"

"Maybe I can do something about why you're sad," Ezra said, gesturing to her unbuttoned jersey.

"No, you really can't."

"I'm looking for a woman in white, blond hair, from the Administrative Zone," Ezra One said.

"I haven't seen her," Ishihara said, lying to protect her stable.

If Ezra One was here to kill someone, she didn't want it to be at the expense of the team. They needed the backing, their dirt bag coach, and everything that came with it to get to the championship game. She could tell by the expression on the Drone's face that he didn't believe her, but at the same time, he seemed to bear her no malice.

"Sorry, I can't help you," Ishihara said, genuinely remorseful.

"A long time ago, people used to make me do things I didn't want to do. I wore a harness similar to what you wear, but it wasn't for my own safety," Ezra One said, turning to gaze down the street.

"What did you do?" Ishihara asked.

"I broke away from it all and took control. I never let anyone use me again."

"What does that even mean?" Ishihara asked, buttoning her jersey.

"You aren't a real warrior if you have no one to protect," Ezra One said, disappearing down the road, the shadows taking him from her sight.

Ishihara sighed, picking up her duffle in time to see Dell walk out of the stable. He grinned at her, his head bobbing back and forth as if to demonstrate how proud he was of what he'd done to her. She just lowered her head as he walked past.

"See you at practice tomorrow. Hope you don't mind staying late again," Dell said, a passenger transport descending to pick him up.

Ishihara watched him depart in the chartered transport, a sign that the administration backing was real. No one but someone who wore white could afford such luxuries. She took the long way back to the Mechanical Zone, along the empty ground transport lanes between zones. She didn't deploy her umbrella, letting the condensation from the biological domes overhead wash over her.

It did nothing to wash away how she felt or the sensation of Dell's roaming hand. It was all different this time, not because the stakes were higher, but because she had genuine feelings for someone. How could she be with anyone while Dell was doing things to her what he'd obviously done to many others? His proclivities are probably what landed him in the teal in the first place, and why he'd been chosen to "manage" a team of women athletes.

She walked back, taking the tram where it was still running. Through it all she couldn't help but feel that there was something obligatory about what Dell had done. Sure, he'd seemed to enjoy himself, but he'd barely looked at her when he came into the locker room initially. If she wasn't his type, why was he singling her out?

Simon's machine shop snuck up on her, the overhead door rolling up as she approached. Simon rolled out some equipment to a pair of miners that had been waiting to have work done. He waved when he caught sight of her. She waved back, half-heartedly.

"How did tryouts go?" Simon asked, beckoning for her to come in.

"You in that much of a hurry for me to leave?" Ishihara asked.

Simon nodded. "You are going to have to go back to your own place, eventually."

"The new owner is some lady in white, Laplace I think was her name, and the coach, he's…"

Simon grabbed her by the arms, his grip strong, fingernails biting down into her skin. "Laplace? Are you sure?" Simon said, startling Ishihara.

"LET GO OF ME!" Ishihara said, shoving Simon hard enough he almost fell.

"Whoa, okay. I'm sorry. What is wrong with you?" Simon said, holding his hands up defensively.

"I'm fine, I... just don't want to be touched right now," Ishihara said, crossing her arms and grasping her own shoulders.

Simon frowned. "Your new coach, what's he like?"

"He's fine. I'm really tired. Can I crash in your bed?" Ishihara asked, lowering her head.

"Yeah, um, you totally can," Simon said, nodding.

Ishihara walked past Aunt Ruth, without a word, heading into Simon's room. She couldn't help but feel safe there, because no one really knew where she was. She knew Simon and Ruth wouldn't sell her out if she wanted to hide. Hiding was all she wanted to do.

Simon had fixed and reinforced the bed. Aunt Ruth had swathed it with fresh linens. She drew the covers up over her head, breathing in the smell, the quiet of Simon's room drowning out the world. She'd been staying in flophouses and community living since she was orphaned as a child. She'd endured every indignity, and every invasion.

It was different when you had something to lose and someone to care about. Dell's voice crept into her mind, his lingering words to her every bit as uncomfortable as his touch. She did what she had done since she was a little girl and tried to just push it all down, hiding it away inside of herself somewhere.

She could hear the click of Simon's leg braces in the next room and Aunt Ruth's worried murmuring. Simon knocked on the door. Ishihara just rolled over, hoping the covers would ward off his questions and his desire for her to leave.

"Hey," Simon said, patting her on the arm.

"Yeah, I'll find a place tomorrow," Ishihara said, as bravely as she could.

"About that, I think you should stay here with us," Simon said, giving her arm a squeeze.

"What? No, I..."

"Most of the community housing is without water and power right now, and the looting has gotten worse. I need to keep working, not for the money, but because the system failures are getting worse. I'd feel better if my aunt wasn't here alone. Please, would you stay with us a few more days?"

Ishihara rolled over, adopting a stern expression. "Yeah, I guess. It's kind of inconvenient with the Entertainment Zone being so far away."

"I'll fly you there, whenever you need. Just let me know your schedule," Simon said, standing up and heading for the living room.

"Yeah, okay, I guess that would work," Ishihara said, dismissively.

After Simon was out of sight, Ishihara flopped back on the bed, relief flooding through her being. Not only could she stay, but Simon would fly her to the stable when she needed to practice. It didn't solve all her problems, but enough of them for now.

She caught a nap before dinner, joining Aunt Ruth and Simon for a family meal, something Ishihara had rarely enjoyed with anyone. She stood at the edge of the small kitchen taking it in, savoring the moment.

"Camille, I really appreciate you being willing to stick around. It's a load off my mind," Simon said.

Ishihara gathered Simon up into an awkward hug, her broad arms squeezing the life out of him. Aunt Ruth indulged a secret smile, focused on her food, doing her level best not to ruin the moment. Simon half-heartedly hugged her back, totally baffled.

"It's fine, glad I could help," Ishihara said, releasing him and sitting down to eat.

"Yeah, okay," Simon replied, shaking his head.

"This is good," Ishihara said, shoveling the stew into her mouth.

"Yeah, eat up. I think your blood sugar might be a little low, weirdo," Simon said, not quite ducking a wooden spoon wielded expertly by Aunt Ruth.

"You take it for granted that you have a nice home, but most folks aren't so lucky," Aunt Ruth scolded.

"This is especially true more recently. Half the calls I went to were for service failures on the grid that I couldn't resolve. At some terminals, the Ares System is there, like you'd expect. In other places, it's like it isn't there at all," Simon said, thumbing through the completed work orders laying on the table.

"What could cause that?" Ishihara asked.

"Well, lots of things, the most catastrophic being the Ares System being offline."

"That's never happened before, even during uprisings in the teal," Aunt Ruth said, clearly dismissing the idea.

Simon nodded. "Given how widespread the outages have become, I can't help but think things are that bad somehow. Maybe the Ares System isn't offline, but it is definitely having problems."

"Wouldn't we all be dead if the Ares System went down?" Ishihara asked. She imagined bodies floating cold and airless in the biological domes.

"Not right away, as system redundancies and server echoes would bounce signals from the Ares System around. It could take days, weeks, or even months for a total shutdown of the colony," Simon said, worriedly.

"That word, 'shutdown.' You make it sound like what happened on Earth could happen here," Aunt Ruth said, unwilling to support such apocalyptic possibilities.

"Laplace. You freaked when I said her name. Want to tell me about that?" Ishihara said, trying to change the subject.

Aunt Ruth just stared at her for a moment, before looking over at Simon. "She's back?"

Simon nodded. "Camille says she saw her at the stable. She's the new owner of the Black Dragons."

"Okay, so you guys know this lady?" Ishihara asked.

"Yes," Simon and Ruth said in unison.

"You want to tell me what the big deal is?"

She could tell by their expressions that neither of them wanted to talk about it. Clearly, it was some heavy news as both her new roommates didn't take to it well. It seemed as if everyone had a problem with the new management at the stable, but that no one could do anything about it.

"The owner... is she going to be at the practices watching? When do you think she'll show up next?" Simon asked.

"I don't know. Today was only my first day back at the stable. Everything is different."

Simon nodded. "Try to find out, please."

"Sure, okay. Do I get to know the big scary secret at some point?" Ishihara asked.

Simon frowned. "She lent me the money for my machine shop. She subsidizes it and our living space."

Ishihara just blinked at Simon, obviously confused. "If that's true, you should have an easier time making contact than me, right?"

"It's all done through the Mining Conglomerate and some company on Earth, Uroboros Financial. We just get vouchers and credits to our operational accounts."

"So? That's pretty much everything on Mars. Even the derby teams all have a silent partner or two."

"She killed my husband, and forced my nephew to lie for her," Aunt Ruth said at last, eliciting an angry glare from Simon.

"We agreed to tell no one about that, as much for our safety as others," Simon said, slightly more harshly than he'd intended.

"We can't do what needs to be done alone. I'm running out of time and you've got partially paralyzed legs," Aunt Ruth replied, quietly picking up the empty bowls.

"How'd she kill your uncle?" Ishihara asked.

"She orchestrated a mining accident. A lot of men died that day."

Ishihara closed her eyes. "That the same day you lost partial use of your legs?"

"Yes."

"Simon, I don't know what you guys are intending to do, but my team needs the backing of this lady. We won't make the championship without steady funding getting us the right matches and greasing the right palms," Ishihara explained.

"You don't get it, do you?" Simon replied, angrily.

"Get what?"

Aunt Ruth sat back down, and took her hand. "This new coach, is he a good coach?"

Ishihara frowned. "No."

"She's going to buy your team into the playoffs, taking in the promotion money. Then, she'll bet heavily against you once you're in and this coach has run the team into the ground. This is what she does. She buys up a deniable or expendable asset, wrecks it, and then she cashes out," Aunt Ruth said, banging a fist on the table.

"No, oh no, that can't happen. I need to win a championship game," Ishihara said, covering her face with hands.

"Then we need to do something about your coach," Simon said.

CHAPTER 6

MARS COLONY, VECK AND TRACE SALVAGE – MECHANICAL ZONE 062

August 8th, 2200

The salvage yard was busy, mostly with scavengers bringing in their meager finds from what the loaders and haulers drop from the flight lanes. Traffic was lower than normal, so the pickings were slim, and the people were desperate. There was shoving and arguments in the lines, this in spite of there being little chance the yard's salvage quota for the day would be met.

Everyone was stressed and life support on the colony seemed substandard even compared to the usual shabby air there was to breathe. It was smoky and humid, the soot of the mines not being filtered well enough to keep it off the skin. People kept their dust masks up and their goggles down as they worked and waited to turn in the scraps they'd spent the entire early morning trying to find.

Simon and Ishihara were in the yard already, working almost entirely alone. Not a single other mechanic was there, with everyone probably out working to keep the colony from falling apart. The duo were not there for that purpose, but with mayhem in mind.

"What are we looking for again?" Ishihara asked.

"Contraband, anything that could get him tossed by the adjusters entering into the arena for the practice session tonight," Simon said, opening a box marked as mining detonation units.

"What are you going to do, build a bomb?" Ishihara asked, fidgeting nervously.

"Not a working one, just something that will make Mars Company security very suspicious. I want that jerk back in the teal behind bars before tomorrow. That way management has six days to find a replacement," Simon explained, loading detonation caps into the satchel Ishihara was carrying.

"I don't like this. If something goes wrong the team could be disqualified for the season."

"If I make the arrest go live on the public network, the shares for the mining company involved in management will dip a quarter percent. There's no way they'll risk dropping someone from the teal in as a coach until the market stabilizes," Simon explained.

"A quarter percent?"

"It doesn't seem like much, but it would represent hundreds of millions of credit vouchers less in holdings and equity against their debt. With Earth mostly dark from the Shutdown, they'd have to either work with less operating capital or borrow from a competitor. Margins are that tight right now," Simon said, pulling up several lengths of threaded pipe from inside a broken transport container.

Ishihara paused, putting a hand on Simon's shoulder.

"How do you know all this? Why would you care what they're worth, and…"

"They killed my uncle. I've been trying to figure out a way to mess with the Mining Conglomerate for years. Economic sabotage has been the most viable option because it wouldn't require killing anyone. I could wreck careers, mess with their golden parachutes, and rub red grease all over their perfect ledgers," Simon whispered, letting the pipe clatter into a sack.

"The Shutdown, you think someone manufactured it? All the vid news programs say it was a computer error," Ishihara whispered, kneeling down beside Simon as he worked to free some components from an engine block.

"Definitely manufactured. There are so many safeguards on the global fiscal system to keep it rigged in the favor of a very few ultra-wealthy individuals. Someone tried to reset it all and something went wrong," Simon said, placing more parts in the satchel.

"Excuse me, do you work here?" someone a little further up the row asked, startling Simon and Ishihara.

They looked to see an odd pair, man and woman, each obviously not from Mars. The man was tall and very pale, his dark hair combed back neatly to meet with the collar of his impeccably pressed dress shirt and tailored suit. He wore leather shoes, an extreme rarity on Mars. The girl had a dark complexion, but brightly colored hair and a flamboyant outfit betraying her as someone from the Lunar Colony. She carried a large designer bag, packed to the gills.

"No, I'm sure Veck and Trace are busy right now. It's the morning, all the scavengers are in there pinching ore and steel for vouchers," Simon explained, taken off guard.

The man had a strange charisma about him and an earnest smile that reminded Simon of family that came to visit when he was a boy. "You're a mechanic in this zone?" the man asked.

"That's 'The Roman'," the woman said, smiling broadly and pointing to Ishihara.

"What, really?" the man said, looking genuinely astonished.

Ishihara blushed. "Simon knows the yard as well as Veck and Trace, he can probably help you."

Simon frowned at Ishihara, then turned back to the odd duo. "Sure, what are you looking for?"

"These," the woman said, handing Simon a data slate.

Simon looked at the data slate, handling it carefully. He'd heard about devices like the one he was gazing at. It housed the equivalent of his local system back at the shop in a form factor the size of a paperback. They were extremely expensive and illegal on Mars without a special permit. Hers was equipped with a full spectrum of wireless and near field communication capabilities. It took a moment for Simon to shove down his envy and even concentrate on the list.

"I can't help you with this stuff. It's all cognitive systems componentry. Regular citizens are not allowed to have anything resembling this kind of technology," Simon said, hesitantly giving the data slate back to the woman.

"Can't or won't, Simon?" the man asked.

"Who are you to even ask me that? You're from Earth and clearly have money. Why don't you just buy the information you need from a white coat?" Simon snapped.

"Because they are corrupt, and they've allowed something terrible to happen to your home. I'm trying to fix things," the man said, checking a sleek mobile device for the time.

"Who are you?" Simon asked, angrily.

"I call myself Silverstein. This is my friend, Taylor."

"Taylor of the Lunar Colony?" Ishihara asked, wide eyed.

Taylor just nodded, smiling politely.

Ishihara gave Simon an intense stare. "She's basically royalty on that Colony. She helps people."

"You're here, searching for things with a purpose. Tell me what you need. Maybe we can help each other," Silverstein said, calmly lighting a cigarette before offering one to Simon and Ishihara.

Simon declined, but Ishihara took a cigarette.

"You've got several of the ECM12 Reactors already checked off on your list. I need one for... a, um, project. Can you shake one loose? Everything else I've just about found on my own and have the vouchers for," Simon asked, certain they would refuse.

The reactors were expensive and very difficult to find. They were also the perfect power source for a suit of Aegis power armor. Silverstein gestured to Taylor and nodded. She reached in her large bag and pulled out the one with the fewest repair tags. Her hair suddenly went white, bioelectric energy arcing off her hand as she sparked the reactor so it functioned properly. The sight made Ishihara jump and Simon stumble and fall backward, his assistive leg braces unable to keep him aloft.

"Sorry about that. She really should warn people," Silverstein said, helping Ishihara get Simon back to his feet.

Taylor smiled, handing Ishihara the reactor.

"It's… uh, okay. I'll make notes to your list, tell you where to go for these things. Most will be from unlisted vendors, and they don't like surprises. Keep…whatever that was…under control while you talk to them and don't tell them I sent you," Simon said, handing the data slate to Taylor.

"What are you giving us?" Taylor asked, looking at the notes.

"Information reserved for union mechanics only," Simon said, worriedly.

"Will these individuals talk to us?" Silverstein asked.

"Do you have money?"

Silverstein nodded.

"Yeah, they'll talk to you," Simon said.

Silverstein shook Simon's hand and went to do the same when Taylor interposed herself and held up her bag. "Hey, could you sign my bag with your old derby name?" she said, holding out a black felt tip marker.

"You're a bigger celebrity than I ever will be," Ishihara said, signing her bag "Killer Katana".

"Not even close, and certainly not on Mars. Here, look at this," Taylor said, navigating to the onna-zumo derby forums on the public network and showing Ishihara.

"Everyone is talking about me," Ishihara said, looking over at Simon.

"You cut an average of fifty seconds off the opposing jammer, per two minute jam, because of how you block. There's huge arguments about whether it's technique or gravity equipment modification that gives you an advantage. When you took up 'The Roman's' name, you went from the sixtieth talked about derby girl to the first in less than a day. You've been the most talked about player for two weeks," Taylor said, scrolling through all the comments made to the public network forum.

"Simon, did you know about this?" Ishihara asked.

"You know I don't watch derby," Simon said, feeling a little guilty.

"I almost quit yesterday," Ishihara said, shaking her head.

"You can't do that," Taylor said, laughing nervously. "You're a hero to working class people on Mars, the Lunar Colony, and Earth where derby is still broadcast. When they see you, they see an orphan that rose to be the most prominent player in the league. Onna-zumo roller derby is huge on the Lunar Colony. Without your gear and your face paint, I almost didn't recognize you."

"None of the girls can afford network access. They live in community housing and get paid enough to barely subsist. She lives with me right now because she has nowhere to go. People like you are entertained by her, but she gets none of the benefits," Simon said, gesturing to the autograph on Taylor's bag.

"Is that true?" Silverstein asked, looking to Ishihara.

She nodded, slightly embarrassed.

"That is not fair," Taylor complained, taking a handful of Silverstein's coat sleeve.

Silverstein nodded, inhaling the last of his cigarette before crushing it out on the ground.

"Simon, are you going to do something about this?" Silverstein asked.

"What difference would it make if I was? Mining Company adjusters move anyone that tries to mess with the status quo to the teal," Simon said, a little frustrated with some outsider telling him his business.

"This is the only Mechanical Zone with facility maintenance that still shows up to work in force. We came here because the union here seems to operate above the tolerances required by the Mining Company Conglomerate. Someone here cares about Mars," Silverstein said, meeting Simon's gaze.

"The 062 is the only self-governing Mechanics Union," Simon said, folding his arms.

Silverstein nodded, understanding. "I didn't know that. So if I need anything, I should keep coming here?"

"If you're smart," Ishihara said.

"He is," Taylor said, winking.

"This is Mars and you still need to watch your back. I don't know why you're here, but you can get dead or dropped in the teal as easy as anyone," Simon said, grudgingly.

Silverstein nodded. "Do you have public network access?"

"It's limited to thirty minutes a day. It's generally all I can do to just log my work and get new work orders before I run out of the time allocated to me," Simon said.

"That doesn't work for me," Silverstein said, pulling out his mobile and removing his individual identifier chip and sliding in a blank one. He handed the mobile to Taylor who began to glow again, hair going white. The screen on the mobile frenetically accepted a complex upload of specialized code heavily encrypting the device. She held it out for Simon, but he refused to take it.

"I don't need anyone else telling me what to do," Simon said, holding up his hand.

"Silverstein doesn't do that and neither do I. Do what you want with it. It'll act as a tether to the public and private networks. You can use it as you see fit, but we believe someone here needs to give working class people access to the same information as people living in the Facility and Administrative Zones. We aren't fond of places that have economic tiers that limit people from rising to their potential," Taylor said, still holding out the mobile device.

"What are you?" Ishihara asked, taking the mobile.

"It's hard to explain," Taylor said, smiling weakly.

"Do I want to know why you two are really here?" Simon asked.

"That is also very hard to explain. You're the only people we've met on Mars who have been willing to help us. I owe you more of an explanation, but for now it'll have to wait. We're on a tight schedule," Silverstein said.

Simon nodded. "Yeah, okay."

They parted ways, Silverstein and Taylor heading back into the yard, Simon and Ishihara heading to the weighing counter. Veck and Trace were both sitting there looking bored as all the scavengers had left. They nodded to Simon and waved him through, not even checking his satchel.

"You guys handing out free salvage today?" Simon asked, confused by the two voucher-pinching tightwads being so generous.

"We are under new management. You're on a list with five other 062 mechanics. Whatever you need for maintaining the zone is getting paid for by a third party. Just leave us an inventory of what you take here," Veck said, pointing to a terminal.

Simon nodded, keying in his inventory. "I should have grabbed more stuff."

Veck shrugged, turning to watch the vid screen. Trace beckoned them over.

"Something is wrong with all this. I don't like it when an off-world suit waltzes in and throws credit vouchers around. It disrupts the flow. This is how we have strikes, unions breaking apart and such," the old scavenger complained.

"I'll take it over the meddling of white coats and jerks that made their money in the teal," Simon said, waving as he walked out.

Ishihara stopped Simon outside the salvage yard, holding up the mobile. "We don't need to get Dell back into the teal. Once I show the girls what's on the public networks about us, we'll have real bargaining power."

"This is still Mars, Camille. Don't let a couple of glitzy off-world folks convince you otherwise."

"I want to handle this on my own. You've already done a lot for me. This is something I want to figure out by myself," Ishihara said, putting the mobile in Simon's breast pocket.

"Okay. I'll keep the stuff around if you change your mind."

The journey back across the zone to Simon's workshop was interrupted by looting and riots at the tram tunnel entrance. Mars Company adjusters had to retreat back to the tram line as furious mining employees threw rocks and trash at them. They were angry that contracts hadn't been renewed, but the adjusters came to collect taxes and tariffs anyway. Ishihara hurled her own hunk of broken masonry, joining in the chaos as Simon looked on.

"Ha, they're running away," Ishihara gloated.

"For now," Simon said, sullenly.

He couldn't remember the last time things were this bad, but the reactor he'd procured might be able to change all that. If he could get the armor back to the Marshal, she could start patrolling again. She might even pay a little more attention to the Mechanical Zones for his trouble. The corruption was getting out of control and with the encrypted mobile as a tether he could collect evidence to that end for more than ten or fifteen minutes a day.

Ishihara came back, dusty with soot and holding her fists in the air. "Got one, right in the back of the head as he was heading back toward the tram. They had to carry him the rest of the way," she said, triumphantly.

"You think it's a good idea to be getting involved, Camille? What if someone recognizes you? You're a big deal, remember?" Simon said, smiling slightly.

"I don't know, honestly," Ishihara replied.

"If you're done, let's head back and check on Aunt Ruth. She's probably got lunch almost ready by now," Simon said, handing off the satchel of parts to Ishihara.

They were almost back to the workshop when they found another body lying in between a moisture recovery unit and a community living spire. It appeared to have been wrapped in plastic, but someone had uncovered it. Simon looked more closely as Ishihara looked the other way to keep watch.

"This body… beaten like the other one. It even looks the same as the other one. This is so strange," Simon said, taking out his cutter.

"The same? What do you mean?" Ishihara asked, looking around to make sure no one spotted them messing with a body.

"Like, as in the same person," Simon said, turning the corpse over to get a view of the back of the neck.

"Like a clone or…?"

"Android, and someone has already removed the data module. I might be able to pull some records from the onboard temporary memory chip, but it'll be messy. Hand me a length of that threaded pipe," Simon said, holding his hand out.

Ishihara handed him the pipe and stood back as he smashed off the top the corpse's skull. Inside was a bluish gel, synthetic skull fragments and a tangled array of cognitive system relays. Simon searched through it for anything that resembled the temporary or short-term memory unit. Finding it, he cut it free and placed it into a pocket on his coveralls.

"Gross, can we go now?" Ishihara asked, looking around.

"I want to know who keeps doing this. Androids don't have the same degree of sapience or awareness as a more advanced artificial intelligences, but they still feel pain. This isn't right," Simon said, standing up.

"These things are expensive, right? It seems like a pretty stupid hobby to go about clubbing these. You'd be in the teal forever paying that off if you got caught," Camille said, waving a hand at the body.

"It has to be someone with Administrative Zone access. You never see the androids anywhere else but there," Simon said, covering the body with plastic sheeting.

The remainder of their journey was uneventful, the quiet streets and walkways mostly devoid of anyone else. Most folks were busy at work or trying to travel to other zones to find work contracts. Scarcity made for a quiet Mechanical Zone after midday. The entry door to the workshop was partially opened, filling Simon with dread. Ishihara rushed ahead, looking inside, but shook her head.

Once they were both able to go inside, they found the shop untouched, but they could hear someone in the living area talking to Aunt Ruth. Ishihara stopped in the entrance mid-stride, almost stepping back into Simon as they entered. Sitting at the small table in the kitchen was Dell, his long scraggly hair hanging down over his teal vinyl suit coat. His outfit creaked slightly as he turned to look at Ishihara.

"Practice is in a couple of hours, I thought you might could use a ride to the stables," Dell said, smiling crookedly.

CHAPTER 7

MARS COLONY, VEDTER MACHINEWORKS – MECHANICAL ZONE 062

August 8th, 2200

"Get out," Simon said, gesturing toward the door.

"Yeah, I can't do that. We all basically work for the same person and, whether we like it or not, we all have a part to play in all of this. She doesn't like it when her pawns go off script, and you guys are way off script from what I'm told," Dell said, trying in vain to adjust his suit coat to more comfortably accommodate his flabby frame.

"What block?" Aunt Ruth asked, stirring the stew and reaching into a drawer.

"What'd you say?" Dell asked, turning around too late.

"I said, what block, convict?" Aunt Ruth said, sliding a long kitchen knife under his chin.

"Bitch, I will…"

"Cut me?" Aunt Ruth said, pressing the blade hard enough to Dell's throat to draw blood.

Dell sat there uncomfortably for a moment, Ishihara and Simon looking on dumbfounded. Aunt Ruth put her cane on his foot and leaned on it, keeping the knife in place. Dell looked at her from the corner of his eyes, finding only the darkest mayhem in the old woman's eyes.

"S Block, for bookmaking, and some assorted decorum violations," Dell rasped.

"I killed a man and a woman and spent only five years in the teal. Do you know why?" Aunt Ruth said, her voice winnowing down to a whisper by the last word.

"You killed for the unions?" Dell said, a lump welling up in his throat.

"I killed for the company," said, her old X Block accent shining through for a moment.

It was how killers sounded after being on that block because of how so many were sequestered for years. A strange dialect inclusive to that cell block arose, one spoken only by killers. Aunt Ruth spoke a few strange words to Dell, pressing the knife in closer until he was having to look at the ceiling.

"You don't understand. The whole time she's been subsidizing you, the company has been collecting rent and letting the unpaid remainder pile up. She owns you, your nephew, me, and that tight piece of derby ass over there," Dell said, smiling.

Aunt Ruth wound her wiry hand around his scraggly hair and pulled backward, sending both of them to the floor. "Everything is in my name. If I die, so does the debt. My husband's living trust protects property for my posterity. I have only a month or two left to live, but I kept that a secret as well, getting my meds like clockwork. You're the one that doesn't understand, Dell."

"Adjusters will come, and they will get what she thinks she's owed, law or not, she's above it all, believe me," Dell said, somewhat frantic.

The old woman rose slowly, grabbing up her cane to steady herself. Dell let out a big sigh of relief, his hand going up to his bloodied neck. Simon hobbled over to steady his aunt, looking down at Dell angrily.

"Like I said before, get out," Simon said, pointing at the door.

"I don't leave unless I have the derby girl with me. I have strict orders," Dell said, turning like a beached whale before staggering up to his feet.

"Works for me," Aunt Ruth said, reversing her grip on the blade.

"No. I'll go with him," Ishihara said, holding up her hand. "Just let me get my gear."

"Let me go, Simon," Aunt Ruth whispered, tugging against his grasp.

Dell tried to backhand Aunt Ruth, but Simon caught him by the forearm, and shoved him back. "Pretty strong for a cripple," Dell said, spitting on the kitchen floor.

"I turn wrenches all day long, what'd you expect? I'm letting you go because I respect Ishihara and this is her play to make. For her, this is about honoring her team. I doubt you know anything of honor," Simon said, barely keeping his aunt at bay.

Dell smiled. "No, I wouldn't. I know how to ruin a pure woman and she can't play unless she's pure. Keep that in mind."

"Dead men don't coach derby teams," Aunt Ruth hissed, flicking the knife into the wall beside Dell's head.

"I will unravel you, and Laplace. It's only a matter of time," Simon said, pushing the parts satchel over his shoulder behind him.

"Yeah, good luck with that, kid," Dell said, shaking his head.

Ishihara came back out of Simon's room with her duffle and derby armor slung over her shoulder. She looked at the ground, Dell grabbing her by the arm and leading her outside. A privately chartered transport descended to the street, meeting them at the curb. Simon watched helplessly as Dell sat beside her, his crooked smile the last thing he saw before the entry hatch snapped shut.

"I hope she knows what she's doing," Aunt Ruth growled.

"I trust her. If she needs us, she'll let us know," Simon said, hobbling quickly into his workshop.

He grabbed the tarp covering the Aegis Armor and pulled it to the floor. It was sitting upright in the repair bay usually reserved for mining exoskeletons, gleaming in the shop lighting in spite of being heavily damaged. Simon swore he could hear it whispering to him, but he couldn't make out what it was saying. Every machine seemed to murmur after a fashion, and had all his life. It was what spurred him to be a mechanic. Still, this armor was different.

He lowered the armor across a canvas cargo net so he could more easily work on the damage to the rear panels. It had to be exacting work, perfect in every detail to get the reactor to provide just the right amount of power. Someone had built the armor with great care, by hand, for someone they loved dearly. The more Simon worked, the more the connection between the armorer and the occupant became apparent. An intense and abiding affection had been worked into the suit.

They were lovers, and the armor was designed to protect that love. Simon shook his head, trying to banish the sensations he felt flowing up through his tools to his hands. Eventually, he stopped trying to fight the sensations and allowed them to guide him instead. The components he'd never seen before seemed to open up to him, exploding in his mind so he could see how they went back together.

Aunt Ruth brought him sandwiches as he worked, putting a cold washcloth to his brow each time. He made the sandwiches disappear as the armor took shape. Sitting down at the grinder he took a slim piece of tin and shaped it into a simply adorned star, placing it where the Marshal's badge had once been. He tried to make it look as official as possible, even shaping a piece of ballistic-grade polycarbonate for the visor as he repaired the cowl.

Hours later, the armor was much as it had been before. Some of the servo-units and actuators had been burned out, so Simon used components from the mining exoskeleton. It made the armor slower, no longer mimicking the exacting reflexes of the occupant, but they would be far stronger. Seals from the exoskeleton made the Aegis suit more than just marginally EVA capable. It would take extreme damage to cause it to lose pressure now.

"What are you doing?" Aunt Ruth said, watching awestruck as Simon shed his assistive leg braces and pulled himself inside the Aegis Armor.

"It won't power up without an occupant I don't think. I'm not sure why," Simon said, letting the visor snap shut.

The armor powered up with a muffled roar, all the actuators firing in their housings as hydraulic cables went taut. The new reactor made the decades old armor hum like it had just been assembled, indicator lights and illuminators shining brightly. The holographic display came up, loading the operating system onboard the suit. The code was dizzyingly complex. It was far beyond the public system interface that was installed at the machine shop.

"Hello?" the suit's internal system intoned, the feminine mechanical voice sounding a little uncertain.

Simon blinked in astonishment, having discovered the system had some sort of artificial intelligence. "Um, hello, I am Simon."

"I remember fighting a very dangerous man with the Marshal but little else before that. Simon, why can't I remember?" the Aegis Suit asked.

"I think the Marshal thought you were...um, killed? She took your core memory unit with her. Your short term memories would still be accessible. Your core programming seems to be intact, but I can't read your directives. The code is too complex," Simon explained.

"Thank you for saving me, Simon," the Aegis Armor intoned.

"How do I return you to your owner? Is there a way to call her or something?" Simon asked.

"I have no protocols to that end. Being separated from the Marshal is, as far as I can tell, unprecedented."

"How would you know that? I just put a fresh memory modules in," Simon asked.

"I have limited onboard data storage and recovery systems for purposes of maintenance and repair."

"I really need the Marshal's help. A friend of mine is in trouble," Simon said, dejected.

"Redundant systems show you were on the tram platform with an elderly citizen during the fight. You saw how I was deactivated. Please, tell me what happened."

"Wow, you have really good sensors to have picked me out of the crowd. The man the Marshal was fighting pushed you into a passing train. You lost power. The Marshal looked sad, well... devastated really."

"And the man?"

"She killed him. She and her friends took the body with her," Simon said.

"Good. I don't remember why, but it was critical that we apprehend or provide street justice for that individual. You and I, we can help your friend," the Aegis Armor said, loading law enforcement protocols from a protected drive to the new memory module Simon had installed.

"I'm a mechanic, not a cop. I've no idea where to even start."

"We will need to get new equipment. I detect no restraints, sidearms, medical equipment, or any of the required inventory for active duty."

"I don't suppose the Marshal has a big warehouse full of everything we need?"

"Yes, there is such a place."

Aunt Ruth knocked on the outside of the armor, waving her hand in front of the visor. Through the doorway, he could see Ishihara returning from derby practice, shoulders slumped. Simon hit the release control, allowing him to slide up and out of the armor. He nearly fell to the floor but caught himself on a nearby work table.

After a moment getting back into his assistive braces, he hobbled stiffly into the living area. Ishihara was lying on his bed, face buried in a pillow. Aunt Ruth patted him on the back, and nodded.

"Go talk to her," she said, heading back into the shop, tobacco pipe in hand.

Simon sat down on the edge of the bed, his leg braces locking up a little as he did. The ceiling fan spun slowly overhead, barely covering up the hundreds of footfalls coming from miners and mechanics returning from work or looking for work in other districts. The murmur of the crowd faded after a few minutes as Ishihara laid on the bed motionless.

"He touches me," she said at last, frowning in disgust.

Simon nodded. "I suspected it was something like that after you shoved me."

Like virtually all Martian Colony citizens, Simon was familiar with it all. In the penal facility, sex wasn't about love or attraction, it was about power. Families held their breath when someone was paroled and released from the teal. Often, they would never be the same and they'd be dangerous to those around them. The cycle of incarceration and probation was neverending.

"Yeah, it sucks. So, how was your day?" Ishihara said, rolling over, her derby face paint streaked slightly beneath her eyes.

"The suit is up and running. Thanks for the help earlier," Simon said, smiling weakly.

"Sure. So, what now? We find the Marshal, give her the armor?" Ishihara asked.

"I didn't think you'd care about that, Camille," Simon said, a little surprised.

"When I told Dell I'd report him, he laughed and said there was no Marshal anymore. If the people on parole living in the orange all begin to believe that, the colony could have a serious problem. Mining Company Adjusters rarely get involved unless it's about money," Ishihara said, lowering her head.

"What about what we've been seeing on the public network?" Simon said, scratching his cheek thoughtfully.

"Dell said I was welcome to try and cause a fuss, but that he could just replace me on the roster and my sway would vanish. I don't know if that's true or if there would be any actual outrage over it," Ishihara replied, putting her hands between her knees.

"We could try it. I could go onto the public network and make a post on your behalf."

Ishihara shook her head. "I need to think about it. There's a lot at stake here for me. What about getting the armor back to the Marshal. Have you figured that out yet?"

"The armor has an artificial intelligence on board, but the Marshal took the primary memory unit. It has some short term memories and a protected recovery drive to reload important protocols. Unfortunately, it doesn't know how to find the Marshal. It does know where she stores her gear, though," Simon explained.

"She might be there. Did you ask the armor if it remembers where the Marshal's office is?" Ishihara asked.

Simon slapped his forehead. "No. I didn't even think about that, Camille. It might not know where the Marshal is, but, like any vehicle with onboard systems, it probably knows how to go home."

"Sounds like something that needs to be done under the cover of dark," Ishihara said, pushing off her onna-zumo armor.

Simon stood quickly averting his eyes while she changed. Once she was properly attired in an orange-colored work suit, they headed out to make some coffee. Aunt Ruth had already retired to her room, but a small covered plate of food was left on the table for Ishihara. The weak colony-issued coffee was better than nothing. Simon and Ishihara drank it in silence to keep from disturbing Aunt Ruth.

"We doing this tonight?" Simon whispered.

"Absolutely."

Donning the Aegis Armor once more, he walked it into the transport, pushing what remained of the mining exoskeleton onto the floor. He locked the armor into the hard points and got back out again. Ishihara helped him descend into his leg braces, wrapping her arms around him to guide him down from the top of the armor. Ishihara didn't let go after he was on the ground and locked into his braces, her arms squeezing him tightly.

He hugged her back. "What's this for?"

"For not being a dick. What you're trying to do for the Marshal is nice. Being a woman on Mars isn't easy, and even with armor, you're a target," Ishihara paused, shaking her head. "What if she's already dead?"

"No way. I've seen her fight. She has a couple of pretty tough friends, a cyborg, and a military grade Ichthyic Metasapient. I'm sure she's okay, but not nearly as effective without her full kit. It'll be better for all of Mars if we can get this suit back to her," Simon said, trying to reassure Ishihara.

"I hope you're right."

Simon took out the encrypted mobile that Silverstein and Taylor had given him and ran a hard wire from it to the systems on board the transport. He routed the Aegis Armor's communication system to the mobile so that it could communicate with the transport via a secure wireless connection. Once the transport powered up, Simon routed control of the transport to the armor.

"What are you doing?" Ishihara asked, seeing Simon head for the armor instead of the pilot's seat.

"We might need me to be in the armor quickly, in case there's trouble. I'm going to try and fly the transport from the armor," Simon said, nervously.

"That sounds like a recipe for disaster," Ishihara said, already nervous about flying.

"Yeah, probably."

"You look at the data thing from the android?" Ishihara asked.

"I have my rapid prototyping unit making a circuit board that should let me access the data. It's an older model, so it takes forever. It should be ready to read the short term memory module by the time we return from scouting the Marshal's office and storage facility," Simon said, checking connection latency between the suit and the transport with an old Mining Company radio.

"Do you think the android really felt any of what was being done to it?" Ishihara asked.

"Yeah, even the oldest models can feel pain. It was a countermeasure to keep them from sustaining damage as they wandered about doing their duties."

"That's kind of messed up. I would think the advantage of being a machine would be that you didn't have to suffer like people do," Ishihara said, frowning.

"This is pretty intense," Simon said, looking at the panel on the radio.

"The wireless connection working?" Ishihara asked, turning in the co-pilot chair to look at the transport control panel.

"Evidently, but the encryption is so high that it jumps frequencies and protocols before I can route to new ones. Even standing here monitoring the mobile device, I can't manually check the latency. Assisted by an automated routing service you could grab a connection, but you wouldn't have it long enough to do anything with it," Simon said, shaking his head.

"Is it a problem?" Ishihara asked.

"Only for whoever tries to hack either the transport or the suit wirelessly. They'll burn a lot of processing power and frustration only to fail unless they have, heck, I have no idea what kind of hardware would beat this," Simon said, blinking in disbelief.

"That girl, Taylor, encrypted the mobile by touching it? She's a mechanic, maybe?"

"I've only ever seen a mechanic work once. It took intense concentration and prolonged contact with a machine. They called him in to open a wrecker line door that had been closed outside of facility protocols somehow. It took him thirty minutes and he had to be rolled out in a wheelchair afterward," Simon said, frowning.

"If she can do this remotely, she can probably track us," Ishihara said, worriedly.

"There's nothing we can do about that. Hopefully, whoever those two off-world folks are, they don't mean us or the colony any harm. I don't know why they would have helped us like that otherwise. Have you ever met anyone like that before?" Simon asked.

"Only you," Ishihara said, smirking.

"Heh, if only I had that guy's money. How about you help me suit up?" Simon asked, laughing.

Ishihara lifted Simon up by his harness easily until he was able to grab the pauldrons on the armor and ease his legs down into the interior. He lowered himself the rest of the way, letting the armor engage personnel clamps so he wouldn't rattle around inside. The clamps were shaped for a woman smaller than himself, but they were still reasonably comfortable and held him in securely.

"You okay in there?" Ishihara asked.

"Yeah, I'm good. Go strap in," Simon said, bringing up remote system control for the transport.

The transport powered up, compression from the engines sending up a plume of ore dust. Ishihara closed her eyes, grasping the restraints with both hands as the transport rose into the air. As the mining company craft entered the shipping lane, it lost power momentarily, the engines sputtering.

"Ahh! What was that?!" Ishihara screamed, closing her eyes even tighter.

"Something in the relays, I'll check it when we set down. Shouldn't be a problem," Simon said over the internal comm.

Simon guided the transport through the shipping lane toward the port, then headed toward the older original part of the colony referred to simply as Zone 1. It had been converted to storage long ago, the majority devoted to stacks of forgotten cargo containers and ancient mining equipment. The Aegis Armor's internal GPS guided him the rest of the way, taking him toward the far end of the zone. It was there that the biological shielding sloped up to meet a high rock ceiling overhead, the whole place cut into the side of a mountain. A mass of containers was arrayed below. Simon wasn't sure where to go, so he set down somewhere in the middle of it all.

It was dark and dusty, showing little sign that anyone had traveled to the location in a long time. Once the transport was down and landing protocols had completed, Simon hit the clamp release and stepped toward the transport access. He activated the cargo door release remotely and stepped out in front of the stack of sealed cargo containers.

"Careful, there could be anything out here. It isn't patrolled or monitored," Simon said, stepping out.

"Great," Ishihara replied, wrapping her arms around herself nervously.

"*This way,*" the Aegis Armor intoned, bringing up a map on the HUD.

They traveled a short distance, rounding several large containers that looked to be sealed up tight. The armor issued a short burst signal that caused the hatch on the largest container to open, revealing the interior. The containers were expertly camouflaged to appear separate but they were actually all connected. The access port opened from behind where welded seals appeared to be, concealing the entrance perfectly when closed. Electromagnetic shielding was built into the interior making it almost impossible to detect with electronic snooping.

Ishihara followed along cautiously, carrying a large battery-powered lamp from the transport. The interior was a nicely decorated living space with a workshop, storage area, and training facility. It had belonged to at least two generations of Marshals, family photos along one wall doing much to tell their story. Simon paused, seeing many parallels between the Rider and Vedter families. Both had sacrificed a lot to be on Mars, with little to show for it.

"She's probably our age, early twenties, and she hasn't been the Marshal for too long. It's hard to believe, having watched her fight. She's a warrior born, a real protector," Simon said, clicking the visor back on the armor.

"I can see why. There's pictures of her training when she was probably five years old?" Ishihara guessed, looking at the photos.

"*Shall we procure the equipment we need to resume patrol?*" the Aegis Suit intoned.

"Wow, it… she, talks?" Ishihara said, startled.

"Yeah, it has some sort of rudimentary AI that helps the Marshal," Simon said, heading toward storage.

"She probably doesn't like being called 'rudimentary,'" Ishihara laughed.

"Aegis, analysis of my assessment of your abilities?" Simon said, smiling.

"*Your incorrect statement does not hurt my feelings,*" the Aegis suit said, deadpan.

"Hah!" Ishihara said, laughing at Simon's startled expression.

"*Go to your left, toward the back,*" the Aegis suit directed.

There were hundreds of weapons, and cases of ancient ammunition waiting to be fired. It appeared to have all been shipped with the original Marshal. Looking through the inventory, he couldn't find machine pistols like he'd seen the Marshal employ before on the tram platform, but there was a single high caliber low-capacity sidearm that seemed to be the closest thing.

"All this for one Marshal?" Ishihara said, gazing back into the dozen containers welded together that housed all the Marshal's equipment.

"Maybe they hadn't intended to send just one Marshal and the plan changed?" Simon replied as he loaded up on ammunition, medical supplies, a police radio, and a custom heavy sidearm with no manufacturing markings.

"You should make sure the gun works," Ishihara said, mirthfully.

"Oh, definitely," Simon said, smirking.

They walked to the interior range and waited for the armor to recalibrate the targeting computer to the new weapon. After a couple minutes, the Aegis system gave Simon the all clear to fire. He held the weapon up with one hand, but the Aegis Suit prompted him to use two.

"I shouldn't need both hands, with as strong as the armor is, but better safe than sorry," Simon said, waving Ishihara back.

She plugged her ears as Simon took aim. The pistol fired a round at such high velocity that it tore the target off the stand. The sound was so loud that Ishihara's ears were ringing even having taken the precaution of covering her ears. Simon walked over to see what sort of damage had been done to the back of the firing range, but found only a handful of light dents in the back.

"Aegis, what sort of rounds are these?" Simon asked.

"Ceramic anti-personnel rounds. They shouldn't penetrate critical enclosures around the station and will have reduced effectiveness on armored targets."

"Are there more than just ceramic rounds in storage?" Simon asked.

"There are seven varieties of ammunition."

"I don't know what she will prefer, so we'll grab some of each," Simon said, heading back to the storage area.

Simon grabbed several magazines worth of each type of round, and a spare set of ear protection for Ishihara in case he had the occasion to fire the weapon again. They looked about the dwelling for any clues that might lead them to the Marshal but found little. It didn't look as though she'd been back in a long time. Simon could relate, preferring to avoid the old Vedter family dwelling in Maintenance Zone. It was just a reminder that he would soon be alone.

"Let's go to her office in the Port Zone, see if we can find her there," Simon said, walking the suit back up into the mining transport.

"More flying. Great," Ishihara joked, following him inside.

The Port Zone was congested with traffic, ore transports waiting in long lines to load either directly to spacecraft or to storage facilities for refining. The streets below were a jumble of job-seekers, protestors, and the black rubber suits of the Mining Company adjusters trying to maintain order. Simon could see the Marshal's office near the port access point, but there was no clear place to set down.

"You seeing this?" Ishihara asked, looking out the cockpit window.

"Yeah, via the external feed. There is nowhere to land unless we want to start a riot or a panic. There's a drop system for mining exoskeletons, but I've never done a cable jump. I expect that would draw even more attention," Simon said, over the internal comm.

"Visor down, no one would know you aren't the Marshal," Ishihara said, mischievously.

"Well, assuming I do the cable jump without falling on my face," Simon said, nervously.

"I can assist you," Aegis intoned, bringing up a menu of directives designed to assist the pilot with controlling the suit.

"That's probably where she is anyway. Hell with it, let's give it a try," Simon said, setting the transport on a course to break from the traffic lane over the Marshal's office.

Once they were in position and at the proper altitude, Simon set the transport to hover and grabbed the winch cable as he unlocked the armor from the housing that had kept it secure. The cargo hatch opened and Simon stepped out, his stomach leaping up into his chest as the armor descended. The cable slowed his descent to the street below, but the armor itself still had to soak up a lot of the impact from the drop.

The landing was rough, the sight of the armor descending enough to scatter the crowd gathered around the Marshal's office. The crowd surged, a number of people holding up digital picture frames of missing loved ones and print outs showing lost wages. They pleaded with Simon for aid, believing he was Marshal Rider.

"She's not there," Ishihara said over the internal comm, observing the scene from above.

"No, her office is locked up tight. I don't want to open it up with all these people down here. There's a crowd of desperate folks, some saying they've waited for days to talk to the Marshal. I wish I could tell them I'm not her," Simon said, sadly.

"Play the part a little, at least look and listen some."

"Yeah, good idea, Camille," Simon said, walking about in the armor looking at the pictures being thrust up to the visor.

Simon made a good show of it, collecting reports and statements, the Aegis system recording the various complaints for him. After he'd listened to nearly sixty individuals, Simon used the winch on board the transport to haul himself and the Aegis Armor back up to the transport.

"That was useful," Simon said, over the internal comm.

"Yeah?" Ishihara replied, incredulous.

"All the complaints are geographically tagged. So I can assume that in a zone with a lot of complaints, the Marshal is not likely to be there," Simon explained.

"True."

Locked back into the transport, Simon turned the transport back to the traffic lanes and made for the Mechanical Zones. In one of the large transit tubes between zones, the transport sputtered again, forcing them to change course.

"The transport feels a little shaky again, kinda like before when we lost power for a moment," Ishihara said, looking blankly at the array of gauges and system reports on the panels in front of her.

"I need to check the relays. The last thing we need is to wreck somewhere and have transit authority checking our authorization to operate. Technically this thing isn't stolen, but I'm using it without proper authorization, which is almost as bad," Simon said, looking for a quiet place to land.

"We're in almost to an Entertainment Zone. Hopefully we don't need parts," Ishihara said, looking out the cockpit and frowning.

Setting down in a mostly empty parking lot of a fight palace, Simon unlocked the armor and strode outside to take a look at the engines. It was simpler than getting out of the armor and the gauntlets had motor control fine enough to open panels and rewire relays, if necessary. He'd opened the first panel when the armor's internal sensors alerted him to unlawful activity.

"*Assault in progress,*" the Aegis Armor said, bringing up a map of the area, and giving direction for the quickest route to respond.

"I'm not the Marshal, Aegis. What do you expect me to do?" Simon said, impatiently.

"You look like the Marshal. All you might have to do is show up," Ishihara joked.

"*Affirmative. A visual deterrent may be sufficient,*" the Aegis Armor intoned.

"Okay, fine," Simon said, turning the suit around and following the path holographically projected inside the visor.

Ishihara followed along, but kept her distance to avoid spoiling the illusion that the law had shown up. They rounded the corner, passing into a walkway between a local fight palace and a dance club. Sensors onboard the Aegis Armor picked up two individuals in the walkway, one male and one female.

A well-dressed man in penal facility teal was standing over an Ichthyic Metasapient woman. She was lying in a pool of her own blood, holding one hand up defensively. The Aegis Armor automatically kicked on a pair of bright illuminators as Simon approached, causing the man to turn and shield his eyes. The Metasapient woman looked to have taken a beating badly, like the man was just hurting her for sport.

"Step away from her," Simon said, struggling slightly to draw the Marshal's sidearm from the protected holster.

"There's no law being broken here, officer. I can do whatever I want to my own Metasapient," the man said, holding up an ID card in a plastic sleeve.

"*He is correct. Assault, rape, and murder laws do not protect Metasapient property from their owners,*" the Aegis Armor intoned.

Simon hesitated at first, but strode forward, weapon in hand. "At minimum, you are littering and causing a disturbance. I'm going to have to ask you to move along," he said, his voice modulated over the suit's PA system.

"Bitch, do you know who I am? You keep the rabble in line, and that's really all you're good for," the man said, dropping the blade he was carrying and using a handkerchief to wipe blood from his hands.

Simon stepped in between the man and the Metasapient woman. The man protested, again flashing his ID card in front of the sensors mounted on the Aegis Armor. His registry popped up on the suit's internal display. He was a Facility Management Executive in charge of refining. He wasn't bluffing when he said he was a big deal, making Simon regret having ever gotten involved.

"Yes, thanks for the warning. I'll take my property and entertain myself elsewhere. Sorry for creating a disturbance," he said, turning his back and walking over to where he'd set the choke collar he'd been using to 'control' his Metasapient property.

As he did, the Ichthyic woman rose, blade in hand, and slashed him along the forearm. Ordinarily, the Aegis Armor would have been fast enough to react. However, the mining suit actuators Simon had installed slowed response time just enough that he couldn't reach the blade in time. He did his best to restrain the Metasapient as she cried out in anguish, the man trying to grab the knife out of her hands.

Ishihara closed the distance and pushed the man to the ground. Without hesitating, she delivered a second solid blow to his head, knocking him out. "Let's get out of here."

"Camille, what have you done?" Simon said, the sensors internal to the Aegis Armor recording everything that had happened.

"Bring the fish girl and beat feet, Simon. If we're lucky, he won't report this to Mining Company Enforcement," Ishihara said, walking quickly back toward the parking lot.

"Yeah, if we're lucky," Simon muttered, catching the Ichthyic Metasapient before she collapsed.

CHAPTER 8

MARS COLONY, VEDTER MACHINEWORKS –
MECHANICAL ZONE 062

August 9th, 2200

Aunt Ruth awoke to the sound of watery gurgling and a clatter of tools being pushed to the floor in the workshop adjoining the living area. Rubbing her eyes, she slid off the couch into some slippers and went to investigate. Ishihara and Simon were doing their best to restrain a frantic Ichthyic woman on one of the work tables. She was hurt badly, panic and shock taking hold.

"You come home with another stray?" Aunt Ruth asked, filling a bowl with warm water from the shop sink.

"He gave her something. She's hallucinating," Simon said, nearly getting overturned by the flailing fishfolk.

Simon and Ishihara were both strong, but the Ichthyic was slippery, both because of her nature and the blood she was continually losing. She had several shallow cuts, but one long laceration in particular was the primary source of blood loss. Aunt Ruth managed to get the bowl of water under her head, instantly calming her down. It took forty minutes for Ishihara to get the wounds stitched up while Simon and Aunt Ruth held her down.

"I'm on fire, it feels like fire," she whispered feverishly, grasping at the gills around her neck.

"We need to move her to the tub," Aunt Ruth said, directing Simon and Ishihara to lift her up.

It wasn't easy to wrestle her into the tub, as she seemed to have unending endurance. Simon had to walk half of the flailing woman on his knees, as his leg braces weren't great at aiding him in lifting much beyond twenty additional pounds. Once she was in the tub, Ishihara held her up so she could roll some industrial tape over the freshly stitched wounds.

"You think that's necessary, Camille?" Simon asked.

"I'm not sure. With regular people, you don't want to submerge wounds like this. Mars water isn't the cleanest," Ishihara said, lowering the Ichthyic woman back into the water.

"Her owner going to come looking for her?" Aunt Ruth asked, shaking her head.

"Definitely," Simon said, directing an uneasy gaze toward Ishihara.

"What? You think we should have left her in the walkway and let that asshole carve her up some more?" Ishihara snapped, giving Aunt Ruth and Simon a clear view of both of her middle fingers.

"Fishfolk aren't people on Mars, they're property. This is theft, and pretty serious time in the teal depending on what type of Metasapient she is. If she's the high class pleasure type, it could be grand theft," Aunt Ruth said, frowning.

Simon nodded. "Camille, I think we should…"

"Get bent? That's what you can both do if you think I'm letting that guy take her back," Ishihara said, kneeling down and taking the Ichthyic's hand.

"That isn't what I was going to say. I need you to steady her while I pull her tracking chip. I'll run it around and ditch it somewhere," Simon said, pulling out a knife and a pair of pliers.

"You are both going to end up in the teal," Aunt Ruth said, shaking her head.

"Not if we do this right. I doubt the conglomerate can spare the adjusters to chase a rogue Metasapient right now given what we saw in the Port Zone," Simon said, patting Ishihara on the arm.

Aunt Ruth gave them both an angry stare that melted away to a sly smile as she turned to leave the bathroom. Simon cut the chip out of the fish girl's arm and walked out with it. Wrapping it in Styrofoam, he dropped it down the drain into running water, excess condensation carrying it quickly away into the colony's underground. When he returned, the Ichthyic was calm and awake, gazing down into the water of the tub.

She was covered in gold and green scales, her delicate features more pronounced now that she wasn't under intense stress. Ishihara sat on the toilet lid beside the tub holding her hand, looking up expectantly at Simon.

"I flushed the chip. Hopefully, they aren't able to derive enough positioning data from it to see that it stopped here for several minutes," Simon said.

"What's your name?" Ishihara asked, looking to the Ichthyic.

"Pearl," she said, her voice shaking in time with her own shivering.

"Why was that guy hurting you?" Ishihara asked.

"Mister Janjigian doesn't like it when I make mistakes, especially when meeting with important clients. I spilled a drink. The client noticed, and the meeting didn't go well. Mister Janjigian was angry. So, so angry, like I've never seen," Pearl said, looking curiously at Ishihara's hand clasping her own.

"You can never go back, Pearl. Do you understand?" Simon said, hoping he hadn't just made a colossal mistake.

Pearl frowned, tears welling up in her eyes. "Mister Janjigian is my owner. If I don't go back, I'll have nowhere to live."

"We'll work on that. Maybe the other Metasapients like you will…"

"They might not take her back. They are all very religious and could view her as having committed too many sins to be saved," Aunt Ruth said, coming back in with a cup of tea for everyone.

Pearl nodded sadly. "I am unclean, a whore."

"There's no atoning for that or whatever?" Ishihara asked.

"What religion do you follow?" Pearl asked.

"Shinto," Ishihara replied.

Pearl blinked, somewhat confused. "Does Shinto have Jesus?"

"No, no Jesus," Ishihara said, smirking.

"The Ichthyic Metasapients have their own version of Christianity and Islam, depending on the underground filtration system in question. The blue collar workers don't have a lot of use for the Type Five pleasure Ichthyic variety that gets shipped in from outside of Mars. They're infidels before they set foot off the boat, so to speak," Aunt Ruth explained.

Ishihara let out a long sigh. "Did we do Pearl a favor by freeing her?"

"Probably not," Aunt Ruth said, drinking her tea.

Ishihara wilted somewhat, looking sadly at Pearl.

"Pearl, you can't go outside, and you'll have to hide when people come by. We'll figure something out for you, but for now you need to keep out of sight. Understand?" Simon said, worriedly.

"I'm good at hiding," Pearl replied, nodding.

"Good, and um… try to make yourself useful," Simon said, averting his eyes as Pearl stood up in the tub, her torn and wet party dress clinging to her.

"And I'll find her some real clothing," Ishihara said, laughing.

The rest of the day was full of awkward moments as Pearl adjusted to her new situation. Simon could see she wasn't terribly bright, having been given little education, but she was good at reading people and guessing what they wanted. She only had to look at Aunt Ruth's face before she headed to the sink to do some dishes. Later, Pearl busied herself cleaning the workshop and living space.

Ishihara found her an orange Mining Company-issue jumpsuit and boots to wear and a matching rain slicker hat that dangled around her neck from a cord. She seemed baffled by the clothing at first, but eventually shrugged it off and continued flitting about the living space. Ishihara and Simon watched her for a while, making sure she wasn't doing anything to open her stitches.

"She's been beaten before, given how quickly she bounced back. Usually, when someone gets roughed up like that, they don't feel like cleaning house an hour later," Simon observed, sadly.

"She does heal quickly," Ishihara added, watching Pearl from the living area sort nuts and bolts at a workbench in the workshop.

"I wonder how she would do if I sat her down at my terminal and let her take some public access classes," Simon said, trying to figure out ways to keep their new roommate occupied.

After some instruction, Pearl took a few of the public education placement and acuity tests. Later, while Simon combed through the results, Pearl tried out the flight simulator he'd used to train himself to fly transports. Ishihara brought dinner that Aunt Ruth made over to a work table and pulled up a stool to sit down.

"You bring me any, Camille?" Simon asked.

"Oh, it's in there. She's got it set up buffet style by the stove," Ishihara said.

"Huh, she hasn't cooked like that in a while," Simon said, shakily rising from his chair.

"Sit, I'll go get it," Pearl said, patting Simon and moving hurriedly toward the living space.

Once Pearl was gone, Simon looked up at Ishihara, a look of defeat crossing his face. "She's not good at anything, Camille. Even if we tried to place her somewhere, these scores preclude even doing most manual labor. She's sort of good at math, but that is it."

"That's not true," Ishihara said, shoveling food into her mouth.

"I don't know what you mean," Simon said, frowning.

Ishihara pointed to the terminal, the scoring screen for the flight simulator laying over a three-dimensional rendering of a commercial transport that Pearl had just landed successfully. Simon traded seats, sitting down at the terminal and began scrolling through the results of Pearl's last simulated flight. He smiled broadly, turning and looking back at Ishihara.

"She's an ace. I've been practicing on this thing for two years and never scored half this good," Simon said, astonished.

"See, everyone has a talent," Ishihara said, feeling vindicated.

"Oh, yeah? What's yours?" Simon teased.

"Kicking snide little mechanics all around their own workshop. I punch faces pretty well, too. Want to see?" Ishihara asked, holding her knuckles under Simon's nose.

"Ha, I'm good," Simon said, holding up his hands defensively.

"This is great. She can help us find the Marshal. You can focus on doing computer stuff or whatever, she can fly the transport, and I'll take a nap," Ishihara said, finishing the last of her food.

"If we put her in a flight suit with a helmet, she'll probably pass casual examination if we have to land somewhere commercial. It could work, if she's willing," Simon said.

Pearl came back in, setting down a plate of food in front of Simon. "How did I do?"

"Oh, um, pretty good I guess. You ever fly a transport before?" Simon asked.

"Mister Janjigian made me learn, for some reason. I've flown nearly everything. I don't know why," Pearl explained, unconsciously scratching at the stitches along her side.

"Would you fly for us?" Simon asked.

"I'll do anything you say," Pearl said, putting on a practiced smile.

"No, no, do you want to fly for us?" Ishihara asked.

"I want whatever you want," Pearl said, maintaining the smile.

"Look, we don't own you. You're like our friend. We're just asking if you want to fly for us while we try to, um, help another friend," Simon explained.

"Sure, whatever you say," Pearl replied, nodding.

"Okay, if you could do whatever you wanted, what would you do?" Ishihara asked.

"Oh, I don't know. I don't want anything. What do you want me to do?" Pearl said, a vacant expression crossing her face.

"I don't feel good about this. Pearl, you don't have to fly for us. We'll try to place you somewhere else," Simon said, standing up.

Pearl snapped, falling to her knees and wrapping her arms around Simon's ankles. "No, please, I'll be good. I'll do anything. Please, don't get rid of me."

"Whoa, no, Pearl. No one is getting rid of anyone," Simon said, grabbing her by the arms and trying to lift her up.

Pearl leaned in, trying to kiss Simon, wrestling with her orange jumpsuit. Ishihara grabbed her and threw her down into a chair with one hand, steadying Simon with the other. Pearl looked up, confused, flinching slightly as Ishihara loomed over her.

"What the heck?" Ishihara said, looking at Simon.

"She's been conditioned to act this way. Apparently, getting rid of her was Mister Janjigian's favorite threat if he wanted something physical out of her," Simon said, frowning.

"We should have killed that guy," Ishihara growled.

Pearl closed her eyes and cried.

"No, we're not killing anyone," Simon said, trying to comfort Pearl.

She passed out, rendered unconscious from the stress. Aunt Ruth looked on from the living space, sipping her tea. Ishihara, feeling a little guilty for yelling at Pearl, picked her up and took her into Simon's bedroom so she could rest.

"I can fix her," Aunt Ruth said, setting her tea cup down on the saucer she held in her other hand.

"How?" Simon asked, leaning over a work table.

"The same way I helped a broken little boy recover from losing eighty-percent of the use of his legs," Aunt Ruth said, wistfully.

"I thought you didn't like the Metasapients."

"That girl stabbed her owner, right? She fought back," Aunt Ruth said, her face adopting a rare and grim expression.

"Yeah, I wasn't fast enough to stop her. She was pretty badly hurt, fight or flight probably kicking in," Simon said, nodding.

"A long time ago, before I met your uncle, there weren't Metasapients to abuse. Like her, I fought back, too. It's why I went into the teal for ten years," Aunt Ruth explained.

"You don't need redemption. Whoever you hurt back then probably deserved it," Simon said.

"Oh, if only that were true. No one deserves to have done to them what I did to the people I killed," Aunt Ruth said, sipping her tea.

"You've never talked about what you did before you came to Mars," Simon said, hoping for a story.

"Not much to tell. I came here alone as a child. My father was a butcher in North America, Northwest Province, old Montana," Aunt Ruth said, gathering up dishes from the workshop.

"And, Metasapients?"

"I don't hate them. I dislike the reasoning for bringing them here. Depraved assholes have been moving to Mars for decades because of the lax corporate regulations and laws on decorum. The Metasapients brought here filled a demand for a particular market, and when they didn't, they got discarded like strays. It isn't fair, but when I see one, I'm reminded by how barbaric humanity has become," Aunt Ruth said, dishes shaking in her grasp.

Simon paused, looking over at the Aegis Armor leaning up beside his heavy equipment workstation. The last few days had been a whirlwind of change and strange fortune. He hadn't considered what he'd do if he couldn't find the Marshal, or if she was dead. His own situation wasn't untenable, but things for Ishihara were difficult, and terminal for his Aunt. Adding someone else to his life was going to make things even complex, especially if Pearl's owner came looking for her.

He went to his room, finding Ishihara lying beside Pearl in his bed. Pearl was sleeping while Ishihara stroked the scales across the Ichthyic's forehead. Pearl would move, almost like she was running or swimming in slow motion. She'd make small gurgling noises, her gills flaring slightly as her eyes moved rapidly beneath her eyelids.

"She's been like this since I put her there. It's like she's dreaming, but can't wake up," Ishihara said, sitting up.

"I have dreams like that," Simon said, yawning and grabbing a blanket.

"Where are you going? You've got me and a former love-slave in your bed, and you're going to take the couch?" Ishihara teased.

"You know that's not funny, right?" Simon said, shaking his head and looking drowsily at the couch.

"Because you're a cripple? That does make it kind of funny," Ishihara said, smiling.

"I let my aunt tease me about it, but she's my aunt. Understand?" Simon said, leaning in the doorway.

"I'm bad at telling people how I feel," Ishihara stated.

"And how do you feel?" Simon said, growing impatient.

"You've been really good to me. I kind of wish you'd be shitty to me, try to take advantage or something. I'd like to not feel guilty about having no way to pay you back for helping me," Ishihara said, letting out a long sigh.

"Whatever, just stop, okay?" Simon said, heading for the couch.

"Okay."

Simon laid down on the couch, kicking his assistive leg braces off to the floor and pulling the blanket up over his head. He slept like a stone, waking up to find Pearl draped across him. He sighed, trying to push her off, but she had a death grip on him.

"Sorry, your place is cold," she said sleepily.

"Off. Get off of me," Simon said, as patiently as he could.

She slid to the floor watching him pull his leg-braces on over his pants. She observed him carefully, moving her hands in a way that mimicked his own. Simon stood up looking for Ishihara but she was already gone.

"She went to derby practice. Dell came by to pick her up again. You slept through it all," Aunt Ruth said.

"Did I miss out on you threatening him with a knife again?" Simon said, rubbing his eyes.

"No, he's marvelously well-behaved around me now," Aunt Ruth said, angrily.

"Did she say when she wanted me to pick her up, or where?" Simon asked.

"She wasn't sure, I guess there's going to be a change of venue. I think she was going to ride back with Dell," Aunt Ruth said.

Simon looked over at the pile of work orders slowly printing out by the office comm, a general apathy overcoming him. He'd lost a lot of work over the last couple of days, but it felt good to have a purpose beyond fixing broken condensers and filtration systems. He knew the other mechanics in the Zone would pick up the slack, glad for the work, but he wondered if he could ever go back to just being a turn-wrench in the Zone.

Pearl was crouched down by his feet, a sad expression hanging on her face. She fidgeted with her webbed fingers, frustrated because she'd broken some of her fingernails in the struggle from the day before. Simon took her hand and led her to the bathroom.

"Let's look at your wounds, make sure they aren't infected," Simon said, helping her get out of the orange jumpsuit Ishihara had given her.

Simon cleaned the wounds, having her lift up her shirt instead of completely disrobing.

"This is nice. No one has ever taken care of me like this before," Pearl said, almost recoiling from the words as she said them.

"This is how regular people act, Pearl. We do things for each other, just because," Simon said, dabbing disinfectant at her cuts.

"Why won't you love me? Do I not please you?" Pearl asked, closing her eyes.

"Sex isn't love, Pearl."

"Then, what is love?" Pearl asked, frowning.

"Oh no, now you've got a really old song stuck in my head," Simon joked.

"Sorry."

"Love is when you do things for others and expect nothing in return. You just like the person and want them to be well," Simon said, putting fresh bandages on Pearl's wounds.

"Okay. I like you, and I want you to be well. Can I fly your ship for you?" Pearl said, smiling.

"Yeah, you can, but I have to go to work. Can you stay here with Aunt Ruth and help her around the machine shop? We can maybe take the transport out tonight."

Pearl frowned. "She doesn't like me."

"My aunt Ruth is sick. I don't like leaving her here alone. Will you please help me look after her?" Simon asked, zipping up Pearl into her orange jumpsuit.

"Yes, I want you to be well."

CHAPTER 9

MARS COLONY, TERATON FIGHT PALACE – ENTERTAINMENT ZONE 113

August 10th, 2200

Ishihara dropped low on the grav-track, skating hard with her team-mates to block the opposing team's jammer, a girl calling herself Hell's Belle. She turned in the grav-lane and dropped her grav-boots to lock up, drawing down heavily on the artificial gravity. Hell's Belle came in hard, but Ishihara all but stopped her with over a minute on the jam.

"Watch the conversion, she's passing the Star," Dell said over their helmet coms, as Hell's Belle passed her Star helmet cover to the pivot player wearing the stripe.

The bout had gone well for the Black Dragons so far, but every time Dell "coached" over the comm, Ishihara would lose her focus. She could feel his wandering hands on her every time he spoke. The other girls on the team covered for her pretty well, but the Onna-Zumo Commission observers were recording every misstep.

Ishihara had been leading the other girls to "goatherd" the best blocker on the other team, but they were barely staying ahead in points. When she'd lock her skates up, she'd often struggle to run back or recycle when she bumped another blocker or jammer out of bounds. She was shaving seconds inside the jam, keeping them from scoring, but the Black Dragon's own jammer and pivot player weren't working together like they should.

The rest of the bout went quickly and, by the time it was over, Ishihara was tired, her arm sore from bringing the whip on the outside to give the jammer more momentum as she passed through the pack. Dell clapped as they skated back onto solid ground, clapping each girl on the back as they came back into the dugout.

"You burn up your quads again, Camille?" Violet Vera asked, coming up behind Ishihara.

"They held this time. None of the blockers with the Wrecker Zone Girls are as heavy as I am, fortunately," Ishihara said, reaching down and patting her grav-boots.

"Yeah, I hear that mechanic you've been staying with takes good care of your gear," Delilah Destroyer teased.

Ishihara brushed off the comment, skating back into the locker room, while the other girls shed some of their gear and chatted about the match. Dell was there waiting for her, leaning up against her locker. She paused in the doorway, powering down her grav-boots.

"Dell, not today, please," Ishihara said, lowering her head.

"You're calling yourself 'The Roman' has to do with your Shinto beliefs. Something about showing gratitude to the spirits so they don't hold a grudge, right?" Dell said, pushing off from the lockers and walking toward Ishihara.

"That's not exactly right, but yeah, basically," Ishihara said, rubbing her sore arm and looking back down the hall at the other girls.

"I'm kinda like that. If someone doesn't show me gratitude, I hold a grudge," Dell said, smiling crookedly.

"Okay, fine," Ishihara said, shedding her quads and harness before walking back into Dell's office.

He pulled the shutters and pawed her while gratifying himself. She shut her eyes the whole time, trying to think about anything else she could. His raspy breathing was nauseating to listen to and his sweaty hands and fingers seemed to have a touch that lingered even after they were gone. It was all she could do not to cry, clenching her fists.

"Don't worry, the fix is basically in. You'll get that championship run and be able to show gratitude to the spirits or whatever. Not sure how pure you'll be by the time you get there, though. You keep playing hard to get, I might have to change our little arrangement here," Dell whispered, before turning away to wash his hands.

"Yeah, okay," Ishihara said, sulking and crossing her arms in front of her.

The other girls were in the locker room now, changing. Dell lingered by the window, leering at them through the shudders. Ishihara consoled herself with the notion that at least he wasn't hassling anyone else. She hoped it would be a pattern that would persist.

"Can I go now?" Ishihara said, reaching for the door.

Dell put his hand on the handle, opening it for her in a gentlemanly manner. "Sure, doll."

A few giggles went up from the other girls, but they ceased when Ishihara emerged. Dell was confronted by a dozen icy stares from Ishihara's teammates. Ishihara looked up from her feet, catching sight of what it was they'd been giggling at before. There was a tall and very handsome man with long dark hair standing in the doorway looking somewhat surprised. The girls were changed and getting ready to leave, duffle bag and totes already slung.

"Who are you?" Cathy Crosskick asked.

"Sorry to intrude. I am a friend of Dell's," the man said with a thick Earth accent that placed him as being from somewhere in Eastern Europe.

"He's the pile of shit over there," Gloria Grande said, gesturing toward the office.

Dell came out, getting ready to light a cigarette, but nearly swallowed it at the sight. "D-Dragos, what an unexpected, um…what are you doing here?"

Dragos smiled, turning to look at Ishihara for a moment. "It's okay, I'm just here to talk."

"Stay where you are, Camille," Dell stammered, putting a hand on her shoulder.

"Dell, I just want to talk to your boss, Cerise Laplace. Tell me where she is and I'll go," Dragos said, taking off his jacket and hanging it from a hook at the end of a row of lockers. He had an obvious cybernetic replacement limb, unlike any of the crude prosthetics Ishihara had seen around the colony. It was sleek and well made, indicator lights just beneath his short sleeves blinking faintly.

"He's been hurting that girl," a woman said from somewhere behind Dragos.

A woman, not unlike Pearl, stepped out from behind the lockers, having quietly entered without being noticed. She was an Ichthyic Metasapient, but she was a wholly different variety. She was pitch black except for a bit of silver around her belly and under her chin. She was wearing a hijab that covered most of her features, but instead of the smooth flat teeth that Pearl had, she had a two rows of sharpened teeth, giving her a sinister appearance in spite of her calm voice.

"That true? Dell, he hurts you?" Dragos asked, looking at Ishihara.

"No," Ishihara answered, trying not to stare at the woman behind him.

"Dell, are you trying to end up in the teal again?" Dragos asked, smiling in a way that made Ishihara uneasy.

"There's no Marshal and no one at the administration level is going to mess with me. I'm protected," Dell said, nervously.

"Protected from me?" Dragos said, waving his hand at Ishihara to move aside, but she wouldn't budge.

Ishihara shoved Dragos backward, hard enough that his back hit the lockers. He came back with his fist raised, but the Ichthyic woman with him reached around his torso and held him at bay. Ishihara was scared, but she couldn't let anything happen to Dell. Without a coach, they couldn't compete and final team selection was coming soon.

"Why, Hashti? If this man is bad to her, why does she protect him?" Dragos said, scowling at Ishihara.

"She has her reasons, and we've no quarrel with her," Hashti said, handing Dragos his jacket.

"If I help you, will you leave Dell alone?" Ishihara asked.

"Bitch, you don't even know anything," Dell said, laughing cruelly.

"Then there's no harm in her helping us," Hashti said, cocking her head to one side.

Dell held up his hands and made for the door, departing hastily. Ishihara stood there, gazing at Dragos and Hashti, waiting to see what they were going to do. She expected that they were mercs sent by one of the mining conglomerates and that she'd stumbled into Mining Company business. She hoped the beating wouldn't be too bad and that she'd still be able to skate by the time the championship rolled around.

"Do whatever you're going to do," Ishihara said, sighing.

"She does know something. She's protecting not just herself, but others," Hashti said, looking at Ishihara.

"How do you know these things?" Ishihara asked, clenching her fists.

"Hashti knows things about people, even if they do not say them," Dragos said, putting his jacket on.

"I'm not going to tell you anything," Ishihara said, folding her arms.

"But, you've heard the name Cerise Laplace before. I could tell by your expression when Dragos said her name," Hashti said.

"So what?"

"You're angry, and she's hurt people you care about. We want the same thing," Hashti said, her sharp teeth extending beyond curled lips.

"If you want justice, you have to get your own," Ishihara said, defiantly.

Dragos nodded. "I like this one. She has fire."

Hashti paused, continuing to look at Ishihara, her cool blue eyes twitching in time as her nostrils sniffed the air. "Indeed."

"Tell us what you want, maybe we can help each other," Dragos said, putting his hands in the pockets of his jacket.

"You're Marshal Rider's friends, right?" Ishihara said, recalling what Simon had told her.

Dragos looked at Hashti, not sure how to respond.

"What if we are?" Hashti asked.

"I need to talk to her. Can you have her meet with me?" Ishihara asked.

Dragos squinted at Ishihara, letting out a long sigh. "What if we did?"

"I need to see her. You bring the Marshal to see me, I'll tell you about someone that knows things about this Cerise Laplace person you're looking for," Ishihara said, hoping Simon would appreciate the risk she was taking.

Hashti nodded. "We'll see what we can do. Come, Dragos. We've other leads to consider."

Dragos turned to go, pausing at the door. "I knew Dell in the teal. He and I worked for same boss long ago. He is not worth protecting."

"I'm not protecting him. I'm protecting my honor," Ishihara said, tucking her derby helm under her arm.

Dragos nodded. "I respect that, greatly. And Dell?"

"When it's time, he'll get his. Mars has its own way, am I right?" Ishihara said, directing her statement to Hashti.

"Indeed," Hashti said, sadly.

After they were gone, Ishihara changed into her street clothes and crammed her gear into her worn sea bag. The fight palace was alive with the usual gambling and "service industry" professionals, but there were Mining Company adjusters as well. Each was dressed in a black rubber suit, a data slate in hand as they went around assessing the property. It wasn't just team management that was changing hands, but venues and real estate associated with derby as well.

She wasn't sure how she was going to get back to the machine shop as the trams stopped running an hour ago and Dell was already gone. The fight palace had rooms, but they cost more for a night than she made in a month skating for the Black Dragons. It would be a long walk. She decided that would be better than trying to sleep on the streets in the Entertainment Zone or any of those adjoining it.

There was a steady stream of travelers taking the pedestrian routes between zones, many carrying all their worldly possessions with them. Ishihara listened to the conversations being held around her as they waited for the zone partition to open allowing foot traffic to move between zones. In these low places, condensation collected at one's feet, dripping down from the domed ceiling overhead.

Union contracts were being held in processing for days when it would usually take hours. People living pay package to pay package were losing their living spaces, forced to move constantly between zones to prevent getting fined by the colony system for vagrancy. Those too old or handicapped from working as a miner had little hope of escaping the teal. Fortunately, few Mining Company adjusters were servicing that traffic.

Ishihara heard people say that the mining company conglomerate was being split up, that the new CEO was already out of the picture and that his heirs were squabbling over his estate. Normally, the Ares System would quickly settle any such disputes, according to old Mars Standard Law, but it had not acted lately for some reason. As the partition opened, water rushed in past Ishihara's knee from the adjoining zone, many more bedraggled citizens of Mars slogging past her in the opposite direction.

"What's going on?" Ishihara asked a passing miner.

"Don't know, the water just started coming up into the streets."

Ascending into the adjoining Maintenance Zone, Ishihara looked around to get her bearings. The lighting that one usually used as a guide was dark, leaving the whole of the biological enclosure far overhead hanging like a dark and starless sky. She walked to a billboard designed to direct visitors to key locations in the zone, gazing across the fading painted surface.

In the distance, she could hear the shriek of metal tearing away from metal, and the rush of some kind of liquid, like a vast waterfall. There was a bright flash as green waste water flowed quickly past her feet. A moment later, the whole zone lost power, emergency lighting coming on sporadically around her. An alarm sounded with a mechanical voice sounding voice accompanying it, saying "Containment failure, please evacuate."

It was panic in the dark, people rushing for the partition. Ishihara chose to climb instead, grabbing handfuls of painted canvas across the billboard and kicking through the backing to create a makeshift ladder upward. Water, and what she guessed was reactor coolant, bubbled up from the street, blowing off the maintenance access ports. The whole lower level flooded along with about ten feet of the street level. Even atop the billboard, water threatened to touch Ishihara's boots.

People surfaced, doing their best to kick off mining coveralls and boots to avoid being dragged down. Several muffled explosions went off underwater somewhere, causing levels to rise even further. Ishihara quickly donned her harness and grav-boots, switching them to work off-track. She knew the power wouldn't last long without being in a fight arena, auxiliary power usually lasting only a minute or so, long enough to descend in an emergency. What she needed to do now, however, was to ascend.

The boots pulsed, allowing her to leap from the billboard to the side of a nearby two-story building. She pulled herself up by a drainpipe, the boots sputtering and flickering as they managed to counteract the artificial gravity just long enough to get her to the top. Once there, she quickly changed back into her boots and looked down at the rising water.

Transports were taking off from commercial access points around the zone, ferrying those fortunate enough to be nearby to safety. None appeared to be trying to pick up survivors from the water. Soon, there would be no escape.

Ishihara was afraid. Even knowing only a little about how the colony worked, she knew that water pressure being exerted against the biological enclosure could breach the containment. If that happened, it would expose everyone inside to the Martian atmosphere outside.

"Shit," Ishihara said under her breath, hugging her knees and watching the water rise slowly.

As emergency power faded, the updraft normal for the colony ceased, life support began to fail. It would take an hour for the air to start smelling stale. Ishihara pulled out her filter mask from her duffel bag, but it did little to help. It wasn't that the current atmosphere was going sour from being breathed, but that the pressure change was causing filtration systems to purge as they lost power. Toxic fumes being pumped from industrial sites to containment areas was leaking out, tainting the whole area.

Ishihara could see lights moving in the flight lane tunnels between zones, but there was a lot of gridlock with automated ore transport services clogging things up. People were lighting flares from the tops of several buildings and they were higher up than the squat two-story structure Ishihara was on. Even if rescuers made it through, she wouldn't be as visible as others. She could almost feel the shame of failing to show gratitude to 'The Roman,' her own place in the hereafter becoming uncertain.

Something came up out of the water in front of her, wastewater dripping off of it in a wide pool as it stood up on the roof. It was a sleek Ichthyic man, wearing goggles and carrying a waterproof satchel. Then, there was another and another until a small cadre of them were standing on the roof, gazing at her quizzically. They chatted in their own strange and silent language and with hand gestures before one came forward, holding out a small crucifix.

"Are you a friend of Jesus Christ, our Lord and Savior?" the fishfolk asked, his green-blue scales glistening in the dark.

Ishihara burst out laughing, but ended up in a coughing fit, breathing too much of the tainted air. "No, no I'm not," she said, feeling light-headed.

"Strange, I was so sure," the fishfolk replied, scratching at the tendrils across his chin.

"Why is that?" Ishihara asked, rubbing her burning eyes.

"I don't... what are the surface world words to explain?" the Ichthyic man asked, turning to a younger fishfolk.

"Pheromone marking ... you've been marked as a friend, by one of us," the younger one replied, waving a webbed hand at Ishihara.

"Pearl. I do have a fish-friend," Ishihara said, nodding.

The elder Ichthyic nodded, waving for Ishihara to follow. "Then, we should get you out of here, and take you to your friend. Surface-friends are very rare, and very precious. My name is Dag."

"I'm Camille. I appreciate the help, but I can't swim or breathe under-water," Ishihara said, shouldering her duffle.

"We can help you breathe. Some of us are trained to release a breath-able stream of air from our gills," Dag said, heading back toward the water.

"So, I hold onto your back, and sip at the bubbles?" Ishihara said, nervously.

"Yes, I know it sounds... counter-intuitive, but it works. It's like drink-ing from a fountain," Dag explained.

Ishihara looked around at the mayhem around her, then the black water down below. "How will I see?"

"It is pitch black down there, you'll have to trust that we know the way," Dag said, jumping into the water.

The rest of the cadre leapt into the water behind him with Ishihara following reluctantly along as well. Once in the water, one of them took her duffle while Dag threaded her arms around his shoulders. He helped her get accustomed to breathing from his gills just below the surface of the water and to look for the breathable air, by touch, with her face.

"What if the water gets so cold I can't feel my face?" Ishihara asked.

"Given what we swam through to find you, I'd be more worried about being scalded," Dag said, making sure she was holding on tight.

"Great..."

The fishfolk swam in a tight formation, at least as far as Ishihara could tell before the water got so dark they couldn't see anything. A school of regular fish followed along with them, occasionally tickling Ishihara's sides and face. The claustrophobia was maddening and it felt like they were under the water for an hour before they came up to give her a break. They were in one of the deep drainage tunnels, debris and rubberized components floating in the dirty water around them.

"Are we lost?" Ishihara asked.

"No, but the way that would lead us to your friend is blocked. We have to wait for the filtration system to cycle and then we can try to swim through," Dag said, pulling Ishihara over to shallower ground.

A sleek and very dark green fishfolk surfaced, a worried expression dominating his face. "Dag, the shift is behind schedule. All is not well."

"Our suspicions must be true. The human's machine God has died and the Christ Father visits upon them a flood in punishment," Dag said, pulling out a Bible from a waterproof satchel.

"Machine God?" Ishihara asked, looking down at the fetid water around her knees.

"Ares, the God of War. He is fallen. A Redeemer, one of the Ancients has brought a Destroyer back from the Stars, a blackened metal God to take his place. There will be a terrible reckoning," Dag said, thumbing through wrinkled pages of his holy book.

"Is all that in the book you've got there?" Ishihara asked.

"Under a certain interpretation, yes, a great deal. It is the portents of our oracles that concerns me most. They can feel the thrum and flow of the Colony and, more recently, a great absence. For a time, our Drone brothers and sisters vanished. We thought they'd been taken, perhaps by a Rapture, but when they returned, they brought something back with them," Dag said, closing the book, his ears quivering slightly.

Ishihara knew there must be some truth amidst the religious babbling, but she couldn't discern fact from misguided religious zealotry. Everyone had their own way of grappling with crisis and, while she wouldn't begrudge the fishfolk their method, she wished she knew more of what was really going on. Whatever it was, it had nearly been the end of her.

"Is there another way to the surface? I need to get home," Ishihara asked.

The fishfolk shuffled about nervously. "Yes, but it would take you through a sacred place. It is not a place we often go, because the entrance generally demands a special occasion."

"What sort of occasion?" Ishihara asked, curious about the fishfolk ways.

"Death. It is where we leave our dead to drift. The sacred waters protect the spirits of those that went on before us."

Ishihara gritted her teeth. "Then, no, we'll wait for the system to cycle. I'm already worried about angering the dead."

Dag seemed impressed by her sentiment, smiling slightly. "You are not like others. You make no demands of us and respect our ways. Pearl must have seen what so many others could not."

"I punched a guy in the face that was hurting her."

The gathered Ichthyic men seemed dismayed at the notion of violence, murmuring quietly.

"Um, Pearl doesn't believe she could ever return because of what the surface-dwellers made her do. Is that true?" Ishihara asked.

"With the exception of the very young born among us, we all suffered similar indignities. Our masters lied to us all, to keep us compliant to their desires. We would welcome her with open arms and help her cleanse of all sin," Dag said, prompting an "amen" from the rest of the cadre.

"She'll be glad to hear that," Ishihara said, smiling.

The tunnel shook, making the water choppy and sending Ishihara down to her knees in the muck. Dag quickly helped her up, but the water began to rise rapidly. Signaling to the others to prepare, Dag turned so Ishihara could cling to his back.

"Hold on as tight as you can," Dag said as water filled the tunnel.

The water was as black and lightless as before. Ishihara struggled to find the air stream coming off of Dag's gills. She could hear metal grinding against metal as the water pressure shifted, shunting them violently through a drainage tunnel. Finally, the tight current fell away as if they had just come into a much larger cistern.

She and Dag were violently separated for a moment as a new and powerful current forced them upward. She held her breath and did her best to limit her movements. Each second without air felt like an eternity, but her athletic discipline served her well in keeping calm. She could feel Dag next to her, bubbles tickling her face once more. She reached out, grabbing hold of him.

The school of fish returned, following along with the cadre brushing against Ishihara as they had before. They were all swimming very fast now, the water almost pressing her eyelids open as they took hard corners and swam at ever higher speeds in the straightaways. Dag didn't feel frantic, each movement and flip of his webbed feet a tightly controlled exercise as though he'd done this many times.

Light surrounded Ishihara. Even with her eyes closed, she could tell they were in a bright place. The water was full of sound, heavy machinery churning in the water as Dag turned hard in the water, one arm reaching up to grasp her hands clasped about his shoulders. The school of fish about her scattered as the jets of water blasted up from below where they swam.

Expanded metal bore them upward, an ancient deep shaft mining elevator bringing them up above the waterline, a well-lit passage above extended to what Ishihara guessed was the surface. Above the sounds of hydraulics hissing and chains creaking as the platform rose, she could hear footfalls and murmuring filtering down.

"Almost home," Dag said, gesturing for one of his allies to give Ishihara her duffel.

"Woo, thanks you guys," Ishihara said, taking the duffel and slinging it over her shoulder.

"Thank Christ, Him we serve," Dag said, smiling.

"Sure, yeah, I totally will," Ishihara said, harboring no plans to actually do so.

The elevator stopped within arm's length of some sort of maintenance access. Dag turned the wheel on the hatch, slowly unlocking it from within. Fishfolk hands held Ishihara aloft until she was able to pull herself upward. She was between two rail lines adjoining a closed tram station in the same Mechanical Zone as Simon's Machine Shop. He wasn't far away now.

"A couple of you should come with me, and meet Pearl," Ishihara said, looking back down.

Dag nodded. "Of course."

CHAPTER 10

**MARS COLONY, REFINING LINE ALPHA 772 –
MECHANICAL ZONE 062**

August 10th, 2200

Simon turned the wrench one last time, making certain the new component rested securely in the housing and waved to the foreman to start the line up again. Within moments, the conveyors were carrying refined ore to be packaged for transport once more. After getting a signature and a promissory for vouchers owed, Simon shouldered his satchel and shambled out the door. His leg braces were low on power, but he didn't want to take the time to change them out in the streets. He'd been trying to build up his lower body strength anyway.

"Thanks again for coming out, Simon," the foreman said, stepping out for a smoke.

"Sure, Jahiem. Sorry it took me so long. Everyone in the Mechanical Union is being run ragged these days," Simon said, wishing he'd been able to avoid this bit of post-work chatting.

"Adjustors came by looking for you," Jahiem said, worriedly.

"Yeah? Am I late on my loan payments or something?" Simon said, playing it as cool as he could.

"They didn't say, but they offered to throw around a lot of money in case you turned up."

Simon froze, wondering how that had played out.

"How long do I have?"

"Pretty sure their bodies are far enough down the line now that it'll be days before they get discovered. You've got friends on the line, but if this had been Bhurge's line, or the guys on 774 you might not have gotten lucky. Whatever you're into, best settle it quick, boy," Jahiem said, his grim face illuminated by the bright cherry at the end of his cigarette.

"I will, thanks."

The foreman nodded and headed back in.

Simon wondered if this was about Pearl, or the transport he'd borrowed, or something else he'd done recently. Regardless, the mining company conglomerate didn't send adjustors unless they were going to take something by force. Simon swallowed his pride and found a bench so he could swap out power supplies on his leg braces. Then he went home as quickly as he could.

The streets were full of mayhem. Public announcement terminals were filled with static as a result of some kind of outage. Whatever was going on, it was hitting the Administration Zones hard. They were struggling to keep order, which made Simon worry all the more about adjustors coming to visit him. If things were that dire, it'd have to be a big deal to shake loose enforcers to hassle a crippled mechanic.

Pearl was outside waiting for him, hands clasped together. Simon covered his eyes, wondering how many people passing by had seen her and reported her presence. She was distinctive enough looking, even for an Ichthyic, that if her owner was looking for her she'd be easy for headhunters to find.

"What are you doing outside, Pearl?" Simon said.

"One of the Maintenance Zones between here and the Fight Palace Entertainment Zone was compromised. At least two zones are flooding with water," Pearl said, somewhat panicked.

Simon stumbled past her quickly into his workshop and switched on his terminal. Aunt Ruth was leaning heavily in the doorway between the living area and Simon's workspace. She looked gravely ill.

"Aunt Ruth, are you alright?" Simon said, rushing over to her.

"Camille, she's not back yet. It's been hours. If she tried to go through Mechanical Zone 059…"

Simon looked down at his terminal and checked the Colony Status updates. He read the screen closely for closures and emergency protocols, trying to figure how much of the flooded Entertainment and Mechanical Zones were still accessible. It was grim reading, as thousands of workers were already listed as missing, including Camille who had checked in at a zone partition currently underwater.

"Pearl, suit up," Simon said, unlocking the Aegis Armor and opening the repair bay.

"Do you think Camille is still alive?" Pearl asked, grabbing a flight suit from a hook by the backdoor.

"If she is, I have a pretty good idea of where to look," Simon said, pulling himself up into the Aegis Armor.

"*Patrol parameters?*" the Aegis Armor intoned, the onboard AI booting up quickly.

"Personnel recovery and disaster relief," Simon said, selecting from one of the many options arrayed in front of him.

"*Acknowledged. Accessing Colony Facility Records.*"

Simon piloted the suit out to the transport, accessing the loading port and locking himself into the transit hold. Pearl was already at the helm, prepping the transport to take off. She donned the old flight helmet Simon had found for her and checked the comm.

"Can you hear me?"

"Yeah, take off as soon as we're ready," Simon replied.

"*We can hear you, pilot.*"

"Who was that? It sounds like another lady is in here with us," Pearl said, looking around.

"It's the armor I'm wearing. It has an onboard AI," Simon explained.

"It has a Machine God? Wow!" Pearl said, bringing the transport up hard.

An alarm went off inside the ship, indicating an unsafe pattern, along with a proximity alert. Pearl disengaged the safety protocols and brought the ship around burying the throttle. Simon held on tight as she flew up through the flight traffic lane, dodging around other aircraft with little regard for their comfort or safety.

"Pearl, take it easy. We need to fly in a way that won't be suspicious," Simon said, gritting his teeth.

"We must hurry, yes?" Pearl said, dropping back into the traffic at a normal pace.

Simon didn't immediately respond, checking the traffic report carefully for official Mining Company vehicles and personnel. The Aegis Armor automatically scanned the various radio frequencies, trying to aid in Simon's search. The search came back negative with only regular colony traffic coming back across the holographic display inside the Aegis Armor.

"Punch it," Simon said, hoping Pearl was as good a pilot as he suspected.

She flew within inches of other transports sitting idle in the traffic lane, coming dangerously close to the top of the atmospheric enclosure and gantries in transit tubes between zones. Throughout the harrowing flight, she never touched another aircraft, retaining wall, or bulkhead. The transport wove in and out like a fish in a school around other slower moving fish, until they managed to squeeze out into the flooded Mechanical Zone.

There were bodies in the water between the buildings and dwellings below, as well as many people huddled on rooftops and balconies above. Habitation spires were without power and the atmosphere outside the transport was deemed dangerous by sensors. Activating searchlights, Pearl brought the transport in low looking for Ishihara amidst the destruction below.

"I don't see her," Pearl said, sounding frantic on the comm.

"Stay calm, go slow over the rooftops. She had grav-boots and she's in good physical condition. She'd have a better chance to survive this than most," Simon said, doing his best to grapple with his own helplessness.

"There's so many other people, why is nobody trying to get them out?" Pearl asked, lingering on a few people huddled on a rooftop.

"I don't know. This doesn't feel like your usual Mining Company insurance fraud. Lock the crew compartment and let's grab as many as we can. Maybe someone will have seen Ishihara," Simon said, unlocking the Aegis Armor from the transit bay.

Simon locked the drop cable to the armor, and opened the cargo bay door as Pearl brought the transport to hover near a rooftop. The people ran toward the transport at first, but hesitated at the sight of what they thought was the Marshal. Everyone wearing teal looked on fearfully for a moment until Simon dropped the visor on the armor revealing his face.

"I'm Simon Vedter from Mechanical Zone 062. Get in right now or I'm leaving you behind," he bellowed, over the roar of the engines hovering VTOL mode.

"You the new Marshal?" a mechanic asked.

Simon looked at the name placard on his coveralls. "Drake, I'm just repairing the armor for her. Figured she wouldn't mind if I used it to grab a few hapless citizens out of this mess."

"How can we help?" Drake asked.

"Plug your radio into the comm on the wall over there. Try to raise the other people in your union. We'll pick them up," Simon said, using the armor to haul up the sick and the wounded from the rooftop.

"Will do. Anything else?" Drake said, plugging into the com.

"I'm looking for someone. Her name is Camille Ishihara, she's a roller derby girl," Simon said, pulling the last of the people inside.

"You mean, The Roman? I heard a couple of guys coming over from E-Zone talking about how they'd seen her," Drake said, setting the frequency on his radio.

"You sure?"

"Oh yeah, she's a big deal, and distinctive enough looking. Not many real Japanese skating in the onna-zumo roller derby," Drake replied.

"Do what you can," Simon said, signaling to Pearl to take off.

"If she's here in the zone, we'll find her. Don't worry," Drake said, dropping coordinates into the com for the other people in his Mechanics Union.

Pearl flew for hours while Simon used the suit and the second drop cable on board the transport to extract as many people as the transport could handle. The radio chatter came back with a few reports of people who had seen Ishihara, but no one knew where she was. They couldn't linger for long and look as many of the people on board were hurt and suffering exposure to the tainted environment.

"Where'd you find your pilot? Never seen anyone hold one of these old Mining Company rigs in VTOL as steady as this," Drake asked, as Simon helped a handful of people in from a balcony.

"You wouldn't believe me if I told you," Simon said, smiling to himself inside the Aegis Armor.

Pearl raced back through the transit tunnel past stalled automated transports, and similar, that were mostly blocking egress. Passengers on the interior watched nervously out the ports as there was barely enough room for her to squeeze by. When they broke out to the other side, there was a crowd in the streets below that included volunteer medical personnel waiting for them.

As the transport set down in the streets, people cheered rushing forward to aid the beleaguered mechanics and their families as they disembarked. Only a few volunteer union medics were there to render aid, the majority of the crowd wanting a glimpse of the mechanic responsible for the rescue. Simon stepped out and, over the armor's PA system began asking people if they'd seen Camille Ishihara, "The Roman." A few said they'd seen her in the flooded Mechanical Zone, but no one knew where she was.

"We going back in?" Drake asked, stepping back out of the crowd.

"You were in there for a while breathing that poisoned atmosphere. You up for this?" Simon asked.

"Someone needs to fly, someone needs to work the winch, and someone needs to run the radio," Drake said.

"True. Just get a rebreather before we go," Simon said.

"Besides, it's not every day you get to fly with a bona fide folk hero," Drake said, smiling broadly and gesturing to the crowd as they stepped back into the transport.

People clapped their hands as the transport went back up into the sky, the street filled with hopeful faces as the lone transport prepped to return to the ruined Mechanical Zone. They hadn't even been to the adjoining Entertainment Zone yet, but reports indicated that flooding was minimal and life support was still on. Simon hoped the situation wouldn't worsen.

"How long do we keep flying?" Pearl asked over the internal comm.

"Until we find Camille, or we burn up the coils," Simon said, closing the cargo bay door.

"That a fishfolk accent I hear?" Drake said over the radio.

"If it's a problem, you're welcome to get out and walk," Simon replied, unapologetically.

"No problem, but you're right. No one would believe it," Drake said, laughing.

They had to push another transport that had drifted into the side of the transit tunnel to get through, a difficult maneuver for an advanced pilot, but Pearl pulled it off easily without damage to either vehicle. Once they were back on the other side, it was clear things were worse. Internal sensors warned of an imminent containment breach and that Facility Control would likely close the transit tunnels soon. They commenced with recovery operations anyway, grabbing up anyone Drake could locate on the radio or that Pearl could detect visually.

"We're getting full again," Drake said, helping people find somewhere to sit or hold onto while standing.

"We can't stay too much longer anyway. Flying in this toxic atmosphere is burning up the coils. The ship was designed for a near vacuum or a cleaner interior colony environment. Pearl, check the engines," Simon said over the interior com.

"They are at sixty-eight percent and declining at seventeen percent per hour, um...I'm not sure how much flight time we have with a full cargo bay," she replied.

"We'll have about ninety minutes before we risk losing one of the engines," Simon said, doing the math in his head.

"These things fly pretty well in the red. The Mining Company always understates operating tolerances," Drake said, continuing to input coordinates to the comm station.

"Would you bet your life on that?" Simon asked.

"There's still a lot of people and families out there waiting for us to pick them up," Drake said sadly.

"Pearl, can you put us down in the water? We might be able to manually purge the coils, give us another couple of hours in the air," Simon said, pulling the cargo hatch closed and pressurizing the cabin.

"Yes," Pearl replied, looking for a rooftop just beneath the surface of the water.

Once the transport was down on a rooftop and partially submerged, Simon remotely activated engineering protocols opening up the coils. Cool flood water poured in slowly soaking the burnt coils, internal scrubbers working to clear collected debris. The evacuees inside shuffled nervously as the transport went silent, the sound of water washing against the outside the only sound.

After a few minutes, Simon purged the coil chambers and set them to power up slowly to burn off any water that remained. Once he was sure they were dry enough, he powered the transport back up again, the interior lights growing brighter as the engines began to cycle. Pearl took them up quickly, clearing the water line and heading toward the next set of coordinates.

"Seventy-nine percent and declining at eight, we should have a little more flight time now," Pearl reported.

"That's good, too good. The water must have been mixed with a heavy amount of reactor or machinery coolant," Simon said, looking worriedly at Drake.

"Good for the coils, bad for the zone...maybe the whole colony," Drake said, knowing that critical facility systems had likely been compromised for that concentration of coolant to be in that quantity of water.

"With it rising to the top, we're talking about surface tension across an entire colony zone. That's a lot of coolant," Simon said, thinking out loud.

"Even if they drain the water, it'll be months or longer before people will be able to return to their homes and workplaces, myself included," Drake replied.

"It'll be good work for people who are EVA certified," Simon said, preparing to grab the next group of people.

"True and we'll both have enough hazardous environment experience to qualify after this," Drake joked, holding his rebreather up to his face.

Drake paused, listening to the radio, pulling his rebreather aside to reveal a smile. "They found her. Someone said they saw 'The Roman' back in M-Zone 062."

"Try to verify..."

"It's real, she's asking for you," Drake said, patching the radio signal over to the suit.

"Where are you, Simon?" Ishihara asked.

"I'm looking for you in the flooded M-Zone," Simon said, greatly relieved to hear her voice.

"I was there. It's pretty bad," Ishihara replied, the sound of people clapping their hands, in the background.

"We're going to grab as many people as we can and then we'll be back."

"Don't do anything stupid, Simon. See you soon," Ishihara replied.

"Will do."

There was a mixed crowd of mining workers and Ichthyic Metasapients at the next set of coordinates, all clustered on top of a flooded refinery. The miners were clearly standing away from the fishfolk, their faces indignant. As Simon opened the cargo bay and set to receive passengers, the miners shoved their way to the front, trying to hedge out the Metasapients.

"Don't let them aboard. Save the space for some real people," the orange jumpsuit clad individual bellowed.

Simon looked over at the terrified Metasapients that were clearly just cooking and cleaning staff at the refinery. Before the first mining worker could step aboard, Simon moved the suit in the way, blocking their pack. The miners tried to push aboard, but the Aegis Armor made Simon frighteningly strong. He pushed them back with ease.

"*These citizens are correct. Hierarchically speaking, they have personhood and the Metasapients are property,*" the Aegis Armor intoned.

With the visor down, only Simon could hear the suit.

"Aegis, in the absence of those laws, would you see a quantifiable reason to protect these miners and not the fishfolk?" Simon asked, looking over at Drake.

"*Negative.*"

"Is that particular law a just law?" Simon asked.

"*I would defer to you to adjudicate such matters.*"

"Great, I'm not leaving anyone behind," Simon said, waiving for the Metasapients to come over.

One of the miners rushed to the side, arms outstretched. "I'm not getting on board with any fishfolk."

"The pilot is a fishfolk," Drake bellowed, laughing at the miner.

"This isn't a sanctioned transport?" the minor asked, dumbfounded.

"No, and no one else is coming. This guy is risking his neck out here trying to help you. You want to stay, that's fine," Drake said, half-yelling over the sound of the engines.

The miners, suitably diminished by the circumstances, boarded along-side the Metasapients. They took up places separate from one another inside the cargo hold, tensions still running high. Simon closed the hatch and switched to the internal comms.

"Pearl, get us out of here," Simon said, wearily.

"There's still room in the hold and more coordinates," Pearl replied, taking the transport up slowly.

"Running power armor takes a degree of physical conditioning I clearly do not possess. I'm running on fumes here," Simon replied, relying heavily on the exoskeletal assistance systems to keep upright.

Pearl pulled the transport up and around the exhaust spires on the refinery to landing area reserved for automated transports dropping off ore. Once the craft was safely on the platform, Pearl opened the pilot compartment and stepped out. She motioned for Simon to sit down and raise his visor.

"You're burning up in there. It's too hot," Pearl said aloud, in front of a group of exasperated miners.

"It's probably the mining suit actuators and components. They're designed for EVA work where heat dissipation isn't an issue. Working in an environment for too long, they'll cook the pilot," Simon said,

"Water, give me your water," Pearl said, beckoning for the Metasapients to come over.

They did, producing several containers of water they'd been hiding. Drake looked on with a concerned expression as Pearl helped Simon drink. A couple of the miners came forward, hands clasped together. Pearl stepped up to meet them, her face uncharacteristically stern.

"About what we said before, apologies. Tell us how to help," the miner said, nodding to Simon.

"Do we need to do the same with the suit as we did with the engine coils? Submerge in water?" Drake asked.

"I can work the service winch," one miner said.

"C'mon, let's hook him up before he cooks in there," another said.

"I'll get us out over the water," Pearl said, heading to the cockpit.

Simon wondered if the miners would actually hoist him back up or just drop the cable and the suit in the water and let him drown. It was all slightly less risky than disembarking from the suit itself. Once they had the winch hooked up, they dropped him slowly into the water as Pearl held the transport in position. The water was extremely cold, quickly cooling the armor and Simon as well.

"Thanks, Pearl," Simon said over the comm.

"Is it working?" she said, engine protocol tones coming back over the comm.

"Yeah. We okay up there?" Simon asked.

"Mostly, hovering like this is hard on the transport."

"I'm cool enough. Pull me up."

As Simon was carried up, a miner passed by him on the way down, thrown from the transport above. As Simon stepped up over the precipice into the cargo hold, it was Drake at the winch controls instead of the miner that had been there before.

"We have a problem?" Simon asked.

"No problem, Boss. Ready to get some more people?" Drake said, nodding to the other miners.

"Yeah, let's get all we can," Simon said, nodding to Pearl.

They gathered everyone they could until Drake could find no one else on the radio. The cargo hold was crowded and hot, but everyone was glad to be there. Old Mining Company jingles were sung as the transport pushed back through the transit tube and through to the M-Zone 062. A larger crowd had replaced the smaller one where Pearl had landed previous. Orange triage tents had been erected and a few meager supplies waiting for those that had been rescued.

The crowd was comprised of miners, mechanics, scavengers, and a few low-ranking Mining Company officials standing about watching the transport come in to land. As the cargo doors opened, a cheer went up from the crowd as beleaguered people exited, holding up their hands, tremendously relieved to have been rescued. Mining Company officials pushed their way to the front, confronting Simon.

"You're in violation of a dozen Colony Statutes. This transport is Mining Company property. Your pilot has a reclamation notice filed on her," the Mining Company official said, eliciting angry booing from the gathering behind them.

"Oh man, what do I do about this?" Simon said aloud to himself, visor still down.

"Tell them you requisitioned the transport via the Marshal's Lawful Authority, under Title 7, Subsection 5," the Aegis suit intoned quietly.

"Um, this is my transport now, under Title 7, Subsection 5," Simon stammered, waving dismissively at the officials.

"And the pilot? Did you know she stabbed her owner?" the second official said, angrily.

"Tell them you witnessed the crime and issued a summary judgement in her favor, ruling her actions self-defense," the Aegis Armor intoned, bringing up the necessary documents for transmission.

"I've got documents already prepared. I issued a summary judgement in her favor. She was defending herself," Simon replied, using the flex monitor to transmit the documents to the Mining Company authority servers.

"Our employee is free to treat his property however he sees fit and…"

The Aegis Armor brought up an obscure law on the display in front of Simon. The law clearly listed Metasapients capable of skilled labor, as protected colony assets.

"He isn't allowed to kill her if she qualified to perform skilled labor. Show them, Pearl," Simon said, gesturing for his pilot to come forward.

Pearl hesitantly unzipped her flight suit, revealing a long and ugly wound stitched up along her side. The gathered individuals gasped and murmured at the sight, making Pearl cover her face in embarrassment. Simon set his comm to transmit only to Pearl's flight helmet.

"Pearl, you did nothing wrong," Simon said, casting an angry gaze at the Mining Company officials.

"So you're the Marshal of Mars, now?" the Mining Company official sneered.

"I guess I am. Unless you have further business in this M-Zone, I'd get going before I ticket you for loitering," Simon warned, putting a hand on his firearm.

"*Also, you are hindering an emergency recovery effort. White or orange, it'll land you in the teal for a minimum of five years.*" Aegis added, over the suit's PA system.

"And them?" the Mining Official growled, pointing back at the crowd.

"Looks like a lawful assembly to me. These people are aiding refugees from zones suffering from flooding. I hope it doesn't turn out to be Mining Company malfeasance at work," Simon said, loud enough for the crowd to hear.

The Mining Company officials were forcibly removed, an angry crowd escorting them to the tram station. Simon made sure everyone had at least some accommodation before stepping back into the transport with Pearl. It was a short hop home from there where Ruth and Ishihara were waiting on the rooftop patio of the machine shop for their return.

"Get me out of this thing," Simon said, once they were safely inside the machine shop.

Ishihara pulled him out, reaching for his assistive leg braces at first, but faltering when she saw the burn marks on his work suit. "Shit. It's Simon's turn to lay in the tub while we do some first aid."

"What happened?" Aunt Ruth asked, grabbing an armful of clean rags from a worktable.

"The suit gets too hot if operated for long," Pearl said, clasping her hands together in worry.

"Shit, shit, shit, shit," Ishihara said, gently lowering Simon into the tub.

"Who are they?" Simon asked, pointing to a pair of fishfolk sitting in the shower stall on the other side of the bathroom.

"That's Dag and one of the fishfolk that helped me escape the flood-ing," Ishihara said, helping Ruth get Simon out of his work suit.

Pearl looked at them shyly, waving meekly.

"Well, these burns aren't too bad. I've seen worse from grav-boot con-tact burns. We can fix this," Ishihara said, opening the first aid kit on the wall.

"I guess it's good that I have limited sensitivity in my legs," Simon lamented.

"Yeah, well, the burns I can treat, but there's nothing I can do for your spindly chicken legs," Ishihara joked.

"Thanks. Thanks for that," Simon said, laughing.

Once Simon was reasonably comfortable, everyone but Ruth retreated to the living area, Dag and his associate picking at Pearl's flight suit. "Do they hurt? These air-breather clothes?" Dag's associate asked.

"No, not compared to a lot of things," Pearl said, eyes firmly on her feet.

"Ishihara told us a little about you. You've nothing to fear, many of us began our lives up here," Dag explained, putting a hand on Pearl's shoulder.

"I stabbed a man. I was going to kill him," Pearl said, sadly wringing her hands.

"He was hurting you. You were protecting yourself," Dag said.

"No, he'd been stopped. I lashed out. He'd been hurting me for a long time. I messed up and he got carried away punishing me. It's my fault," Pearl said, shaking her head.

"Are you penitent? Do you reject whatever sin of the hands or mind you may have committed?" Dag asked.

"I still harbor dark feelings for him. If I ever got the chance, I don't know that I would spare him. My anger is great," Pearl explained.

"This sounds like the truth you speak, a sign that you are penitent even if you aren't willing to forsake the sin," Dag said, nodding to his associate.

"It sounds like equivocating to me," Pearl said.

"Perhaps. What good have you done?" Dag asked.

"I flew a transport that rescued lots of people from flooded zones," Pearl said, smiling a little.

"We rescued but only one, and only because she'd been marked as a fish-friend. You were not as discerning, helping anyone that would climb into your transport. Your deeds speak to your good heart more than a few dark thoughts. Come with us, sister," Dag said, beckoning.

Pearl looked up, the sadness in her face returning. "Marshal Simon needs me. He needs someone to fly."

"Perhaps we should let him make that decision? Does he want you to?" Dag said.

"Even if he doesn't, I want you to stay. Simon is a shit pilot compared to you, Pearl," Ishihara said, chiming in.

Pearl laughed.

"Look, Pearl, Simon and I won't tell you what to do, but you are wanted here. It sounds like Dag and his people want you, too. Revel in the choice, it's rare on Mars you get any kind of choice to decide your fate," Ishihara said, heading back into the bathroom.

"Well?" Dag said, holding out his hand.

"If I go with you and I don't like it, can I leave?" Pearl asked.

Dag hesitated for a moment. "Ours is a secret place and we'd need to come to trust you before we could let you leave."

"Then I'll stay here for now. At least until the job is done," Pearl said.

"Will it ever be done?" Dag's associate asked.

"I think so. Once we return the armor to the real Marshal, Simon won't need me to fly," Pearl said.

"He is not the real Marshal now?" Dag replied.

"I don't know," Pearl said, confused.

"Maybe you can find out who you are, together," Dag said, smiling.

CHAPTER 11

MARS COLONY, SECURE UPPER MANAGEMENT BUNKER, ADMINISTRATIVE ZONE

August 10th, 2200

"Have you given any consideration to what will happen if this does not work?" Octavo muttered, looking up at Cerise.

"Of course. You won't get your revenge on Dragos Dalca and Ouroboru wrests control of the Mars Colony from us."

Octavo paused, looking at the android arrayed in front of him. It looked back and, even though it was all in pieces, it was still willing to serve. Cerise approached and grasped the hand he'd been using to guide the cutter to disassemble the android in a wakeful state.

"Some sacrifices have to be made. We can't build our collective facility maintenance entity without testing their tolerance to pain and their mechanical threshold to continue functioning in spite of it," Cerise said, pressing her other hand across Octavo's scarred face.

"They're like children," Octavo said, frowning.

"Sounds like you're soft for these machines. They aren't real people. You know that, right?"

"Even if they were, I wouldn't care. I did a lot worse to get into the teal for the stretch you rescued me from. Dragos broke the orbital around my eye. It took the medic hours to put me back together and I still can't taste anything on the right side of my mouth," Octavo said, resuming to inflict agony on the android.

"Then what is the problem?"

"Children are unpredictable. You think you've broken them, but they can go and surprise you when you least expect it," Octavo growled, recalling how he ended up in the teal in the first place.

"I've some…particular experience in that area. Motivating synthetic children is something I've done before and can do successfully again," Cerise explained, walking around behind Octavo.

"You'll need it if this Ouroboru guy has a real Omega class, facility-grade artificial intelligence. This collective we're building won't even be able to compete for colony control," Octavo said, shrugging off Cerise's advances.

Cerise grabbed up a wooden chair and broke it over Octavo, sending him to the ground. The android on the table gasped and gurgled in surprise, whining pitifully. Cerise grabbed Octavo by the hair and held him fast while she straddled him on the floor.

"It's hard to go on without your confidence, Octavo. Why do you want to hurt me like this?" Cerise said, twisting Octavo's hand around up to his face, still clutching the surgical cutter.

He knew better than to fight her when she was like this. If he fought her, she would really hurt him. Cerise began to fumble with the zipper on Octavo's jumpsuit but paused, a sad expression crossing her face. She rose, letting the cutter drop to the floor a little too close for Octavo's comfort.

"I miss Archie. He would at least try to hurt me back, make me really feel something," Cerise said, more to make Octavo feel inferior, as opposed to genuine longing.

"Yeah, we all miss someone," Octavo said bitterly, sitting up and pulling the zipper on his jumpsuit back up to cover his narrow frame.

Cerise lit a cigarette and walked over to the table where the android lay disassembled. The android turned and looked up at her, face half in pieces from Octavo's meddling. She smiled up at Cerise, her programming telling her to appear compliant and friendly.

"This is not unlike what I will do to the colony itself and our enemies. I will tear them apart for our own purposes. They will thank us for the opportunity to serve," Cerise whispered, holding the burning end of her cigarette over the android's eye.

Octavo batted Cerise's hand aside. "Not the optic assembly. I need all of them intact as they are they have the most efficient data relays."

Cerise laughed, walking over to the terminal and flicking it on with a finger against the touchscreen. Her few agents appeared to all be doing as they were supposed to, messaging her as they accomplished certain tasks. She was particularly proud of the way onna-zumo roller derby would work into her plans.

It had become the most popular sport across Mars and had gained a large audience there, as well as Earth, before the Shutdown. The girls were idolized and adored by the public. Because the players had been kept poor, they probably only had an inkling of the sway they had over public sentiment. Dell was the perfect patsy because he and Dragos Dalca had met at least once in the teal.

"Cortex collapse," Octavo reported, gesturing to the android on the table.

"Do her like the others," Cerise said, waving dismissively over her shoulder.

"Okay…"

"Wait, no, I have a better idea," Cerise turned around scrawling something on the back of a piece of paper.

"Like the others, but I want to start dumping them in more… creative places."

Octavo just shook his head, taking the scrap of paper. "Okay, whatever."

Cerise left the cybernetics laboratory for the living quarters of her private bunker. She laid down on her bed and looked up at the ceiling, imagining Silverstein and Marshal Rider busying themselves above in the Mars Company corporate offices. It amused her that she was basically hiding in a very secure basement that was off the municipal blueprints and grid.

Dell knocked at the door a few moments later. She waited until he'd started to walk away to call him in, delighting in causing him any degree of inconvenience. He entered, swallowing hard and keeping his eyes low.

"You wanted to see me?"

"You haven't reported in for a day. I thought something might be wrong," Cerise said, sitting up and crossing her legs.

Dell hesitated, never seeing her act this casual, and having never talked to her anywhere that wasn't an office or official company vehicle. "Dragos Dalca paid me a visit. He and his fishfolk friend tried to muscle me into giving you up. I spent a day making sure they didn't know about any of our other operations. I'm sorry for the radio silence, but I'm afraid it was necessary."

Cerise smiled broadly, her perfectly white teeth coming out from behind curled lips.

"What?" Dell said, having never seen her be anything but a very formal Mars Company politico.

"Out of everyone in Archie's portfolio, aside from Dragos Dalca, you're the only one he didn't end up killing at some point. I'm starting to see why," Cerise said, sliding off the bed to the floor.

"Um, thanks?" Dell said, fidgeting, gaze locked on the floor by his feet.

"Have you been keeping the videos as I asked?"

"Yeah. I don't know why you'd want video of that, but here they are. These are the only copies," Dell said, laying a trio of survey visual records on the dresser.

"We'll release them a day before the match, it'll boost the ticket sales, get more people in the seats at the derby championships," Cerise said, walking over to the liquor cabinet and pouring herself a drink.

"Let me guess, you're going to have mercs hit the ticket office and you've got someone working the other team as well? You bet against the favorite and cash in on the upset, am I right?" Dell said, wondering what his percentage would be.

Cerise laughed, knocking the drink to the ground. It wasn't a mirthful laugh or the sort Dell would have expected from a woman who barely look thirty. It was the laugh of someone spiteful and ancient, a cackle that made Dell cringe down to his soul.

"I can't override an Omega AI that is installed as facility maintenance for the colony. No matter how many androids I have Octavo stitch together, our collective is still just a bunch of half bright robots running support systems," Cerise said, shaking her head as if to scold the fallen brandy snifter.

"Then the money? You're going to use it to buy influence in the new regime?" Dell posited, scratching his chin.

"Ouroboru had a major controlling share of the debt and equity in Earth's global economy and squandered it trying to put something right that can never be. Anyone he appoints as guardians of the new Omega AI isn't going to be for sale," Cerise said, delighting in how dumb Dell was.

Dell just looked at her, hands held out to his sides expectantly.

"In the event of a crisis, the facility maintenance AI will award majority control of the colony to the highest ranking Mars Company official. Secretly, that is me thanks to a winding paper trail that will take Marshal Rider too long to decipher from the few coded documents the Marshal has been able to find and transcribe," Cerise explained, offering Dell a drink.

"We lost a Maintenance Zone, that should have been enough," Dell said, taking the drink.

"Should have been, but our dear Simon meddled in our affairs. He rescued a couple hundred workers from the disaster, spurring others to do the same. Also, his mechanical union is efficient, preventing many of the failures and accidents that should have boosted my numbers. I haven't been able to achieve a great enough mining colony personnel loss to trigger a crisis event in the system," Cerise said, swirling the brandy around in her glass.

"Okay, so what do we do?" Dell said, drinking the finest alcohol he'd ever tasted.

Cerise smiled sweetly. "We create the most anticipated derby championship run in Mars Colony history, throw a little scandal into the mix with a popular player, and then kill everyone in the stadium during the first jam."

CHAPTER 12

MARS COLONY, MARS COMPANY ADMINISTRATIVE ZONE - ARCHIVES

August 11th, 2200

Marshal Rider sat in the shadow of her new Aegis Armor at a large table surrounded by plastic totes filled with physical records. They were piled up on either side leaning up against both walls, leaving little room to walk. As the Marshal tapped through the physical records, she transcribed authorization codes, control numbers, and accounts that were needed to free the colony from Mining Company control.

She sipped tea and scrolled through each entry on the terminal, the only source of illumination in the room. It was blessedly quiet except for the soft hum of an automated record digitizer in the background. Ezra One slept sitting up, perched on one of the stacks of boxes, his eyes twitching back and forth beneath his eyelids, his pointed ears quivering slightly to the light noise around him.

"What time is it?" Ezra One said, opening his eyes.

"Late morning, a little after ten," Marshal Rider replied, gesturing to the hot tea pot beside her.

"I didn't mean to sleep so long, but I've been having dreams," Ezra One said grasping the teapot and pouring himself a small cup.

"Long? You were barely asleep a couple of hours."

"Drones only sleep a full eight hours once a week or so, sustaining ourselves the rest of the time on thirty minutes at a time. The only time I ever dreamed before was in a chemically-induced sleep while traveling between Earth and Mars," Ezra One said, sipping the tea.

"Any luck finding the Drone working with Cerise Laplace?"

"No, he's from Earth, like me," Ezra One said, finishing his tea.

"You saying we've got inferior Drones here?" Marshal Rider joked.

"If by inferior you mean peaceful enough to not have fought a civil war with each other. Drones from Earth fought a bloody war. The Elders and the Sodality battled over corporate edicts like they were religious commandments. You learned to hide from other Drones if you wanted to survive," Ezra One said, walking his cup out to the drinking fountain in the hallway.

Marshal Rider watched him, standing on his tiptoes to reach as he rinsed out his cup. She'd seen only a few pygmy Drones, more than most having lived on Mars, but none seemed to retain their wonder about the world. Most had seen too many conflicts and too much war in zero gravity over the dozens of other small outposts throughout the solar system.

"Thanks for letting me chill with you. Silverstein and Taylor have been needing more time alone of late," Ezra One said, placing the cup back beside the teapot.

"Anytime. I know the feeling. I'm kind of a third wheel with my friends right now, too," Marshal Rider said blandly.

Ezra One just nodded, exchanging a knowing look with Marshal Rider.

"I'll be back in a few hours. What do you want from the noodle stand?" Ezra One asked, taking out a menu from his jacket pocket.

"Rice with the imitation pork and the murgi ki chhoile."

"Again?"

"Yeah, that old man makes it how I like it."

"I'm bringing you something else. It's for your own good," Ezra One joked, pocketing the menu.

"Don't you dare, and make it spicy. I need all the help I can get staying awake over here," Marshal Rider said, laughing.

"You got it," Ezra One said, holding up a hand in farewell.

It would be almost noon before she would again have visitors. She could hear them talking in the hallway as they approached. It was the sort of warm conversation and laughter two people would share if they were closer than friends.

Dragos came in, opening the door into a stack of boxes. "Ah, there are even more of these records now?"

"Did you find her?" Marshal Rider asked, continuing to look at the terminal.

"We hoped you'd found something in your search of the records," Hashti said, hesitantly, lingering in the doorway.

"These assholes hid in plain sight among the rest of humanity for eight thousand years. Do you think she just left a clue to her secret holdouts somewhere in the Mining Company records?" Marshal Rider replied, trying not to sound as sarcastic as she was exhausted.

"There may be another way," Hashti said, nodding to Dragos.

"Do tell," Marshal Rider said, looking up from the terminal briefly.

"We need you to come into the street with us, talk to someone," Dragos said, beckoning.

"Don't you think I'd already be out there if I could? Question them yourself. You can be scary, too. Sort of," Marshal Rider said, smiling mischievously.

"They ask for you, and they said Cerise Laplace by name. They knew someone that knew someone," Dragos stammered.

Marshal Rider sighed. "Silverstein needs all the administrative metadata pulled from these records. It's written in Hebrew with orthography matching the regional Mars Colony dialect. You know another Jew from Mars that can take my place for a couple hours while I chase what sounds like a dead lead?"

Hashti shifted uncomfortably.

"You believe this person?" Marshal Rider asked, looking to Hashti.

"Yes, she thought we were Mars Company enforcers, there to rough her up. She's in some kind of trouble," Hashti explained.

"Who is she?" Marshal Rider asked.

"Her jersey said 'The Roman' on the back," Dragos said.

"What? Where was this?" Marshal Rider said, rising from her chair, handguns clacking against the armrests.

Dragos fished around in his pockets. "Black Dragon … something, I have address. Tracked Dell to that location and…"

"Wait, Cerise Laplace is messing with my favorite derby team?" Marshal Rider growled.

"It… seems that way?" Hashti replied, never having seen Marshal Rider so angry before.

Marshal Rider quietly stood, turning to switch her armor on. "I should have killed her when I had the chance."

"Over a game?" Dragos asked, unaccustomed to seeing anything disturb the Marshal's unrelenting calm.

Hashti seemed to brace for impact, looking on worriedly as Marshal Rider turned a hard gaze in Dragos' direction.

"All Mars imports is debtors and dirt bags. All we export are rocks, corpses, and onna-zumo roller derby. It's watched back on Earth, and the Lunar Colony. Without it, the Mars Colony would have probably been forgotten. It's our only source of pride, the only thing Mars did half right since the first lander," Marshal Rider said, relating her ire with a harsh tone Dragos had rarely heard before. Usually, when Marshal Rider spoke that way, people died.

Dragos hurriedly pulled out his notebook and thumbed through it. "Maybe we could bring her here, get some clarity?"

Marshal Rider didn't respond. She stood looking at the flex monitor she'd disengaged from her armor. The armor booted up, indicator lights going from orange to green, the internal AI whispering to Marshal Rider through an earpiece. Her anger quickly faded, yielding to bewilderment.

"I'm already out there," she said, a look of bafflement crossing her face.

"What do you mean?" Dragos said, sidling up beside her to gaze at the flex monitor.

On the screen was video shot in what looked to be a mechanical district. A Mars Company exoskeleton deployment vehicle landed amidst a crowd of cheering individuals. When the hatch opened, someone stepped out in her old armor. The individual used the assistive strength to lift people out of the vehicle to the ground as quickly as they could.

"That's a man," Hashti remarked, pointing to the screen.

"What? How can you tell?" Dragos asked.

"Men walk funny. Also, see how he lowers the children from the transport in the same way he does everyone else? A woman would handle the children differently, even if just a little," Hashti explained.

"This was shot by a miner with an ore survey monitor and limited public network access. It's all over the colony now, where the network isn't down, anyway," Marshal Rider said, checking the log signatures on the video.

Marshal Rider tapped around on the flex monitor, looking through associated entries to the video. She stopped on a report filed by two Mining Company officials that were ejected from the Mechanical Zone after trying to recover Mars Company property. A smile spread across Marshal Rider's face as he read the details beneath the report.

"You read too fast. What did it all say?" Dragos said, squinting at the flex monitor.

"Allegedly, this guy borrowed a transport and conscripted a missing Ichthyic Type Five as the pilot. He took both to the Maintenance Zone that went into full mechanical failure yesterday," Marshal Rider said, shaking her head at Dragos.

"What, okay? He is nice, save people, yes?" Dragos said.

"He, or someone he knows, repaired my old armor. The Marshal's Star is very similar to mine."

"How can that be?" Hashti asked, furrowing her brow.

"They'd have to have met me before, seen me up close. The transcript says that while he was helping people, he was looking for 'The Roman,'" Marshal Rider said, stepping back into her Aegis Armor, the mechanical bulwark snapping shut around her.

Marshal Rider led the way through the sprawling administrative complex, pushing past busy white coats to the security checkpoint. There was a long line in both directions as Silverstein had made coming and going difficult, at her direction. She checked the log as she always did at the security terminal for any familiar or troublesome names.

The terminal flashed red for a moment, security protocols suddenly getting tripped by someone coming through the checkpoint ahead. A small quake shook the building as the whole place lost power. The magnetic locks holding up the two huge blast doors that allowed access to the building failed, sending thousands of tons of steel crashing down. Workers waiting in line ran in both directions, most clearing the gap before the doors fell, but not all.

"What just happened? Taylor, Silverstein, are you there?" Marshal Rider asked, tapping her comm.

There was only silence over the other comm as darkness blanketed the area. Illuminators on Marshal Rider's Aegis suit activated, granting the checkpoint area some dim illumination. Dragos brought up his rifle as Hashti squinted into the dark around them, frightened people huddled around the checkpoint kiosks. Baffled security personnel fished around in cabinets for flashlights as a lone individual walked through the crowd toward Marshal Rider.

"Marshal Rider, hello!" Octavo said, flattening out his teal jumpsuit as if to make himself look more presentable.

"Octavo Floros, I've been looking for you," Marshal Rider said, drawing her sidearms.

"And I, you, but only to find Dragos," Octavo replied.

"Do I know this man?" Dragos said, training his rifle on Octavo.

"He's the mechanic that shut down my armor in the teal. You kicked him in the face," Marshal Rider whispered, watching Hashti melt into the crowd to flank Octavo.

"Oh yes, him," Dragos said, nodding.

"This isn't exactly ideal, but I think we can still make this work," Octavo said, keeping his hands out where the Marshal could see them.

"Yeah? You want to turn the lights back on?" Marshal Rider said, moving her fingers from the guards to the triggers.

"Oh, that's going to be hard from the inside. We'd hoped to trap you all in here, but Ezra One is harder to track for some reason. Even our people in the underground aren't sure if he's in here or not," Octavo said, smiling broadly.

"We?" Dragos asked, nodding to Hashti who'd worked her way around to the back.

Octavo had been walking slowly forward, coming more into the light. At thirty feet, one should have been able to see the tight network of scars across his face where Dragos had kicked him. But, his face was strangely pristine. At twenty-five feet from the Marshal, the HUD in her armor began to flash, warning her that bomb residue had been detected somewhere nearby.

"HASHTI! GET AWAY FROM HIM!" Marshal Rider yelled, panicked, cycling concussive ammunition into her sidearm.

"Not exactly ideal, but good enough," Octavo said, remotely using his telemechanical ability to trigger the detonator for his bomb harness.

CHAPTER 13

MARS COLONY, MARS COMPANY ADMINISTRATIVE ZONE - ARCHIVES

August 12th, 2200

"You've broken the prison code, the unwritten law of the teal," Aunt Ruth explained, looking weakly over at Simon.

That morning, she'd been unable to rise from her bed. Everyone in the household was somber, the fishfolk offering up their prayers. Ishihara was in the kitchen, doing her best to figure out how to make food for everyone. Simon sat beside Aunt Ruth, bandages wrapped tightly about his legs.

"Because I put on the star and armor?" Simon asked.

"That armor is a cop and you asked it for help. If you ever go into the teal, it'll be bad for you. As much as I ever told you to stay out of trouble, it's vital that you listen now," Aunt Ruth said, sipping her tea.

"The Marshal helped us that once, on the tram. Wouldn't that be the same sort of trouble?"

Aunt Ruth shook her head. "That guy was showing his bits to anyone that would look, ducking decorum, and we didn't ask her for help."

Simon nodded, understanding. "What if I have to put the armor on again?"

"You want to end up being the Marshal?" Aunt Ruth asked.

"Not really, but the mining conglomerate isn't doing anything to protect regular people. They never really have, but this is going beyond negligence. They would have just left all those people to drown, or freeze, or suffocate in that failed Maintenance Zone," Simon whispered, rubbing his eyes.

"On Mars, you look out for yourself."

"And where has that gotten us? It's so bad here my parents never sent for me because they thought I was tainted by this place. The family that did accept me, got cut in half by a greedy corporate politico, and we took the hush money. Now you're sick and there isn't anything we can do about it," Simon said, utterly losing his temper.

"Your parents were fools that came into a little money on Earth and cut everyone off for political ambition. It had nothing to do with you," Aunt Ruth said quietly.

"That's not how it feels. I can't help but take this personally."

"So, you're going to don that armor, prove them wrong? Show them what a good guy you are?" Aunt Ruth said, frowning.

"After the Shutdown on Earth, I've no idea if they are even alive or my sister for that matter," Simon said, leaning back in his chair to let the circulation flow back into his legs.

Ishihara stepped in placing some blackened toast, slathered in butter on the nightstand.

"It's all I could figure out how to make," she announced, obviously frustrated.

"You made yourself plenty of food before. Remember when you basically ate it all?" Simon retorted, reluctantly eating his buttered carbon slice.

"Not breakfast. Before I was staying with you guys, I slept until noon, two zones over. Seriously, I don't even think I knew what morning was until a week with the Vedter clan," Ishihara related, mournfully eating her own blackened bread.

"This is terrible," Aunt Ruth said, pushing the toast aside.

"The fishfolk seem to like it. Maybe I'll open a burnt toast stand near a manhole cover and trade scrap with them," Ishihara joked.

Aunt Ruth and Simon laughed, as much at the mental picture as Ishihara's funny grin. Aunt Ruth rose from her bed with some help and walked about, finally finding the strength to make a proper breakfast. Simon returned to his workshop and began working on the Aegis Armor, taking actuator assemblies apart. Ishihara watched, handing him tools while he worked.

"Where is Pearl?" Simon asked.

"Out praying with the other fishfolk. I think they'll head back below soon," Ishihara said, handing him an air tool.

"I'm going to need some things from the scrap yard, but I don't want to aggravate my burns walking all that way. Could you get me some things?"

"Any excuse to skip practice is a good excuse."

"Don't let Aunt Ruth hear you say that, she's got high hopes for you to win the championship, start strong in the first bout," Simon said, pausing to look at the actuator assembly arrayed on his work table.

"I don't think I can let Dell touch me again. I hate it."

"You ready for Plan B?"

"No, getting him tossed back into the teal won't fix this. This Cerise Laplace lady will just assign someone else, someone worse."

Simon bristled at the mention of the name. "I wish we could get her sent to the teal."

"Marshal Rider's friends, the cyborg and the scary fish lady came to the stables. They tried to press Dell for her location."

"She's in hiding?" Simon said, looking up from his work.

"They called themselves Dragos, and Hashti. I kept them off Dell, and I thought they'd hurt me, but they left after I offered to make a deal with them," Ishihara explained, wringing her hands.

"What deal?" Simon said, hesitantly.

"I agreed to help them find Cerise Laplace if we got an audience with the Marshal," Ishihara said, knowing Simon would not approve.

"We don't know where Cerise is. What if they come looking?" Simon asked, angrily.

"We have the Marshal's armor, and you're fixing it up. You've got history with this Cerise person. Just tell them what you know," Ishihara said.

"Camille, I can't believe you did that," Simon said, covering his face with his hands.

"I couldn't let them hurt or kill Dell. No coach, no championship," Ishihara said, frowning.

"I understand, I just... the Aegis Armor isn't safe to operate right now, and what I know of Cerise Laplace goes back a lot of years. I don't know if it would even be useful," Simon said, drawing an assembly diagram on a chalkboard beside his worktable.

"No information is useless with people like Cerise," Ezra One said, rising up out of a shadow beside the entry door.

Simon and Ishihara scrambled for cover, seeing the small Drone carrying a rifle. "What do you want?" Simon bellowed, hoping his aunt would hear.

"You. You sent Dragos and Hashti to the stable. You're their scout," Ishihara said, recalling their earlier meeting.

Ezra One pushed his rifle around to his back and looked up at the Aegis Armor, unpleasant memories flooding his mind. Aunt Ruth came in and, catching sight of Ezra One, quickly produced a long steak knife. Ezra One seemed to ignore it all, holding a slim mobile in one hand and comparing what he saw to Simon.

"I'm not here to hurt anyone. We're just trying to find Cerise Laplace," Ezra One said, sliding his mobile into a breast pocket.

Aunt Ruth squinted at Ezra One. "We?"

"Yes, we all work with Silverstein," Ezra One explained.

"Don't you mean, work for Silverstein?" Simon asked, frowning at his workshop being intruded upon.

"No," Ezra One said, folding his arms.

"I don't know what any of you are talking about, but I don't like Drones in my home," Aunt Ruth said, still clutching the knife.

Simon nodded. "Yeah, not a fan of them, either. We can't help you with Cerise, so you should just go."

Ezra One nodded. "I understand. I'll go, but my friends will come instead. If you're working for Cerise, I'd recommend finding a new employer soon."

"Silverstein doesn't sound any better. Like Cerise, he employs mercenaries and Drones to do his dirty work," Simon said, waving Ezra One toward the door.

"Cerise has...Drones working for her?" Ezra said, cocking his head to one side.

"At least one, but like everyone else working for her, he's probably being coerced," Simon said, ruefully.

"No one forces me to do anything. Why do you think the Drone is being forced to cooperate with her?" Ezra One asked, placing a hand on the entry door.

"He told me, long ago, that if I ever got the chance, I should kill her," Simon explained.

Ezra One frowned, looking back at Simon for any sign of deception. His heart sank when he saw none. It sounded the way a Type One would speak. Worker class Drones would never suggest killing anyone as a solution. The only Type One Drones on Mars were former allies and soldiers from Earth. The Drone working with Cerise had to be someone he knew.

"You said your friends were coming here. Tell them not to bother, we'll be long gone," Simon said, loading tools into a satchel.

"This is why I hate Mars. No one can trust anyone else," Ezra One said, disappearing through the doorway.

Simon hobbled to the door and looked out, making sure the Drone was truly gone. "I don't like this. We should pack up and leave until this Silverstein and Cerise have settled whatever beef they have with each other."

"Agreed, none of us need to be caught up in the middle of white coats having a pissing contest," Ruth said, walking slowly back toward the living area of the workshop.

Pearl walked back in, a broad smile dominating her face. "Caught in the middle of what?"

"We're going to pack up and leave for a while. Would you like to come with us?" Ishihara asked.

"In the transport? Are we going on a trip?" Pearl asked.

"Yeah, something like that," Simon said, smiling.

"Where will we stay?" Pearl asked.

"I'm not sure. Likely, we'll be sleeping in the transport until we find a good place to hide," Ishihara said, already trying to figure out how to get Simon's bed to fit.

"Oh, well, I know a place. It's nice," Pearl said, gathering up her few possessions.

"You do?" Simon said, surprised.

Pearl nodded, smiling vacantly, eyes wide.

"Heh, okay, what should we bring?" Simon asked.

"Just some clothes and whatever tools you need to work on the armor. Everything else should already be there," Pearl said. She headed out the back toward the transport.

"Why do I have a bad feeling about this?" Aunt Ruth said, barely able to lift a small satchel of clothes.

They loaded up into the transport, taking a change of clothing, the Aegis Armor, and some tools with them. As the transport powered up, Simon locked the shop up tight, turning his terminal off so that no work orders would be sent to him. He hoped the Mechanical Zone would be okay for a few days without him.

Pearl flew slowly through various zones, taking the tubes slowly and blending into traffic until they reached one of the more affluent Entertainment Zones. There were spires that reached from the street to the biological enclosure overhead. Most of it was dark, a dream of better days when the Mining Conglomerate hoped to expand Mars into a tourist attraction.

There were nicer transports carrying administrative white on their sides lazily making their way to the portions that were lit for business. Pearl flew the transport to the glitzy area beyond, toward a large fight arena that only had flight warning lights active. She drew close, making Ishihara wince, then tapped in a code on the onboard terminal. The hanger doors for the parking area opened, allowing Pearl to fly inside.

"Pearl, what is this place?" Simon asked, looking over her shoulder through the viewport.

"Mister Janjigian owns a suite in this building. He uses it for meetings with clients and private gatherings," Pearl explained, setting the transport down in an empty docking port.

"Your old owner? What if he comes here? I punched him in the face, remember?" Ishihara asked, worriedly.

"Ha, I don't remember much from that night. And no, he shouldn't come here until January and again in April of next year for the administrative conference and the reporting cycle meetings," Pearl explained, smiling.

"With luck, no one will think to look for us here, at least for a few days," Simon said.

They loaded up the Aegis Armor with satchels and bags, Simon piloting it through the winding Martian resort until they reached the private suite belonging to Pearl's former owner. She used her own biometric signature to open the door, allowing them access. Once inside, they found a large private dwelling with many beds and rooms, a place to entertain guests, a full kitchen, and a balcony looking out into the Entertainment Zone beyond.

For Ishihara, Simon, and Aunt Ruth, it was luxury and extravagance they'd never experienced before. Even the air they breathed was carefully filtered and sweet smelling compared to the cloudy and particulate laden Mechanical Zone.

"While Simon gets the lay of the land, I think I'll take a rest. Camille, help me find a bed," Aunt Ruth said, looking around at the many doors and hallways.

"Yeah, let's do some exploring," Ishihara said, taking Aunt Ruth's hand and heading toward some back rooms.

Simon picked up a facility manual on the dining table and flipped through it. "There's even medical facilities here. There might be something that could help Aunt Ruth or at least make her more comfortable," Simon said.

"It's possible, but Mister Janjigian only ever sent me there to pick up more... recreational drugs. There's lots of other machines and a pharmacy. It's automated, though, and only responds to orders keyed in at the terminal," Pearl explained.

"Where's the terminal?" Simon asked, looking around bewildered.

"Ha, it's right here, silly," Pearl said, tapping her hand on a mirror.

The reflective surface vanished as the room dimmed slightly. A terminal display appeared beneath the glass, a menu of options waiting for the user's input. Simon walked up to it and looked across all the facility options and features.

"Pearl, this is really nice. I know you probably don't have many happy memories of this place. And, your owner is probably still looking for you," Simon said, scrolling through the security features for the resort facility.

"My owner has probably already replaced me and moved on with his life. He wasn't one to dwell on things long," Pearl said, walking toward the balcony.

"Still, given what happened in the alley, he might not pass up a chance at revenge. We shouldn't stay here too long. I'll try to find somewhere else for us to go tomorrow," Simon said.

"You're so nice to me and I don't even know why," Pearl said, walking behind the bar to fill a pitcher with water.

"I know it's strange, but this is just how people are supposed to act."

"You think I'm 'people'? No one else does," Pearl said, thoughtfully.

"What's important is how you see yourself. When I lost most of the use of my legs, I had to stop thinking about what everyone else thought. I could never get people to see me as anything but a burden most of the time, so I focused on how I saw myself. I decided to be a mechanic, so that's what I became. The more I saw myself that way, the more others did as well," Simon explained, looking through the cabinets for some glasses.

"I like to listen to you talk," Pearl whispered, pressing against Simon, her face brushing against his.

Simon hugged her somewhat awkwardly, trying to keep things platonic. Pearl didn't return the hug, but laid her head on his shoulder and gurgled softly. Ishihara suddenly appeared in the doorway, announcing her arrival by clearing her throat. "Aunt Ruth could use a drink of that," she said, gesturing to the pitcher.

"Oh, there's some glasses here," Pearl said, reaching up past Simon to a cupboard.

"Wow," Ishihara said, holding up the glass, tilting it slightly to agitate the water.

"Right? There's nothing floating in it," Simon said.

"I'll take it to her," Pearl said, grabbing up the glass of water.

Pearl smiled, glad to help but, like Simon, she worried her owner would come. She didn't want to go back to doing what he wanted. Thinking back to the night she met Simon and Ishihara, she still couldn't understand why he'd been so angry or why the woman he was meeting with was so important.

"You guys are getting cozy," Ishihara teased, watching Pearl disappear into the backrooms of the suite.

"Can you blame me? She is gorgeous. Cripples can't be choosy," Simon countered, winking.

"Seriously though, what's up with her?

"I think that whenever she's heard a man's voice, it's been scolding her or telling her to do things she didn't want to do. Anyone that treats her even decent comes off like an angel," Simon said, frowning.

Ishihara sighed. "How do we fix that? I don't want anyone taking advantage of her. I know your Aunt Ruth has been working with her, but it's just…"

"Kinda sad?"

"Yeah."

Simon nodded. "I think that we're used to a certain degree of nonsense being a worker and a performer. The affluent can afford to be blind to their own."

"Speaking of bullshit, Dell will be looking for me in about four hours if I don't show to practice. The first bout is in a couple of days," Ishihara said, sulking.

"Tell me you're going to win the championship," Simon said, folding his arms and leaning up against the counter.

"Assuming the colony doesn't fall apart? We totally could, we've got a really good team this year. Why? I didn't think you cared about derby."

"My aunt does, and I think she's staying alive to see one more season. You're her favorite player."

Ishihara frowned. "Shit, no pressure or anything."

Simon smiled. "She's been watching derby since I was little, but I've never seen her this excited. I would expect other people are as well. Derby is the only thing that doesn't suck on Mars."

"Do you really think Aunt Ruth will just drop dead in the stands after the championship?" Ishihara said, shuddering.

"Naw, not until after she's stabbed Dell in the face with her favorite kitchen knife."

Ishihara laughed.

"She's sleeping now," Pearl said, returning to the kitchen.

"Is there food in this place?" Simon asked.

"And booze?" Ishihara added.

Pearl nodded, smiling as she walked over to the terminal. "The room service cart is automated. It'll bring whatever we want."

"It's still just freeze dried Mars food, right?" Simon asked.

"This time of year, yeah, but it's the best kind. You can get Salisbury steak and carrots," Pearl said, scrolling through the options.

"Haha, order me two of those," Ishihara said, clapping Pearl on the back.

Pearl ordered food that came within thirty minutes, a small automated cart appearing in the hallway outside the suite. Pearl opened the stainless steel door and lifted several plates of hot food to a push cart before opening the cooler section and grabbing several bottles inside. Once empty, the cart beeped and sped off back down the hallway.

"Pearl, let me help you with this stuff," Simon said, helping her set the table.

"I'm supposed to do this," Pearl said, frowning.

"No, we're all the same here. We split the labor," Ishihara said, grabbing bottles from the cart.

"You'll need a bottle opener for those," Pearl said, looking toward the kitchen.

"No, I won't," Ishihara said, palming the top of one of the bottles, her powerful hand twisting it off easily.

Pearl laughed, letting some of her decorum slip away, no longer feeling like a servant.

"I've never sat at this table. I've only ever stood beside it and waited for people to tell me what to do," Pearl said, smoothing the table cloth with her hand.

"Never do that again," Ishihara said, holding out a bottle to the center of the table.

Simon clinked her bottle with his. "Never."

Pearl followed with her glass of water. "Never-never."

The Aegis Armor chimed, a red light flashing on the holographic HUD inside. Simon paused, mouth still full of food then rose to check it out. He lifted the visor and read the backwards text quietly to himself. Ishihara and Pearl sat expectantly, having never seen the armor do something like that.

"The armor's most recent upload to the Ares System failed. Aegis, is your link to the transport still active? Are we too deep in the resort for your radio to reach?" Simon asked.

"There are relays in the building, all functioning nominally. The transport is functioning properly, and transmitting to the colony relays in zone. Administrative Control is listed as temporarily unavailable for maintenance."

"Pearl, open this terminal for me. I need to check something," Simon said, scratching his chin and thinking deeply.

Pearl began to get up, but Ishihara pushed her back down, issuing Simon a stern look.

Simon sighed. "Please?"

"That's right, you talk to my friend with respect," Ishihara said, winking to Pearl.

Pearl giggled. "Yes, I'll open the terminal for you."

Once Simon had access, he tried to engage rudimentary civil resources that would be available to anyone on the public access grid. There was nothing. It was as if the Ares System was not there. Simon tried for another couple of minutes, before the civil resources reappeared.

"That was weird. Aegis, are you able to upload now?" Simon asked.

"Yes."

"Don't, delay the upload until further notice," Simon replied, walking over to the armor.

"I'm sorry, Simon. I've already uploaded the files."

"It's okay, we're behind pretty heavy encryption, but don't transmit again until I've checked some things out," Simon said, walking back over to the table.

"Acknowledged."

Simon headed back to the table and sat down, feeling sick with worry. The Ares System had never done anything like that. Usually there were redundancies that would pick up the slack, the general populace never aware of any maintenance, if it ever happened. That every available relay would ping the same was disconcerting, the same as if one looked into the sky and the stars were suddenly not there.

The Aegis Armor suddenly stood upright, visor snapping shut. It tried to draw the sidearm on the right hand side, but Simon hadn't put the actuator assembly back together. The arm jerked, unable to comply with the directive. Instead, it reached out with a left gauntlet and staggered toward the table.

"Simon, run, get away," Aegis intoned over the PA system installed in the suit.

CHAPTER 14

**MARS COLONY, MARS COMPANY ADMINISTRATIVE ZONE –
CENTRAL SECURITY ACCESS**

August 12th, 2200

Ezra One sat cross-legged in front of the massive blast doors that had fallen sometime earlier in the day, trapping his friends and an untold number of civilians inside the Mars corporate complex. The whole Administrative Zone was on emergency power and the communication relays were down. He checked his mobile again, looking for a signal as he had every ten minutes or so for the last hour.

"She was right, this murgi ki chhoile is good," Ezra One whispered to himself, trying the food he'd brought for Marshal Rider.

The smell of bomb residue in the air told Ezra One that something bad had happened, but that it had happened inside the security partition, and after the blast doors fell. The magnetic seals weren't functioning, which meant that if the zone failed, everyone inside the complex would probably lose atmosphere as well. The place was a tomb now, unless Ezra One could figure out a way to open the doors.

He turned, hand on his rifle, as his ears picked up footfalls in the distance. It was too quiet to be a human and it wasn't an Ichthyic Metasapient, not fishy enough. Ezra moved back into the overflowing duracrete jungle of office buildings taking refuge up high, where condensers and life support apparatus changed the direction of airflow. No Drones should be out this far from the Tribehome, and if they were, they weren't up to any good.

When Athos One arrived, there were two half-eaten bags of food, still warm. He stooped over, holding his hand over the rapidly cooling noo-dles, then looked around warily. There was nobody and, while he could smell what he thought might be another Drone, he couldn't tell where they went. Athos One cursed himself for being careless, as this might have been his only chance to intercept Ezra One.

He pulled out his compact rig radio and switched to a hidden Mars Conglomerate frequency. He used it to send out a request for service and waited. "Hello?" A woman's voice came across faintly on the radio.

"He's gone. I missed him by a few minutes. You should have shaken loose a transport to get me to the Zone edge," Athos One complained, looking up at the darkened rooftops.

"If Janjigian had delivered my off-record pilot, it would be simpler to move things around. How is Mister Janjigian?"

"He and his staff are floating with the rest," Athos One replied, his voice betraying deep revulsion.

"Avery One gets to breathe for another forty-eight hours. If this issue with Ezra One isn't dealt with in that time, I'll shut her cyberware off."

"I'll find him, Cerise," Athos One said, shutting the rig radio off.

Athos One took a deep breath and raised his hands slowly, turning to face Ezra One. He had his rifle trained on him and likely loaded with high velocity ammunition. Ezra One's face was like chiseled marble, impassive behind dark highly advanced optics clamped on over his normal Drone-is-sue goggles.

"So, now you know," Athos One said, sliding his own goggles back, an act of submission among Drones.

Ezra One moved his finger from the trigger to the guard, trying to figure out a way to save his friend. Back on Earth, he and Silverstein pulled Taylor from the server interface, saving her life and damning millions of people to darkness. He couldn't help but feel he'd be a hypocrite if he pulled the trigger, and a traitor if he didn't.

"How do I get my friends out?" Ezra One said, calmly keeping Athos One in his sights.

"You don't. Not until Cerise Laplace has institutional control of the Mars Colony."

"She wasn't sending you to kill me," Ezra One said.

"No."

"What if I'd been caught inside?"

Athos One smiled. "I gambled that you wouldn't, to save Avery One."

"You guys… are together?" Ezra One asked, lowering his rifle slightly.

"I've never told her how I feel," Athos One admitted, looking at the ground, hands still raised.

Ezra One slid his rifle around to his back and crossed his arms. Confused, Athos slowly lowered his hands, genetically programmed guilt ravaging his conscience. He'd betrayed another Drone, someone assigned to his original EVA combat team. He didn't have the scout's six, and it was killing him, right alongside the notion that he may never speak to Avery One again.

"Let's play this out. If I opted to work with you and Cerise, what's the next move?" Ezra One said, pulling out his mobile, and checking the signal strength in the area.

"That won't work, you'll need a rig radio to call out."

"What's Cerise going to have us do if I joined up?" Ezra One growled.

Athos One sighed. "Accompany one of her contacts, someone named Dell, to get her off-record pilot, a derby girl, and sequester someone named Simon Vedter. There's a transport and a team of Mars Company collectors waiting for me, or us, if I was able to convince you to help."

Ezra One nodded. "How is she holding Avery One hostage?"

"She's got a guy named Helmet that built the cyberware back when Avery One went into survival stasis. He's been providing maintenance for her cybernetics and has the ability to shut them off remotely," Athos One said sadly.

"Have you seen this Helmet guy recently?"

Athos One thought about it for a moment. "No, and he's always with her. I haven't seen him for a couple of weeks."

"That's because he's locked up in a teal temporary status holding cell in there," Ezra One said, pointing back at the duracrete fortress where his friends were trapped.

Athos One blinked in disbelief. "She's been playing me."

"The individual we're holding isn't the original Doctor Gorshteyn Helmet. He's a replica. Yeah, he is extremely dangerous, gone delta enough to kill."

"Would he hurt Avery One?"

"Using cyberware to hold people as hostages runs counter to the original Doctor Helmet's ideology. Doing it to a Drone, beings he considers to be like his own kids…" Ezra One said, shaking his head.

Athos One shook his head. "Every time she made the threat, the Doctor wasn't in the room. We'd be watching him conduct the maintenance on Avery One on the other side of environmental shielding, or out in the waiting room."

Ezra One pushed his goggles back, sliding his optics into a pouch on his tactical harness. "So, what do you want to do?"

"What I should have done long ago," Athos One whispered, patting the rifle hanging at his side.

"You should have come to me with this the moment I set foot on Mars. Making me drag it out of you wasted a lot of time," Ezra One said, pointing and then holding out his hand for the rig radio.

Athos one shook his head. "I'm sorry," he lamented, handing the radio over.

Ezra One ran a connection cable from the rig radio to the second mobile he was carrying. He set the mobile to boot while he walked toward the duracrete partitions outside the Mars Conglomerate offices where his friends were trapped. Ezra One rolled out some grey putty, usually reserved for explosives, and affixed the rig radio and mobile to the wall behind some narrow pipes carrying communications and data cable into the building.

As soon as the mobile booted, Ezra's personal mobile chimed. "Silverstein?" he answered.

"I assume you're outside?" Silverstein said, the sounds of frantic people murmuring in the background.

"Yeah, your worst case scenario prediction was pretty much right on. You were right about her having a Drone working with her. You were right about everything," Ezra One said, turning a stern gaze toward Athos One.

"I'd hoped to have everything in place to avoid this. There just wasn't time. It's a good thing we've got you as a countermeasure," Silverstein said, appreciatively.

"Everyone okay?" Ezra One said, fearing the answer.

"Marshal Rider, Dragos, and Hashti were on their way out when it went down. I knew there would be some retaliation, which is why I tried to keep them inside and busy."

"Tell me, Silverstein. Just tell me," Ezra One said, bracing for the worst.

"Someone calling themselves Octavo Floros entered the building intent on killing Dragos. He had a suicide bomb harness on and detonated it in the checkpoint. Hashti jumped on him to absorb as much of the blast as she could."

"Is she dead?"

"No, but she may not live through the night. She leapt on him from behind, pushing him face down. Most of the explosive load and the ball bearings went into the ground. There were two people on the security detail injured, but everyone else is just a little deaf after the blast," Silverstein said.

"Athos One and I are going to accompany Dell and some Mars Company collectors to grab up Cerise's other assets. I'm going to do what we discussed if something like this happened, with a couple of revisions," Ezra One said, angrily.

"How can I help?" Silverstein replied.

"I need to know if the cyberware keeping Avery One has been compromised."

"I'll have Marshal Rider and Dragos question Doctor Helmet. They are both grappling with some supreme helplessness right now and could use something to do. Anything else I can do?" Silverstein replied.

Ezra One ran his hand over the jacket Taylor had made him, fingers lingering on the "Slayer" band patch on the sleeve. "Nothing. That's it. I'll call again when I can."

"I am genuinely sorry this has fallen on you to fix. I'm really bad at predicting just how completely insane the people in my tribe have become," Silverstein said.

"I can relate," Ezra One replied, looking at Athos One disapprovingly.

"Heh, for sure, but I am no less sorry about all this."

"It's going to be fine, friend. I'll have you out of there in a few hours, and we'll fix this together."

"Okay, Ezra. Thanks."

Ezra One ended the call and gathered up the relay he'd put together, pulling it from the wall. He handed Athos One his rig radio and pocketed the mobile he'd used as a relay. Athos took out a little food from his pack and nibbled it, looking mournfully at his feet.

"There's still some food in the bags," Ezra One said, nodding to the Indian food cooling on the street.

"I never developed a taste for surface food," Athos One said, giving Ezra One a half-smile.

For Ezra One, that meant Athos One never really worked with Cerise in the way he worked with Silverstein. They weren't friends and Cerise had been taking advantage of Athos One for years. Most Drones didn't show their age, appearing much as they did when they left the factory their entire lives. Ezra One could see the wear and tear in every crease and wrinkle on Athos One's face, making him look far older than most Drones.

"When you're ready, lead the way. Let's make the meet with Dell and play this out," Ezra One said.

"Thanks for not killing me." Athos One said, cramming the last of his black bread in his mouth.

"The day isn't over yet, Athos."

They traveled by foot to the lift that slowly carried equipment and personnel from the lower habitation zones to the mining facility above. The elevators were huge, powered by perpetual power engines and would likely continue to crawl up and down the Martian mountain long after the colony was gone. They caught the number two elevator making a descent, the platform gathering speed the further down the slope it got, then slowing within a mile of the receiving station below.

They stepped off the massive platform as it lingered for a few moments before slowly moving back up the mountain. The maintenance facility was bustling with workers, some fighting for ore contracts in the streets. Athos One led them up high, to the service gantries and substructure of the environmental dome. Ezra One paused at a high point, condensation from the dome raining down around him from above. He wondered if the people below, fighting for a few vouchers, knew how close the colony was to an apocalypse.

There were almost two dozen collectors wearing black rubber suits and carrying machine guns loaded with caseless ammunition. There was a portly and slovenly man waiting along with them, constantly checking his watch. Athos One and Ezra One did their best to portray the expected appearance, approaching at ease while still having their rifles at the ready.

"Took you long enough. You tunnel rats took your sweet time figuring who the winning team was," Dell said, laughing.

"Yeah, well, he's not exactly happy about all this, and neither am I. Mobilizing armed response this deep is going to draw attention, Dell," Athos One said, gesturing to the numerous collectors standing by next to a chartered transport.

"Oh, not where we're going. The pilot fled to Janjigian's private suite at the resort. This time of year, there will be nobody around and we'll be a mile high," Dell said, smirking.

"I thought we were taking everyone alive. What's with all the lethal armaments?" Athos One complained.

"The mechanic actually got the Marshal's old armor up and running and he's outfitted it with an Earth LE issue sidearm. I've been assured by Octavo that we don't have to worry about it, but I like being careful," Dell explained.

Athos One squinted. "I heard Octavo blew himself up."

"Don't believe everything you hear," Dell said, smiling.

They loaded up into the transport, Ezra One strapping himself in beside Athos One and opposite from Dell. Dell had a bemused expression, his gaze lingering on Ezra One for a moment. Ezra ignored him, looking over at the collectors, carefully observing them with great interest.

"From what I'd been told, you're supposed to be some serious operator, the premier Drone soldier. Type One Drone, full EVA training, hundreds of kills and some kind of legend back on Earth. All I see is a little kid, dressed up in tactical gear and carrying a subcompact rifle," Dell teased, gesturing dismissively toward Ezra One.

"Dragos says you know a lot about guns, that he got a rifle inside the teal from you," Ezra One replied, calmly dismissing Dell's tone.

Dell looked startled. "That's right, he was going to off the Marshal, needed high velocity rounds."

"This Octavo fellow, he's more than a mechanic, he's a tele-mechanic, a shaman?" Ezra One asked, his gaze still fixed on the collectors.

"You ask a lot of questions," Dell said, his crooked smile fading.

Ezra One nodded. "It makes sense. If she was going to kill her whole portfolio, wipe out any trace of her actions, this is how I'd do it too. Maximum deniability."

Dell pulled out a handkerchief and wiped sweat from his brow. The transport began to climb, ascending to the travel lane and heading toward the adjoining zone. The collectors were silent, not a one uttering a word or exchange in conversation. They sat with an identical and rigid posture, holding their weapons at the ready.

"What are you saying?" Dell said, nervously.

"Nothing, just that if I were Cerise, and I wanted to tie up all my loose ends, this would be a hard opportunity to ignore," Ezra One said, turning his silvery eyes toward Dell for a moment.

Ezra One slid his goggles down, keeping his other hand on the restraints at his chest. Athos One sat silently, doing little to comfort Dell or dispel his growing paranoia. The transport began to pick up speed as it entered the travel lane. The portholes high in the passenger compartment flashed as other transports went by in the opposite direction, the engines humming quietly.

"You're just messing with me. Tunnel rats, you can't trust them," Dell said, shaking his head dismissively.

"I was able to reach my friends on the inside. They said someone named Octavo blew himself up at the checkpoint," Ezra One said, Athos One just nodding quietly beside him.

"It had to be an android, made up to look like him," Dell whispered, fidgeting.

"Like all these guys?" Athos One said, gesturing to the collectors quietly riding with them in the compartment.

Dell looked over at the collectors nervously.

"You smell bomb residue?" Athos One said, sniffing the air.

"Not enough to trip bomb detection sensors on a nice chartered transport like this, but the plasticizer used to manufacture old school C-4? Definitely," Ezra One said, pulling out his mobile and playing with it with his free hand.

Dell looked stricken for a moment, eyes wide, and breathing too quickly.

"Calm down or she might set it all off early," Ezra One hissed.

"Oh, God…" Dell said, clasping his hands together and rocking back and forth.

"Relax. Tell us what Cerise told you to do after you went to the resort to pick up her other assets," Athos One whispered, leaning forward.

"She needs that Ichthyic pilot for something. I don't know what, I swear. She's going to use a controversy with the derby girl to pack the fight arena and then kill everyone. With a big enough disaster, and loss of personnel, she'll get assigned emergency control of the colony. She's got the holdings to carry her through the selection process," Dell stammered, sweating profusely.

"What about the mechanic, Simon Vedter?" Ezra One said, keeping his eyes on the collectors.

"Grab him, drop him at his shop in one of the Mechanical Zones. She wants the armor he repaired brought back. Octavo wants it for something," Dell explained.

"What does he want it for?" Athos asked.

"I don't know. He's… kind of weird about machines with any artificial intelligence. He likes to hook up to them and then hurt them. It's messed up," Dell said, shakily.

Ezra One stopped playing with his mobile, switching it from speaker mode to default. "You get all that?"

CHAPTER 15

**MARS COLONY, MARS COMPANY ADMINISTRATIVE ZONE –
CENTRAL SECURITY ACCESS**

August 12th, 2200

"Yeah, I got it," Simon said, somewhat baffled.

"Will you wait there for me?" Ezra One asked.

"Yeah, I'm sorry I didn't trust you before," Simon replied, hanging up.

Simon paused, looking at the mobile that Taylor had given him just four days ago. He couldn't help but feel that their meeting at the scrapyard was not an accident. The luxury suite was in shambles. Minutes before, the Aegis Armor had plowed through walls, trying to kill him. In the struggle to pull the central memory core from within the pilot compartment, Ishihara had gotten some scrapes and bruises. Worse, his assistive leg braces were damaged.

"Can you fix them?" Aunt Ruth asked, dabbing at a fresh gash over Ishihara's eye.

"Yeah, but not here. I don't have the parts," Simon replied, looking down at his half useless legs.

Pearl sat beside Simon on the floor leaning back against the wall. It had all been quite a fright for her, getting tossed aside by the Aegis Armor as it went on a rampage. It had made her feel safe before, but she shivered now to look at it. Even laying on its side, half through a wall and wedged between two support beams, she was afraid to take her eyes off it, in case it started moving on its own again.

"Was that really Ezra One like the caller ID said it was? That little guy that showed up at the shop before we came here?" Ishihara asked, wincing as Aunt Ruth cleaned her wound.

"He's got a pretty distinctive voice and he was interrogating Dell," Simon replied, looking mournfully over at the Aegis Armor.

"Interrogating him? Man, we need to get out of here," Ishihara said, covering her face with her hands.

"He asked Dell about Cerise Laplace. Apparently, Pearl was supposed to be delivered to Cerise, but…"

Pearl burst into tears, surprising everyone.

Simon put his arm around her. "We're not going to let her take you. We'll figure it out."

"It's not that. That night he tried to kill me, he was angry. I spilled a drink…"

"I remember, why was that such a big deal?" Simon replied, trying to calm her down.

"The woman, the client, she said if I couldn't carry a tray of drinks, how could I be steady enough to fly a transport to do what needed to be done," Pearl said, sobbing.

"Do what? What needs to be done?" Ishihara asked.

"I don't know." Pearl replied, covering her face.

"It doesn't matter. It isn't going to get done, regardless. She should have given you a chance to fly. You're the best pilot I've seen," Ishihara said, laughing.

"Really?" Pearl said, looking at Ishihara.

"Yeah, even Drake commented on how steady you held the transport when we were rescuing people from his union," Simon said.

"What did the lady look like? What'd she say to Mister Janjigian that night?" Aunt Ruth asked, washing her hands in the kitchen sink.

"She wore all white, light colored hair, pretty, really pretty. She was cruel, said she wouldn't pay for clumsy," Pearl said, leaning into Simon.

"That had to be Cerise. That tightwad white coat didn't want to pay full price and Janjigian probably didn't want to haggle given what a Metasapient like you costs," Aunt Ruth said, shaking her head.

"So, because Janjigian didn't give Cerise the Mining Company employee discount, her plans are all messed up?" Simon said, smirking.

"Rich people and their greed," Ishihara muttered.

"Never assume you really know what conglomerate politicos are up to. We should load up and be prepared to leave in the event this Drone is lying to us," Aunt Ruth said, heading to the bedrooms to gather her things.

"I don't think he was lying," Simon said, shaking his head.

"No harm in being careful all the same. Here, I'll be your legs," Ishihara said, helping Simon to his feet.

They used a damaged luggage lift to move the deactivated Aegis Armor to the transport and lock it in along with what little else they'd brought with them. Simon rode on Ishihara piggy-back between the transport and the suite, making certain they'd covered their tracks. Pearl was downcast through most of the process, but seemed to look a little happier once she was in the transport, hands on the controls.

"I'm not going to fix my braces. Camille is a perfectly good set of legs," Simon joked.

"Yeah, until you break my back. You'd think there would be at least one wheelchair in this place," Ishihara said, grunting as she collapsed into the passenger seating on the transport.

"Off! Off! You weigh a ton!" Simon said, pushing on Ishihara.

"Oh? I weigh a ton?" Ishihara laughed, doing her best to press her back into Simon.

"You guys should just get a room," Aunt Ruth said laughing, sitting down beside Pearl in the crew compartment.

Ishihara rolled over to the seat next to Simon and looked out the open cargo door. There were at least fifty places to land transports. She didn't think there could be that many people in the whole colony that could afford a place in the resort district and there were at least a half dozen buildings like the one they'd stayed the night in.

"Speaking of rich people, where are they?" Ishihara asked.

"What do you mean?" Simon replied, leaning back in the crew seat, stretching his legs.

"The resort district isn't a Class C zone, it's as big as any of the other habitation zones. Hundreds, maybe thousands of people could stay here. Where are they?" Ishihara said, leaning forward on her knees.

Aunt Ruth cleared her throat and turned around in the comm station seat. "Before either of you were born…"

"Here we go," Ishihara teased.

"Shut your hole and listen, you might get the answer to your question," Aunt Ruth scolded.

"I like your stories," Pearl said, smiling warmly.

"Okay, well, after the second attempt to overthrow the Wardens and sever their control of the teal, Mars had something of a revival. There was a massive attempt to attract tourism here. If the Lunar Colony was Disneyland, they wanted Mars to be the Las Vegas of the solar system," Aunt Ruth said, pausing to sip tea from a paper cup.

"You were saying something about this before, I think," Simon said, nodding.

"Derby was huge on Earth, as big as international football. If you bothered to count, there's twice as many fight arenas as teams right now. It was going to be the main draw to get the wealthy and advantaged to not just visit Mars, but move here. It's why the Mars Conglomerate finally merged with Prison System Enforcement to provide the workforce," Aunt Ruth said, each word coming out slower than the last.

"That all happened, right? I mean, that's why Mars is the way it is," Ishihara said, nodding.

"There were three union organizers. They were powerful and had every intent to protect the contracts they had with the mining conglomerate. Mining company officials were greedy, and back then it took a year in order to prepare transport and travel from Earth to Mars. They needed the union organizers to go away," Aunt Ruth explained.

"What happened?" Pearl whispered, sitting on the edge of her seat.

"I killed two of them," Aunt Ruth said, lowering her head.

Simon and Ishihara both snapped forward gazing down the aisle to the crew compartment.

"What?" Ishihara said, eyes wide.

"One was Marshal Rider's father. He thought he was meeting with someone from the company to discuss terms. They convinced him to come to the Administrative Zone without armor or weapons as a gesture. I took him by surprise, stabbing him to death," Ruth said, tears in her eyes.

"Holy, shit," Ishihara said, frowning.

"Why are you telling us this?" Simon said, covering his face.

"When you give that girl her armor back, you should tell her the truth. I doubt she knows why her father died and she should know. There's a file under the floorboards beneath my bed. Give it to her," Ruth said, shakily setting her tea down on the console.

"What about the other two organizers?"

"Angelica Preston, a fight organizer. She was going to unionize the derby teams and make sure the girls had good representation. The company couldn't let her live or they wouldn't be able to rig the betting system and keep the profits for themselves. No one knows she's dead, but the file will help Marshal Rider fix all that," Aunt Ruth explained.

"What do you think the Marshal will do to me when I tell her all this?" Simon said, worriedly.

"Nothing, she's a good person, like her father. She'll do the right thing."

"What about the third organizer? There were three," Pearl asked, barely able to contain herself.

"I couldn't kill him. I helped him go underground and, for my betrayal, the Company had me committed to work in the teal for a few years. When I got out, the heat was off and we got married. His name was Shane Vedter," Aunt Ruth said, taking out a small photo and gazing at it.

Simon lowered his head. It was like a bomb had gone off, destroying everything he thought he knew about his family on Mars. Ishihara sat in stunned silence, while Pearl clapped quietly, glad for the interesting story. Aunt Ruth just smiled at Pearl, glad some of what made her innocent had survived all she endured.

Simon collected his thoughts, and did his best to sit up. "What else is in this file, Aunt Ruth?"

There was no response. When Simon looked down the aisle to the crew compartment, Ishihara was solemnly picking up Aunt Ruth's limp form out of the comm seat. She carried her back over to where Simon sat, laying her down in Simon's lap so he could have a few last moments with her. Pearl and Ishihara stood over Simon while he held his aunt.

When she was gone, Simon looked up at Pearl and Ishihara, tears in his eyes. "They're all gone now. I've no family left on Mars."

"You have us," Ishihara said, nodding to Pearl.

"Thanks," Simon said, brushing his hand over his aunt's face to close her eyes.

Camille nodded. "We need to get that file, set things right for her."

"Yeah, we do. Should we just go, or wait for Ezra One?"

Camille and Simon both looked to Pearl.

"We should wait, but I'll keep the transport powered up. If things are bad, run inside and we'll go. That's what Aunt Ruth said we should do," Pearl said.

Simon set about repairing the structural damage to his leg braces so he could at least limp along. They'd be unpowered until he could fix the circuitry, but they'd allow him to at least stay upright if he had to. Camille pulled a long parts bag from the back of the transport and laid Aunt Ruth down inside of it with her belongings. She paused for a moment before zipping the bag up.

Death was a constant on Mars and life was cheap. Any kind of attachment tended to be dangerous, and painful. Ishihara was starting to understand why. The sadness and anger she felt was unbearable. Something had gone wrong long ago, pushing the destiny of Mars in a bad direction. Ishihara resolved to find the truth of it all, even if she had to violently shake every person in administrative white to find it.

They didn't wait long before the chartered flight landed a few port spaces over. When the cargo bay doors opened, two Drones, one large, one small, exited with Dell, his hands zip-tied behind his back. Shell casings rolled out onto the flight deck as they exited, just before interior cabin lights clicked on. The interior looked like a massacre, dead collectors in rubbery black suits strewn about all over the place. The chartered flight didn't even wait for the cargo door to close before it took off.

"You could have killed us all!" Dell bellowed, staggering forward.

"What are you talking about?" Athos One asked, a broad smile on his face.

"You said they were rigged with bombs! Shooting the androids could have set them off," Dell said, panicked, turning to look at Ezra One.

Ezra One smiled slightly, shaking his head at Dell, while Athos One covered his mouth to laugh.

"You played me, there were no bombs...Cerise wasn't going to kill us?" Dell said, looking very pale.

"When you're trying to rattle someone who jumps at shadows, it's pretty easy for guys like us to be the shadows," Ezra said, shoving Dell forward.

Simon and Ishihara waited a few paces from the cargo door of their transport, watching the drama and quietly delighting in Dell's discomfort. Athos One held Dell down on the ground, putting his knee in the middle of his back. Ezra One gave him a nod, then walked forward to talk with Simon.

"You guys okay?" Ezra One said, looking around warily.

"I waited for you. What do you want?" Simon asked, impatiently.

"Where is your aunt, and Pearl?" Ezra One asked.

"My aunt passed away," Simon said, leaning on Ishihara.

Ezra One nodded, taking off his knit cap and holding it respectfully. "I'm sorry for your loss."

"What do you care?" Ishihara said, folding her arms.

"I care whenever a fellow soldier passes," Ezra One said.

"What makes you think she was?" Simon asked, genuinely curious.

"You can tell a lot about someone by how they hold a knife. What's it going to take to catch a break with you people? What do I need to do to earn your trust?" Ezra One asked, shaking his head.

"You can give us Dell, that'd be a start," Ishihara said, gesturing to her coach.

"And, tell us what you want. No cloak and dagger, just tell us what you want," Simon said.

"Dragos told me you want to meet with Marshal Rider in exchange for information about Cerise. I'm here to broker that deal," Ezra One said, motioning to Athos One to let Dell up.

"Thank you!" Dell said, running forward.

Ishihara smiled warmly and nodded to Dell before punching him hard and low in the gut. He gasped for air for a moment, Ishihara bending over to meet his gaze. He opened his mouth to cuss her out, but she laid him out with a swift left hook before he had a chance. Simon nearly fell in the exchange, but Ishihara steadied him as she rolled Dell over on his stomach with her foot. Ezra One and Athos One watched impassively, pausing to squint at Dell and make sure he was still breathing.

"Marshal Rider and most of my friends are trapped in the Mars Company complex. The whole zone lost power a couple of hours ago and they'll suffocate if we don't get them out. The magnetic seals holding up the security partitions failed, sealing everyone inside. I need help getting them out if you want to have your meeting," Ezra One explained.

"And you think we can do this for you?" Ishihara said, smirking.

Ezra nodded. "Yes, I do."

"We can do it, but I need to go back to my machine shop," Simon said, eliciting a shocked expression from Ishihara.

"That's too dangerous right now. Cerise is going to be aware something has gone wrong very soon, if she doesn't know already," Ezra One said, shaking his head.

"There's a file implicating the Mars Company Conglomerate in murder and conspiracy, and it explains how and why Marshal Rider's father died," Simon explained.

Ezra looked back over shoulder at Athos One. "Do you need us to open the security partitions?"

"No, Camille and I can handle it," Simon said, nodding to Ishihara.

"Athos One and I will get the file, and meet you at the Administrative Zone," Ezra One said, pulling out his mobile and checking the time.

"It's under the floorboards, beneath my Aunt Ruth's room, it's…"

Ezra nodded, and turned to go. "I can find her room by scent, we're going to get rolling."

"You don't want a lift to the zone edge?" Ishihara asked.

Ezra One paused, looking back over his shoulder. "You'd give us a ride?"

"No, but it's odd that you wouldn't ask," Simon said.

"Cerise is thousands of years old and more dangerous than you can imagine. Very shortly, she is going to want Athos One and me to be very dead. I've every confidence she has the resources to try and make that happen. You're in enough danger already. I don't want to compound it with my presence," Ezra One explained before waving to Athos One to take point.

"Good to know, I guess we'll do our best to steer clear," Ishihara said, helping Simon limp back to the transport.

Once inside, Ishihara helped Simon to the comm seat. They watched the Drones vanish into the maintenance access leading down into the rest of the resort tower. Dell, still face down on the landing platform, twitched and choked on the blood pooling around his face.

"Are we really going to let them go through the workshop and just take stuff? I want to know what's in that file," Ishihara said, walking slowly out to pick up Dell.

"No, we'll get there first, grab up the file. Drones are good at detecting deception and I needed them to believe we were on board with whatever nonsense they're mixed up in," Simon said, frowning.

"That story, about Cerise being thousands of years old?" Ishihara asked, dragging Dell into the transport.

"There are Ichthyic Metasapients that have lived to be more than a century. I guess that's different than being thousands of years old," Pearl said, doing her best to help.

"Drones are also known for being very literal, but Type One military grade individuals are clearly capable of deception. They managed to trick Dell it sounds like," Simon said.

"Tricking Dell doesn't make you a master of social subterfuge. Let's be clear, he's not a genius. Speaking of genius, how do you know all this stuff about Drones?" Ishihara muttered, dropping Dell on the cargo bay floor like a sack of potatoes.

"It's in the core policing manual loaded onto the Aegis Armor. I read a lot of it between picking people up while I was looking for you."

"They looked sad," Pearl said, tapping her fingertips together.

"Who?" Ishihara asked, strapping in.

"Athos One and Ezra One. I don't think they were sad for the same reasons, either. Are we going to help their friends?" Pearl asked.

Simon looked to Ishihara, shrugging. "Pearl, is that what you want to do?" Simon asked.

"Yes, I want to help them."

"Okay, but we're only going to do it because you want to," Ishihara said, hitting the cargo door latch with her fist.

Pearl took them up, flying fast through the empty travel lanes, and skirting the large resort towers and infrastructure. There were unused monorail systems and other attractions that were all dark. The whole zone was like a slumbering dream of what Mars could have been. Ishihara was glad to see it get small behind them as they merged into the dense Mining Company traffic that would be their company on the way home.

Dell slid around on the floor unconscious, gently coming to rest under the personnel seating on the far side. Simon worked to reconnect the Aegis before they landed and to check the status of whatever had hijacked her systems before. As they were making their landing behind the workshop in the Mechanical Zone, the Aegis booted up successfully after two failed attempts.

"Aegis, do you have control of all systems?" Simon asked, speaking to her through the comm station.

"*Negative. Foreign intrusion detected.*"

"Tell me how to resolve it, if you can," Simon said, looking through the front port warily for trouble.

"*Physically disabling my communications array would sever the connection. However, I will have no way to communicate with the Ares AI, or the law enforcement servers, relays, or databases.*"

"I could hook up the mobile Taylor gave me as a relay, but it would leave our ship vulnerable to similar intrusion. If only there was a way to get both our transport and Aegis on the other side of the encryption it is providing us," Simon said, scratching his chin.

"What if we asked her for another mobile?" Pearl asked, smiling.

"I think Taylor is one of Ezra One's friends trapped at the conglomerate administrative complex," Ishihara said, opening the cargo bay door and looking out.

Pearl sulked. "Oh."

"It's a good idea, Pearl. If we had another mobile with similar processing architecture, I bet we could clone it. Then we would have two," Simon said, nodding.

"That sounds hard," Pearl said, frowning.

Simon patted Pearl on the shoulder. "Well, the hard part will be finding a mobile like this one. You don't see very many of them on Mars. No one can afford them."

"We could ask the free Ichthyic folks that live under the teal," Pearl said, watching Ishihara circle around the workshop and check things out.

"Do you really think they'd have one?" Simon said, astonished.

"You'd be surprised what people lose down the drain. When Mister Janjigian needed contraband, and the teal couldn't provide it, he asked me to go to the fish market and look."

"Fish market?" Simon said, quizzically.

Pearl smiled. "Well, that's what humans call it."

Ishihara stepped back in and abruptly threw Dell out onto the ground outside.

"We good, Camille?" Simon asked.

"I don't know. Something doesn't feel right," Ishihara said, looking around nervously.

"Okay, help me grab a few things and we'll get out of here," Simon said, struggling to his feet.

They grabbed what Simon thought he would need from his workshop and located the file under his Aunt Ruth's bed. Ishihara placed Aunt Ruth on the couch reverently, taking a moment to look around. Simon made quick work of the repairs to his leg braces, joining Ishihara in the living space.

"We should go, Camille," Simon said, tugging on Ishihara's arm.

"It's weird to have her gone. It's weird to miss her, or anyone, I guess. Never been cozy with anybody like I am with you guys," Ishihara said, pulling Aunt Ruth's favorite blanket over her still form.

Simon swallowed. "Yeah, it is."

When they stepped outside, Dell was sitting up, looking about bleary-eyed. "What have you done, Camille?"

"Shut up, Dell," Ishihara said, walking past him to the transport.

Dell reached up and grabbed Simon by the arm as he walked past. "This shit won't land only on me. It will land on us all."

Simon jerked free, shoving Dell to the ground even as he struggled to rise. "Don't touch me."

"Do you think she will just let you roam free?" Dell bellowed, struggling to right himself.

"With my aunt gone, she's got no more leverage, no one to take from me," Simon said, stepping up into the transport with Ishihara.

"There's always more to take," Dell said, watching the transport slowly ascend.

CHAPTER 16

MARS COLONY, VEDTER MACHINEWORKS – MECHANICAL ZONE 062

August 13th, 2200

Dell watched the transport rise up past the habitation spires and vanish amidst the pollution drifting just below the environmental dome. He started to check his mobile for a signal, but thought better of it. He tried the handle on Simon's shop and found it unlocked. Letting himself in, he looked around for a rig radio he could use, only to find the terminal was locked out. There was an older one, but he would have to wait for it to charge.

In the next room, Ruth opened her eyes and took a deep breath, willing her lungs to operate normally again. Taking out a shiv, she slowly cut herself out of the zippered bag and sat up. The house was empty, but could hear Dell cursing and pacing back and forth in the workshop. He was too preoccupied with whatever dilemma he was facing that he didn't hear her enter.

She approached swiftly, hitting him across his right leg with a pipe, crushing the lateral femoral nerve. He went down, crying out in agony. Before he could rise, she hit him again in the same place on his left leg, eliciting an even more panicked scream. Grasping both legs, he turned over to see Ruth standing over him.

"You're dead, they put you in a bag," Dell said, through clenched teeth.

"Yeah, I needed a little time alone with you, and a couple other folks. Thanks for making it easy to find you," Ruth said, kneeling down beside him and dropping the pipe.

"What the hell do you want?"

"It was a thing I practiced in the teal, in case I ever needed to get out quickly. You had to be quick or lucky to avoid getting pushed out an airlock. You'd be surprised what you can learn in that place if you aren't too busy making book," Aunt Ruth said, twirling the shiv around in her hand.

"My legs, they won't work right," Dell complained, trying to rise.

"It'll pass. Did the kids just leave you outside?" Aunt Ruth said, laughing.

"Yeah, they took off in a hurry," Dell said, trying to rub feeling back into his knees.

"Where's Cerise, Dell? How do I get close to her?" Ruth asked, patiently.

"Go to hell. I'm probably already in deep for talking to those Drones. If any of the androids on board were online and wired for sound, I'm done."

Ruth nodded, understanding his predicament. "When I was in the teal, there was a rat that talked to the Warden Authority about the Company. I vivisected him. You'd be surprised how much you can take someone apart and still keep them alive. You have to have a heat source, cybernetic suspensions drugs, and a few other things that are pretty hard to get in prison."

"Yeah, so?"

"I have pretty much all that stuff just laying around here at the shop, Dell," Ruth said, pressing the point of her shiv to his nose.

"I'm not telling you anything."

Ruth smiled. "I was hoping you'd say that."

CHAPTER 17

MARS COLONY, MARS COMPANY HEAVY EQ HQ – COLD STORAGE UNIT

August 13th, 2200

Sleeping in the transport wasn't ideal, but Pearl managed to land on the inside of an exhaust duct outside one of the larger refining plants. Simon hoped it would make them invisible to both regular visual detection and other electronic detection methods. Smoke billowed past the portholes, the thrum of the refinery shaking the transport at regular rhythmic intervals.

"You look in the file yet?" Ishihara asked, looking up at the ceiling of the cargo bay from her bedroll.

"No, be my guest," Simon said, gesturing to the thick packet of paper on the crew seats.

"I'm nervous. If Aunt Ruth was a company operator, everything in there is going to be spooky," Ishihara said, frowning.

"Why do you think I haven't looked at it yet?" Simon said with a chuckle.

Pearl sat nearby, having slept less than an hour, but it was all she ever seemed to require. She was playing with a hotplate, trying to figure out how to set it up to make tea or at least some oats. Simon was in his bedroll on the opposite side, thumbing through the mobile Taylor gave him.

"How is it that you can't figure out a hotplate, but you are an ace at the controls of a transport?" Ishihara said, sitting up and gesturing for Pearl to hand the small device over.

"I don't know," Pearl said, sulking.

"See, you turn this knob here to set the time, this lets the fuel travel up to the burner, and this is the sparker that you use to start it," Ishihara explained, showing Pearl how to work the hotplate.

Pearl smiled, setting a small pot of water on the hotplate. "Thanks."

"It's probably about time to get rolling. I'm dying to know how you're going to restore power to the Administrative Zone so the security partitions can be raised," Ishihara said, standing up and looking for her pants.

"I'm not going to restore power to anything, it'll take too long. Those people are going to be pretty hungry by now," Simon said, sitting up and sliding into his leg braces.

Ishihara gave him a funny look. "Each one is tons and tons of duracrete. We just going to go down there and lift?"

"With a very large front loader from the yard below us, yeah," Simon said, smiling wickedly.

"You're going to just clip one from the yard, drive it to the elevator, and drive off once we're at the administrative district?" Ishihara asked, raising her eyebrows.

"Yes," Simon replied, his smile widening.

"It won't fit down those narrow walkways and streets in the Administrative Zone. You'll make a colossal mess."

"I know," Simon said, his mischievous smile only getting more crooked at the thought.

Ishihara sighed. "Cool, I'm in."

"Me, too," Pearl said, handing out small cups of boiled oats.

The cold storage yard was full of ancient mining equipment. It was too expensive to repair some of it and the cost of removing it from Mars was slightly more than building more environmental domes to house them.

Simon had to climb in and out of several front loaders before finding one that was minimally functional for his purposes.

"What's wrong with this one?" Ishihara said, holding Simon up on her shoulders.

"The sifter is broken, but everything else works, including the radio. It's perfect. I bet the reactor still has half a charge, more than enough for the mayhem I have planned," Simon said, unplugging his diagnostic tool from the maintenance port on the front loader.

Ishihara pushed up until Simon was standing on the palms of her hands. It was just far enough he could grab the bottom rungs of the ladder that would allow him to access the cockpit. He pulled himself up, hand over hand, until he was at the cabin door. Using a pry bar, he popped the lock on the door and slid into the pilot seat. The front loader started right up, causing the enormous rubber tires to jerk, sending a decade of red Martian dust to fall on Ishihara. She coughed, shaking a fist at Simon.

"Simon, come down here so I can punch you!" Ishihara bellowed.

Simon looked back out, holding a finger up to his lips. "Quiet, this is supposed to be a heist," Simon said with a wink.

"We'll shadow you with the transport. Keep the cockpit locked and expect a punch when we get to the top of the mining elevator," Ishihara said. She turned and ran back toward the transport.

Simon dropped the huge front loader into gear and spun it around through the cold storage lot. He had to push past a couple of other pieces of machinery, but the security fence was designed to keep people out. The front loader rolled over the top of it with ease, the tires more than twice the height of the chain link and barbed wire.

"Maybe I should have driven the loader," Pearl joked over the radio.

"You'll get your turn after I'm done," Simon said, dropping it into high gear.

Pearl followed him from the air, staying high in the refinery smog as it drifted toward huge exhaust fans at the top of the environmental dome. From the air, it looked like black tentacles reaching up from the ground. Pearl wove around them to maintain good visibility on Simon, flying slowly to match his speed.

Fortune continued to favor them as they reached the elevator. It was making the descent, empty on the return trip down the mountain. Simon was able to just drive aboard and park, taking up the entire span of the elevator in the process. Pearl followed him up, using the directional thrusters to keep the transport at a steep angle while ascending slowly, something few pilots could do for very long.

"You could have taken the flight lane, it would have been easier," Simon said over the radio, looking back down the elevator shaft.

"You said to follow you," Pearl whispered, the majority of her focus on keeping the transport steady.

"I think you both just like to scare me with your driving," Ishihara said, eyes closed, sitting at the comm.

"That, too," Pearl said, smiling faintly, and making several micro-corrections to the course.

At the top of the elevator, Simon fired up the front loader again and headed toward the security checkpoint outside the Administrative Zone. The front fence had already been ripped off, but there were new concrete partitions that formed a barrier. Simon hit them squarely, the tires on the front loader slowly rolling over the barriers, crushing them.

The power was off throughout the zone. It was evident that it had been that way for hours as the loader began pumping stagnant air into the cockpit. Simon switched on the spotlights and set them to roam up front to give him as much visibility as possible. He'd expected that some of Ezra One's story wouldn't be true, as the Administrative Zones tended to have so many redundancies and safeguards.

He sounded the horn, rolling toward the most direct route to the Mars Conglomerate offices. While the area was mostly deserted, a few people darted out of buildings before Simon slowly rolled through. The front loader ground the decorative façade off the fronts of the various shops, offices, and dwellings, narrowly missing supports as long as Simon kept the loader straight. A pair of dwellings were not so fortunate at each of the turns he had to make.

As he got near the conglomerate offices, he could see the partitions were down as Ezra One said they would be. The usual line of people coming and going was absent, only two sacks from a noodle cart sitting side by side adorned the street out front. The lights of his transport appeared overhead as Pearl began to circle in front of the building, looking for a place to set down.

"Stay in the air," Simon said, over the radio, worried there could be trouble on the ground.

"We'll grab you from the cockpit of the loader if things get dumb down there," Ishihara replied.

Simon dropped the forks on the front loader and lowered them to the ground, gouging the carefully manicured concrete walkway. Simon felt a moment of panic as the loader fought the weight of the partition to even get the clearance for the forks. Finally, the threshold gave way, allowing the forks to grind under. Simon dropped the loader into high gear, hoping the hydraulics would hold under so much weight.

"Here goes nothing," he whispered, the load control shaking violently in his grasp.

The front loader hesitated at first, lifting the security partition up a couple of feet at a time before finally getting it high enough that the magnetic locks clicked in to hold it up. It wasn't a moment too soon as hydraulic cables burst, sending jets of black fluid down at a velocity high enough to cut up the street below. The front loader jerked, automatically powering down as the internal sensors detected an unsafe operating condition.

Weary and relieved people began streaming out of the building. None were wearing Mars Company black rubber and only a handful of security personnel appeared to be armed. Simon waited for a moment, making sure it was safe to disembark before climbing out to stand on one of the wheel wells of the loader. He waved to the transport, signaling for Pearl to set down.

Simon climbed down the ladder and dropped to Ishihara's waiting arms. Pearl disembarked as well, but with her flight helmet still on. There were many questions, particularly about the Aegis Armor sitting in the cargo hold of the transport. Simon and Ishihara ignored the bureaucrats and building security personnel, making their way back to the transport.

Ezra One and Athos One dropped from the undercarriage of the transport, crouching down to walk out from beneath it. "Thanks for the ride," Ezra One said, walking past toward the open security partition.

"Well, now I know why I had a funny feeling back at the shop. How'd they beat us there? Should we just go?" Ishihara asked.

Simon shook his head. "The Marshal might be here. I want to give her the Aegis if she is."

"And the file?"

"I don't know, Camille. Let's see how this plays out," Simon said, nodding toward Silverstein and Taylor as they emerged from the security checkpoint.

Taylor started over first, her million-watt smile almost shedding real light. Silverstein walked beside her, a disarming ease about him as he placed his hands in his pockets, fishing around for his cigarettes and lighter. The two had traveled a couple hundred million miles together and it showed.

"You're early," Silverstein said, looking at an ancient timepiece on his wrist.

"Early? You were expecting us?" Simon asked.

"It's a thing he does. Everything is just math and probability to him," Taylor said, smiling.

"Did you even need me to come and open the security partition? Is this some kind of game?" Simon asked, a little angry.

"Definitely not. I couldn't predict what Cerise would do exactly, only that it would be bad and involve her assets, specific people in her employ. Your intervention on our behalf is as timely as it is appreciated," Silverstein said, growing more serious.

"He means to say thank you, but he's kind of bad at it," Taylor said, taking Simon and Ishihara's hands.

"You moon-folk are kinda touchy," Ishihara said, pulling her hand away.

Simon gave Taylor's hand a squeeze and let go. "I guess you must have seen all kinds of things on your way to Mars, being so cool about all this."

Taylor laughed. "No one grieves more for Mars than I do, but we have to carry on, yes?"

"Is the Marshal here? I'd like to talk to her. I have something that belongs to her," Simon said, nodding.

Silverstein nodded. "She is, but we need to…"

Dragos broke through the crowd, carrying Hashti and looking frantic. There was little of her not wrapped in makeshift bandages, most soaked through with blood. Ezra One and Athos One flanked him, both wearing grave expressions.

"She's not breathing," Dragos said, his words strangled by panic.

"We need to get her to the medical facility, see if someone there can help," Taylor said.

"Can I charter a flight?" Silverstein said, looking at Simon.

"She won't make it like this," Pearl said, removing her flight helmet and stepping forward.

The congregation stopped and stared at Pearl for a moment. Ignoring the odd looks, she beckoned anxiously for Dragos to bring Hashti. "Please, tell us what to do," Dragos pleaded.

"I need that equipment locker," Pearl said, pointing up metal box bolted to the front loader.

Dragos clambered over to the side of the front loader, Ezra One quickly leaping up past him. With two quick swipes of his claws, Ezra One cut the bolts holding the equipment box. Dragos used his bionic arm to rip it open, finding nothing inside. He looked at Pearl, but she had already sprinted inside the Mars Conglomerate checkpoint. Within moments, she came running back pulling a firehose along with her.

"There's nothing," Dragos said, holding up the equipment locker.

"That's good. Use something to plug the bolt holes and set it down over here," Pearl instructed.

Ezra One pulled out some detonation putty and stopped up the holes. Once he'd done that, Pearl used the firehose on low pressure to fill the equipment locker with water. After it was half full, she began frantically removing Hashti's bandages. Silverstein knelt down beside her and helped until all of Hashti's terrible wounds were revealed.

"What are you doing?" Dragos said, covering his face.

"Camille, grab all the salt packets from the sack of food I brought with us," Pearl said, pointing back to the transport.

Silverstein helped Pearl gently lift Hashti into the equipment locker, letting her slide beneath the water. Dragos ran forward to stop them, grief and extreme emotional distress making him irrational. Athos One and Ezra One grabbed him by the arms, holding him back. Ishihara ran back from the transport, carrying a large bag of salt packets.

"Help me," Pearl said, tearing open a salt packet and dumping it into the water.

Silverstein and Ishihara ripped packets open, one at a time, until Pearl stopped them. "Okay, that's enough. We don't want too much."

Hashti jerked, bubbles rising up from her face as she began using her gills to breathe the water. Hashti couldn't open her eyes and the confined space of the locker caused her to panic and struggle feebly. Pearl reached down into the water and put her hand on Hashti's face trying to soothe her. She weakly clutched Pearl's hand. Feeling the scaled skin of a fellow Ichthyic Metasapient, she calmed down.

"You were hurting her. The bandages and exposure to the air was keeping her from being able to heal," Pearl explained.

Dragos covered his face, distraught. "I didn't know."

"It's not your fault. I've never seen a Sphyraenic Metasapient like her. They are usually larger, and... very scary. They are not as lovely as she is," Pearl said, smiling as she reached down into the water to smooth Hashti's hair out of her face.

"Thank you. I have so few friends, to lose even one..." Dragos said, bowing his head.

"I know. I know how that is," Pearl said, looking over to Simon and Ishihara.

Pearl lowered the water pressure and placed the hose into the equipment box so that fresh water continued to flow. "You should leave her in there until she wants to come out."

"Yes, I will stay with her," Dragos said, taking the hose and kneeling beside the equipment locker.

The gentle hiss of hydraulics and footfalls of powered armor made the gathering outside the checkpoint go quiet. A pair of illuminators swayed in the darkness just beyond the raised security partition, a familiar shape appearing in the gloom. Marshal Rider strode out in her new Aegis Armor, badge shining in the spotlights of the front loader as her sidearms clicked at her hips.

"Disperse. Return to work and wait for power to be restored, or go home. Either way, you can't be obstructing the checkpoint," Marshal Rider ordered, the crowd parting for her as she walked forward.

She paused at the sight revealed before her as bureaucrats returned to their offices to work by lantern light. Security personnel took up their positions inside, doubling up behind the one door that was open. Ishihara walked forward first, with Simon and Pearl walking along beside her.

Marshal Rider looked past them to Hashti and Dragos. "You put her in the water. Of course, why didn't I think of that?"

"Pearl did that. My friend Simon has something he'd like to say," Ishihara said, nudging Simon.

Marshal Rider's visor slide back revealing her face. "Thank you, Pearl. Hello again, Simon. How is your aunt?"

"Heh, you remember me?" Simon smiled.

"It is not a day I will ever forget." Marshal Rider said, taking a deep breath.

Simon nodded. "I've done my best to repair your armor. I didn't realize you had a second Aegis."

"Thank you. I didn't, until very recently."

Simon sighed. "I've some other information, about your father, and how he died."

Marshal Rider looked incredulous at first, narrowing her eyes. Simon held up the file, showing her the thick stack of yellowing paper. Marshal Rider reached out, turning it over in her hand and looking at the markings and the numbers on the tab and exterior.

"Have you looked inside?" Marshal Rider asked.

"No, I've been afraid to," Simon admitted.

"This looks like several physical archive files, missing from my father's records. He generated these during the weeks before he was assassinated," Marshal Rider said, her lips tight and thin.

"My Aunt Ruth confessed before her death that she was the assassin, operating on behalf of Mars Company and the Conglomerate. She killed Angelica Preston as well. This file has something in it about all that, and my aunt had it stashed away, probably as insurance," Simon said, unsure of how Marshal Rider would react.

"My father must have had the file with him when he went to the meeting. Your aunt must have had her reasons for not turning them over to Mars Company," Marshal Rider said.

"She was a nice lady. There must be more to the story," Pearl said.

Marshal Rider smiled. "Probably."

"You're being really cool about all this. He just told you who killed your dad and why," Ishihara said, observing Marshal Rider's calm demeanor.

"There is no other way to be. Until we figure out who ordered the assassination contracts, it's just another case that needs to be worked."

"So, what happens now?" Simon asked, offering the file to Marshal Rider.

"Those documents are fine where they are. I have a security detail to work, something important to the entire colony," Marshal Rider said, holding up an armored hand.

Simon blinked in disbelief. "I… don't understand."

"You need to work the case and follow all the leads. Find out who gave the orders to have my father and Angelica Preston killed," Marshal Rider said.

"Um, what? Why me?" Simon said, eyebrows crawling up his forehead.

"Work the case, Deputy Marshal Simon Vedter, and report back to me when you've got enough to make an arrest or execute summary judgement," Marshal Rider said.

"What? Whoa, wait a minute. What about your armor?" Simon said, pointing a thumb back toward the transport.

"It wasn't designed for Law Enforcement. My grandmother made it to help someone like you, someone who got hurt. She'd be glad it was helping someone like you," Marshal Rider explained, pointing to Simon's leg braces.

"No, I can't. It's priceless hardware and part of your family legacy."

Marshal Rider shook her head. "Yes, you can. That's your Aegis now, Deputy Marshal Vedter. Take good care of her, and she'll take care of you."

Simon just blinked, not sure of what to say, then looked fearfully at the file in his hand.

"My aunt said I broke the prison code when I put the armor on, that I would always be on the outside of the teal or something," Simon said.

"Now, you're starting to understand. The moment you decided to put that armor on and help all those people, you were branded blue. You'll never be able to wear Mining Company orange or prison teal and have it mean the same thing again," Marshal Rider said, tapping the star riveted to her armor.

Simon sighed. "I wish someone had told me that beforehand."

"Would it have changed anything if someone had? Would you have left Camille Ishihara out there to drown or freeze to death?" Marshal Rider asked.

Simon looked over at Ishihara. "No, but she didn't end up needing my help. She managed to get out of there on her own. It would have worked out."

"Not for all the people you ended up pulling out of there. You took a big risk for a bunch of strangers."

"I don't know. All I've ever done is keep my head down, turn wrenches, and take care of my aunt."

Marshal Rider stepped in close and lowered her voice. "I won't make you wear the badge. Your aunt was right, though. It isn't safe for you on Mars if you don't. I thought I could walk away from it. That my father being a Marshal wouldn't blow back on me. I found out the hard way that Mars doesn't work that way."

"I'm not sure I could look down the sights of a gun and kill someone. I fix things, that's what I try to do."

"That is never easy, and doesn't get easier. For now, just find the bad guys, we'll worry about what to do with them after you've figured out who they are," Marshal Rider said, pointing to the file.

"What about Pearl? She helped me while I wore the armor," Simon asked, looking over at Pearl, worriedly.

"I'd keep her close, at least until you figure out why your aunt stashed that file."

"That works for me. I'd like to know more about this anyway, as it involves my family," Simon said, tucking the file under his arm.

"Oh, before I forget." Marshal Rider said, fumbling with a pouch on her duty belt, pulling out a ticket book and pen. Then, she held it out to Ishihara, expectantly.

"Uh, what's this for?" Ishihara asked, taking the ticket book.

"Can I have your autograph? And could you sign it as the 'The Roman'? Might be my only chance before the championship game."

CHAPTER 18

**MARS COLONY, MARS COMPANY ADMINISTRATIVE ZONE –
CENTRAL SECURITY ACCESS**

August 13th, 2200

"Simon, are we really going to track down these people? People that can call hits on union organizers?" Ishihara said, sitting down beside Pearl in the crew compartment of the transport.

Simon nodded. "Whoever it was, they messed up derby for decades. Angelica Preston would have kept the sport honest and given all the girls representation. You do want to know who that was, right?"

"I do."

"Then why are you...?"

"I want to kill whoever did it," Ishihara said, wrapping an arm around Pearl and taking a bite of her sandwich.

Pearl looked over astonished. "Kill?"

"Yeah, and I'm wondering if you're going to go all white hat on me. Are you going to forget where we come from?" Ishihara said, gesturing to the Aegis Armor in the cargo hold.

Taylor was in the cargo hold as well, hands pressed to the outside of the Aegis Armor. She'd been there for about ten minutes, communing with the artificial intelligence within. Silverstein sat nearby, reading a book.

"It's my prerogative... if I decide to be a Deputy Marshal. When Marshal Rider said 'summary judgement' before, that's a fancy word for killing a criminal," Simon said, looking longingly at Pearl's sandwich.

Pearl sighed, breaking off a corner of her sandwich and handing it to Simon. "We shouldn't kill anyone."

"Yes, we totally should," Ishihara said, standing up and leaving the crew compartment.

"Pearl, remember when you were so angry you wanted to kill Mister Janjigian?" Simon said, taking a bit of sandwich.

"It's like that?" Pearl said, frowning sadly.

"Yeah it is, except that whoever it is didn't hurt just one or two girls. They hurt hundreds over the years," Simon explained.

"It still feels bad to me," Pearl said, looking over at Ishihara as she paced the cargo hold.

"Me, too," Simon admitted, not sure he wanted to kill anyone, no matter how bad they were.

Taylor pulled her hands back from the suit and opened her eyes. She blinked away the augmented reality she had been experiencing a moment before, delving through Aegis's relays and circuits. When Silverstein saw that Taylor was finished, he slipped the book he'd been reading into the breast pocket of his suit coat and stood up. He lingered by the cargo hatch, checking the time on his mobile.

Taylor smiled and patted the armor. "It should be free of intrusion now. It will be far more difficult the next time Octavo tries anything like this again."

"Should be? Octavo?" Ishihara said, pausing to fold her arms and look worriedly at the Aegis.

Taylor blushed. "Octavo is the name of the tele-mechanic that was messing with the armor remotely. I don't really know how my abilities work. I've been told it is better that I don't."

"I thought all you tech-shamans were world class coders and hackers," Ishihara said, squinting at Taylor.

"Thank you for doing this," Simon said, giving Ishihara a stern look.

"It is the least I could do after you got us out of that building," Taylor said, looking through a large bag she carried with her.

"Sure, hopefully I can get the union down here to figure out why the power is out," Simon replied, looking up from the monitor.

"Don't worry about that, I've got it handled," Silverstein said, gazing at the glowing screen on his mobile.

"What are you really doing here?" Simon said, shaking his head at Silverstein.

"The Ares AI institutional governance system has been damaged beyond repair. I'm installing a new institutional grade AI that will be able to take the place of Ares."

Simon looked around in shock. "That's why everything is going haywire and work contracts aren't being renewed?"

Silverstein nodded.

"Well, all those weird parts you asked me about at the scrapyard make more sense now," Simon said, worriedly.

"Thanks for that, by the way. Your assistance helped to guide us to some crucial components," Silverstein said, smiling.

Simon nodded, glad he'd decided to help. "Sure, I…"

"She's putting a lot of trust in you," Ezra One said, stepping up into the cargo hold.

"Who?"

"Marshal Rider, don't let her down," Ezra One said, meeting Simon's gaze.

Simon looked down at Ezra One, then over at Athos One. "I'd be more worried about your friend over there."

"They already know everything," Athos One countered, holding up his hands defensively.

"It took me a minute to remember who you were. I guess I should thank you for going into the wrecker line to get me when I was a kid. Somehow, that doesn't feel right, all things considered," Simon said, bitterly.

"We're all on the same side now. Simon, I'm sure you can appreciate what it's like to be under Cerise's thumb. Athos One was no different," Silverstein said, trying to diffuse the situation.

"With all due respect, it is very different if Athos One was the one that set the explosives that killed my uncle and left me partially paralyzed," Simon said, glaring at Athos One.

Silverstein nodded. "I agree. You deserve to know what happened that day."

Athos One opened his mouth to speak, but nothing came out. He let his hands drop to his side before walking away, obviously as sad as he was conflicted. Ezra One watched him walk away for a moment before turning back to address Simon.

"Maybe you should tell us more about how you're mixed up in all this."

"Why don't you ask your buddy out there?" Simon said, sitting down in one of the crew seats.

Pearl came up beside Simon, glaring at Ezra One. "You are upsetting my friend. Get off my transport. Now."

"Simon, let me know if we can help," Taylor said, taking Silverstein's arm and walking with him down the ramp.

"Thank you, I appreciate it," Simon said, taking a deep breath.

Ezra One held fast for a moment before Pearl comically shooed him off. Once they were safely down the ramp, Pearl bumped the button to the cargo bay door, closing it. Ishihara clapped Pearl on the shoulder and looked over at Simon.

"Your transport?" Simon said, looking at Pearl and raising an eyebrow.

Pearl smiled shyly. "I did say that, didn't I? I didn't mean anything by it."

"As far as I'm concerned, this is your transport," Ishihara said, wrapping an arm around her.

Simon nodded. "Agreed. We might have stolen it, fair and square, but you're the one flying it."

"And hopefully making the sandwiches," Ishihara added.

"Yep. That pretty much makes it yours in my book," Simon said, laughing.

Pearl bawled, covering her face with one hand and patting the interior of the transport with the other. "I've never owned anything, ever."

"It'll take money to keep and maintain it. We'll figure it out," Simon said, taking a deep breath.

"Well, if you decide to be the Deputy Marshal, you won't be hoofing it around the colony. You'll need a dedicated chartered transport," Ishihara said, smiling knowingly.

"Yeah, even with the assistive tech in the armor, walking too far will be rough. Not even sure I've got the heat issue compensated for. How about it, Pearl? You up for it?" Simon asked.

"Yes!" Pearl said, excitedly.

"No, not unless you agree to do the maintenance and pay her a daily," Ishihara interrupted.

"Whose side are you on, Camille?" Simon said, laughing.

"Representing my girl is how I earn a few free rides, hopefully."

"The transport is nice, my new friends are better," Pearl said, hugging both Ishihara and Simon.

"Speaking of transport, where do we go from here? I don't think I thought much past today and none of it went how I thought it would," Simon said, putting a hand on the Aegis Armor.

"Somewhere quiet, crack open that file, figure it out," Ishihara said, sitting down in a crew seat.

"What about Silverstein and Ezra One?" Pearl asked.

Simon bowed his head. "Everyone I've ever met from Earth or the Lunar Colony has been bad news. My family basically gave me up. I think they thought I'd lived on Mars long enough the stink of it would never leave me."

"You're tight with Marshal Rider. She's from Mars, like us. That's probably all that matters," Ishihara said, nodding to Simon.

Simon hit the cargo bay door button, and headed out. He walked back across the street to equipment locker where Hashti was recuperating. Dragos stood up, nodding to him as he approached.

"Who did this to your friend?" Simon asked.

"You asking me as a cop?" Dragos said, frowning.

"I can't. Metasapients don't have the same Mars Colony protections that other citizens do."

"But you have your own Ichthyic friend. You know how it would be, to have her hurt."

Simon nodded, feeling uncharacteristically angry. "Yeah, I know how that would be."

"His name is Octavo. I kicked him in the face in the teal. He's a tele-me-chanic, and very dangerous. He sent in a robot or something. It looked like him. It was rigged to blow up," Dragos explained.

"I keep hearing that name. I've already got a couple good reasons to look for him. What's he look like?"

"He's older, probably fifties, bald, green eyes, thin as hell, K-block tat-toos, and a matching accent," Dragos said, calmly relating all he knew.

"Thank you. Don't worry, he'll get his," Simon turned and headed back toward the transport, a cold feeling in the pit of his stomach.

Ezra One and Athos One were waiting there, a disapproving Pearl standing in the cargo hold glaring at them. Simon slowed his pace, stop-ping beside the ramp without looking at either of them. Ezra One nudged Athos One.

"I didn't set the explosives on the wrecker line. I swear, I had nothing to do with it. She calls me to clean up messes, not to make them. I don't expect it means much, but I am sorry about your uncle and your legs," Athos said, voice shaking.

"I know it wasn't you," Simon said, his gaze drifting up to the armor in the cargo hold.

Ezra One pushed his goggles up to the top of his head. "What, you just figured it out in the last five minutes?"

"Yeah."

"Are you going to do something about it?" Ezra One asked, putting a hand on his rifle.

Simon glared at Ezra One.

"You don't trust Athos One, and so you don't trust Drones, any Drones. I get it. For one second, consider the possibility that we might have a common enemy," Ezra One said, meeting Simon's gaze.

"I guess you'd just ride on the undercarriage if I tried to ditch you again?" Simon said, grinning.

Ezra One sighed. "Just to ride along, what do we have to do?"

Simon looked back into the transport at Ishihara and Pearl, both shaking their heads "no".

"My friends don't like you. Either of you," Simon said, walking up the ramp.

"Even if you figure out where they are, you won't be able to get in without a familiar face," Athos One said.

"What do you mean?" Simon said, pausing at the top of the ramp.

"Every place I ever met Cerise was a bunker, heavily fortified and monitored. After dropping Dell, she's going to know you, Camille, and Pearl have all gone rogue and become a threat to her plans," Athos One said.

"You probably think you can play me like you guys played Dell," Simon said, folding his arms.

"Dragos and Hashti were supposed to bring Cerise in. You saw what happened when she got wind of that. Please, Simon, let us help you. Think about your friends," Ezra One said, nodding to Pearl.

Simon shook his head. "How do I know that 'wind' you're talking about isn't Athos One?"

Ezra One frowned. "Cerise had leverage. Marshal Rider has that leverage locked up in a cell."

"And, if she didn't?" Ishihara said, coming up to stand beside Simon.

"Ezra One would have killed me, yesterday," Athos One said, grimly.

"Shit," Ishihara said, shaking her head.

Pearl squeezed Simon's arm, nodding toward the Drones.

"What'd she have?" Simon asked.

"The woman I love. Cerise had a guy that could kill her remotely. He's locked up," Athos One replied.

"All these years? Ever since you pulled me from the wrecker line when I was a kid?" Simon asked, incredulous.

"Cerise doesn't age and she doesn't stink like the people that take gene therapy to extend their lives. I don't know how she does it," Athos One said, pacing back and forth.

"And Octavo?" Simon asked.

"He ages like a regular person."

"It doesn't feel right. My aunt can't set things right with the one lifetime she had. Cerise has more time than anyone it sounds like and all she does is harm. For what?"

"Like everything, it started out as something noble. In the end, it corrupted nearly everyone involved." Ezra One said, disdainfully.

"And you're just involved because you're one of the good guys?" Ishihara said, smirking.

Ezra One sighed. "I hate Mars. I just want to go home. The quicker the new AI is installed and Cerise is locked up, the sooner I can do that."

"What about the fight arena, the one Dell was talking about?" Simon said.

"What's this about a fight arena?" Ishihara said, perking up.

Ezra One shook his head. "Silverstein doesn't think it's real. She'd have Mars Company control, but no authority over the teal. Her plan is either vastly more complex or Dell is just part of a trail of breadcrumbs designed to mislead us."

"What are you guys talking about?" Ishihara said, giving Simon a concerned look.

"The phone call from earlier, I meant to tell you, but it was upsetting Pearl. Dell says Cerise is going to try to grant herself emergency powers by having a large enough people killed. A packed fight arena is allegedly the target," Simon explained.

"You're just telling me now?" Ishihara said, rolling her eyes.

"Hey, we've been kind of busy."

Pearl stepped down out of the transport and crouched down beside Simon, as if she was carrying a heavy burden. "How would she do it?"

"I'm not really sure. Like I said before, Silverstein doesn't think that's real," Ezra One said.

"You sound pretty confident in Silverstein," Pearl said, smiling.

"He's as old as Cerise, came up in the same village and he's rarely wrong about anything. We need to find Cerise," Ezra One said, growing impatient.

Simon let out a long sigh. "Okay, give me a minute. There may be something in this file that can lead us to her."

They stood outside the transport, Mars Company offices looming overhead, contemplating their next move. Ishihara paced while Simon read the Marshal's Office archive file with Pearl looking over his shoulder. The Drones quietly conversed nearby, somatically communicating with a few gestures and facial expressions.

"Where's he going?" Ishihara asked, watching Athos One walk away.

"He's going to check the tunnels, make sure the Tribehome is okay. He will lead a crew down to check the tunnels beneath the fight arena for the season opener," Ezra One said, nodding back over his shoulder.

"What if we need his face to get into Cerise's bunker?" Ishihara asked.

"We won't," Ezra One replied, heading up into the transport to find a seat.

Simon watched Athos One disappear down a drainage access tunnel. "You don't trust him, either."

"No," Ezra One said, squinting behind his goggles.

"What are you going to do?" Ishihara said.

"Like he said before, if he's still working an angle with Cerise, I'll kill him."

Simon handed off the archive file to Pearl. "There's a list of physical assets, properties in the colony that are connected to whoever ordered the assassinations. It was all managed through Mars Company trusts, listing the Board of Public Development as the managing department."

"We could look through all the pages in that file or we could find Octavo and squeeze him. Guess which option would make me feel better," Ezra One said, folding his arms.

"Sure, do you know where he is?" Simon asked.

"I have a pretty good idea," Ezra One said, looking at his mobile. "Taylor was able to narrow it down to a specific cell block in the teal, K-203."

"She did that by just touching my Aegis Armor?" Simon asked.

"Yeah, look, I know it's hard to believe she can do those things, but believe me, she really can and a lot more. She and Silverstein aren't going to let anything happen to the Mars Colony," Ezra One explained, showing Simon the message he'd just received from Taylor.

"How does she do it?" Ishihara asked.

"You wouldn't believe me if I told you," Ezra One said, pocketing his mobile.

"Try me," Simon said, more insistently.

"She steps into an airlock specially modified to mimic the cold and a vacuum similar to outer space. She's a quantum-capable, terrestrial artificial intelligence. When she was nearly killed on the Lunar Colony, she discovered her abilities work better when she's subjected to a vacuum and the cold," Ezra One said, quietly delighting in their collective looks of astonishment.

"Wow, okay, that makes a sort of crazy sense if she's quantum capable, but how does she survive?" Simon asked.

"The first time, she nearly didn't. A friend built her a special suit to wear. It's still very uncomfortable and she can't persist in the vacuum chamber for very long. Fortunately, she doesn't need that long in the chamber to do amazing things," Ezra One said, quietly reflecting on the first time he'd watched Taylor step into the vacuum chamber.

"You care for her," Pearl said, nodding.

"She brought color to my Tribehome, greatly improving the lives of my family. She makes everywhere she goes a better place. What she does is important," Ezra One said, deflecting.

"I can get behind someone like that," Ishihara said, strapping herself in beside Pearl.

Pearl powered up the transport, while everyone else made themselves comfortable. Taking a trip to the teal wasn't out of the ordinary for regular folks with visitation passes. K-block was a little different, in that it was considered minimum security and the inmates could mingle freely with regular civilians. The gate was still closely monitored and every inmate had an implant to keep them from wandering.

"How will we get in without a visitor's pass?" Ishihara asked.

"I have a badge and a gun," Simon said, a hint of remorse in his voice.

CHAPTER 19

MARS COLONY, THE TEAL –
K203, GENERAL POPULATION CONTROL

August 13th, 2200

Pearl watched sadly as her friends departed for the teal. The huge bulwark separating the industrial orange from institutional green parted for them slowly. Security personnel waved them through. She'd elected to stay with the transport on Simon's advice, not sure how inmates would react to a Type 5 companion model Metasapient.

Ezra One went in fully armed, expecting trouble. Ishihara tagged along hoping to get a glimpse of the person responsible for messing with the Roller Derby Union years ago. Pearl wasn't sure any of that would come to pass or that they'd find what they were looking for in the teal. She didn't know that they wouldn't. Only a few minutes would pass before the huge stone gate would open once more, emergency lighting and a soft siren sounding to warn people to get clear.

A very slender woman walked back out, cane in one hand. She looked familiar to Pearl, but she couldn't place her, the viewing port on the transport wet with condensation. As she drew closer, she recognized Aunt Ruth's clothing and gait. Pearl's mind reeled at the prospect of Aunt Ruth being alive somehow, rushing to unlock the cargo hold.

The ramp descended to the empty receiving lot outside, the ground scarred and pebbled by inmates dragging leg irons to and from prison transports. Aunt Ruth stood outside looking up at Pearl with a grave expression. There was an awkward silence, Pearl staring at Aunt Ruth with her large eyes.

"Are you going to invite me aboard? We need to talk," Aunt Ruth said at last, trying to sound polite.

"How are you alive?"

"I'm a company operator. I have implants that allow me to self-administer performance enhancing drugs. The first thing you learn is how to make yourself look dead to avoid recovery by competing corporate entities."

Pearl blinked. "What does that mean?"

"I can play dead, like a possum."

"What's a possum?"

Aunt Ruth sighed loudly. "Pearl can we continue this conversation in the warmth of your transport?"

"Oh, sure," Pearl said, helping the elderly woman up the ramp.

Once Aunt Ruth was settled into a crew seat in the hold, Pearl closed the cargo hatch and went over to her makeshift kitchen to make tea.

"We haven't time for that, Pearl. I need your help to protect Simon".

"There's always time for tea," Pearl said, waiting for the filter to dispense water.

Aunt Ruth rose from the crew seat, taking a firm hold of Pearl's arm. "We have to hurry or Simon, Ishihara, and their new friend will never leave the teal alive."

"Okay, okay, what do we need to do?" Pearl asked, rubbing her arm.

"We need to get to the port and deliver a package. I have it here with me," Aunt Ruth said, doing her best to shoo Pearl into the cockpit.

"But they'll think we just left without them. I'm sure Simon will want to know you're alive."

Aunt Ruth shook her head. "Trust me they'll know, once we've worked this all out."

It felt wrong to Pearl to just leave, but Aunt Ruth had been kind to her and helped her mend after being attacked. She could sense Aunt Ruth's anxiety about making the delivery. Clearly, whatever she was bringing to the port was very important. But the port was on the opposite side of the orange industrial zone from the teal, requiring almost an hour to travel through the various transport tubes between zones.

Pearl tried to reach Simon using the onboard comms, but the walls around the teal blocked almost all except frequencies bounced to a satellite and back. Such was beyond Pearl's expertise, so she did the next best thing. Taking a piece of chalk, she went out to the landing platform and wrote in the receiving lot "be right back" and signed her name with a curly "P" beside.

"Okay, we can go now," Pearl announced, taking the pilot's chair and powering up her transport.

"Good, please hurry," Aunt Ruth said, sitting at the comms beside her.

Pearl flew as quickly as she could while being safe, operating like a Mars Company transport in the tubes where monitoring was allowed. Aunt Ruth closed her eyes, waiting patiently for them to arrive at the port, the sound of the engines almost lulling her to sleep. As they drew close, Pearl roused her, pointing out at the blinking lights beyond the atmospheric shielding.

"Almost there," Aunt Ruth said, patting Pearl on the arm.

Pearl turned toward the Mining Company landing zones, but Aunt Ruth chimed in saying, "Head for the common traffic zone, the one adjoining the A docks."

"Simon says that's conspicuous. He has sort of borrowed this transport, but I don't know how to explain that to someone if they ask," Pearl said, worriedly.

"If we make this delivery, none of that will matter," Aunt Ruth said, trying to reassure her.

"Okay," Pearl said, reluctantly.

She pulled the transport in over the loading yard, lift trucks darting about below moving cargo and baggage between different loading bays. The commercial yard was busy, but the private lot beyond was empty. Private travel to Mars had all but ceased following the Shutdown on Earth, and there wasn't even a customs official monitoring the private landing area adjoining the port.

Pearl stepped out first, to better assist Aunt Ruth down the ramp before they made for the port access bridge. It was dark and looked to have been untraveled for months. The airlock granting access parted with a quick swipe of Aunt Ruth's Mars Company ID card. The interior was vacant, blue carpet with LED lighting embedded along the edges to guide people to their flights.

Older pop music played softly in the background as they made their way to a boarding passage at the far side of the private terminal. Pearl kept looking over her shoulder, feeling as though they were being followed. Each time the hallway was empty, the dim floor lighting casting a faint dusting of illumination over the walls, railings and access ports nearby.

As they rounded the corner, Aunt Ruth took firm hold of Pearl's arm, holding her fast to the spot. A woman dressed in white business formal-wear stood beside a half-dozen stripped down android frames that had been outfitted with tactical armor, automatic rifles, and sentry AI-box upgrades replacing their heads.

"We just give this lady the package and leave, right?" Pearl asked, nervously as the woman in white approached.

"Sort of. You're the package, Pearl. I'm sorry," Aunt Ruth replied, giving her a rough shove forward.

"You're the client, the one that was going to buy me from Mister Janjigian," Pearl said, recognizing Cerise Laplace as she drew closer.

"Why pay for something you can just get for free?" Cerise asked, smiling and holding her hands out to her sides, as if to put her cleverness on display.

"My friends are going to find me, they went to deal with Octavo. They'll find me," Pearl protested, covering her face.

"I doubt they'll learn anything from Octavo," Cerise said, looking to Aunt Ruth.

"Dell and Octavo didn't know anything critical to the real operation. If they did, they certainly won't be telling anyone," Aunt Ruth said, handing Cerise a small data module.

"Athos One, he and the other Drones will find the bombs. They'll stop you," Pearl said, looking about for some avenue of escape.

Cerise laughed. "There are no bombs, Pearl. All that was designed to properly distract Silverstein and his allies. I needed them to believe I was as crazy as some of the rest of our fallen tribe, get them to spread their resources everywhere but to the one place I needed a little privacy."

"I don't understand," Pearl said frowning.

"It's not hard to explain. I can only take whoever is listed as my spouse and property of a certain value, not including a single Metasapient servant, with me to Mexico. I'll need a pilot once we're on the ground and someone to take care of some day to day tasks," Cerise said, nodding at Aunt Ruth.

"You and Aunt Ruth are married?" Pearl asked, mystified.

"On paper. Our arrangement is somewhat simpler in that regard. Ultimately, we both just want to leave and start over," Cerise replied, beckoning for them to follow her.

"But, Mister Janjigian...he..."

"Mister Janjigian was greedy, and while I could easily afford to pay him, serendipity kept leading Simon to cross your path."

Pearl blinked, sadly following along. "Serendipity?"

"Manipulating people, making them believe that happenstance is providence, is what I do best. Picking the right people to manipulate is important. Greed and idealism are the easiest weaknesses in a person to that end. It's been my careful hand guiding everything," Cerise said, entering a code into the airlock door.

Beyond, in a large hanger, a strange vessel hovered in the air above them. It was more creature than ship, but easily as big as a commercial vessel capable of travel within the solar system. Pearl gazed up at it in wonder, trying to comprehend what she was seeing. It was beautiful and otherworldly, serene and terrifying in equal measure.

"What...what is it?" Pearl asked, fearfully.

"My people, the Cabal, called her The Dragon. It's the alien vessel Silverstein and his allies used to reach Mars. We're going to steal her, go to Earth, and vanish into the Mexican Protectorate after paying off the proper officials," Cerise said, smiling broadly.

"Steal?" Pearl asked.

"Well, not exactly. Silverstein thinks he's the only one who can command the ship, but he couldn't be more wrong. Golgotha used her to heal my wounds after she disemboweled me. I went back to commune with her as Silverstein did, for thousands of years. It was delicious to watch the rest of the Cabal fruitlessly search for The Dragon, when I knew all along where she was," Cerise said, lovingly putting a hand on the ship.

"Can the ship heal Aunt Ruth? Or fix Simon's legs?" Pearl asked.

"Her understanding of the human anatomy was crude back when she healed me, but it had to learn in order for her to eventually extract Golgotha's brood from the Cabal. It's been a process, but we've been able to get her to do some marvelous things," Cerise said, running her hand across the side of the alien vessel as she walked beside it.

"Is this why you betrayed Simon? Lied to us?" Pearl asked, looking at Aunt Ruth.

"I don't even know how to explain all that has happened, or all that I did, in the last three decades to lead me to this moment. I began this journey long before Simon, Ishihara, or you came into my life. Believe me, this isn't personal and nothing bad is going to happen to Simon or Ishihara, that was the deal," Aunt Ruth said, hobbling toward the alien vessel on her cane.

"But bad things did happen to them. Simon's legs and what Dell did to Ishihara. Bad things did happen," Pearl said, clenching her fists.

"This is Mars, Pearl. You, better than anyone, know that bad things happen here," Aunt Ruth said, doing little to console her.

Athos walked into the hanger, his hands draped over a rifle hanging in front of him from a strap. His goggles were down, but they did little to hide his disdain for the android frames standing guard nearby. He paused mid-stride, stopping to look at Pearl.

"Why is she here?" Athos One asked, looking at Pearl's frightened expression.

"Worried she's going to take your place on the ship?" Cerise teased.

Athos One frowned. "I was never going to go with you. I have a hard time seeing her being here of her own volition."

"That's a shame, I could really use someone with your talents in Mexico."

"You'll just have to make do without me, and her," Athos One said, gesturing to Pearl.

Cerise smiled wickedly. "Look who's grown a soul. We'll need a pilot when we get to Earth. I invested a lot of resources into this Ichthyic Metasapient, it…"

"It?" Athos One replied, cocking his head to one side.

Aunt Ruth gave Athos One a severe expression. "Remember those assurances you wanted? You'll have them with us gone. That girl you like will be safe."

"Yes, I remember," Athos One said, pushing Pearl around behind him.

"What are you doing?" Cerise said, her smile fading to a scowl.

"What I should have done long ago," Athos One replied, pulling his rifle back into his shoulder and pulling the trigger.

CHAPTER 20

MARS COLONY, THE TEAL – K203, CELL 990-B10

August 13th, 2200

Simon stepped through the trash and debris around the cell, flanked by Ishihara and Ezra One. There were a pair of thick-necked goons standing outside barring their way, each unimpressed by Simon's Aegis Armor and Deputy Marshal's badge. The goons sneered, looking up at the gathered convicts only just beginning to appear on the ledges overhead.

"Go away, Octavo is taking a private meeting."

Simon, keenly aware that a brawl in the cellblock would only delay them, did his best to be diplomatic. "We'll wait until he's done."

"We will?" Ishihara said, already wanting to answer some of the catcalls and whistles with a fist.

"Doesn't matter either way," Ezra One whispered, sniffing the air.

"You got something to say little man?" one of the goon's said, stepping forward, a heavy pipe in one hand.

"Your boss is dead. Can't you smell that?" Ezra One said, switching his goggles to close quarters targeting mode.

The goon frowned, looking back at the other guard and nodded. The cell and the door itself had been tethered with sheet metal and other materials to make the interior private. The goon knocked on the door, and when there was no answer, he peered inside.

He went sheet white, staggering away to throw up on the floor nearby. The other had a very similar reaction with only a casual glance inside. Both hurriedly scurried off, presumably to let others know the balance of power in K Block had suddenly shifted.

Ishihara and Simon both went to look, but Ezra One slid around in front of them, barring their path. "There's nothing in there you'd ever want to see. Let me."

"Shit, if you say so," Ishihara said, waiting patiently.

"I need to see, especially if there's been a crime," Simon said, determined to find out what was going on.

"Suit yourself," Ezra said, slipping through the gap into the cell.

Inside was Octavo, stretched out across the cell by wires, hooks, and whatever else the person that had attacked him could find. He'd been vivisected down to his bones, across his limbs, chest, and with the majority of his internal organs. It was as gruesome and terrible a death as Simon could imagine and it sent his mind reeling.

"What the...? Why? Why would someone do this?" Simon said, letting the Aegis Armor take video for documentation.

"Company Operators are highly trained cyborgs. Long ago, a handful were trained to use their own cybernetic stasis drugs, the chemicals that allow their body to tolerate implants, for torture. There are a few that got really good at it. Rumor has it there was one on Mars that could take you completely apart like this, while you were still alive. He or she was a ghost, vanishing two decades ago," Ezra One said, looking around the cell for clues or evidence.

"They... wanted information? Or just to hurt him?" Simon stammered, averting his eyes while the Aegis continued doing automatic visual evidence collection.

"If anyone else in the cell block knows anything, you can be sure they won't be talking either. It had to be someone Octavo knew, someone he wasn't threatened by, and could get this close to him," Ezra One said, looking through the stacks of prison contraband that lined the room.

Simon walked back out of the cell trying to banish what he'd seen in the cell from his mind.

"That bad?" Ishihara asked.

"Someone took Octavo apart while he was still alive," Simon said, trying to catch his breath.

"Heh, well don't throw up in your armor, that'd really suck," Ishihara joked.

"I'm trying, haha," Simon said, feeling a little better.

Ezra One walked back out, shaking his head. "There's nothing. Rare to run into this kind of professional. I'm not even sure how she got out of there."

"She? How can you be sure?" Ishihara asked.

"Something about the way those guards said their boss was in a private meeting. Also, the reaction to you by the rest of the cellblock was somewhat subdued," Ezra One said, turning to leave.

"Like I wasn't the first woman they'd seen walk through today? That's pretty thin," Ishihara said, laughing.

"Totally, just a feeling. We should get you guys back to wherever you belong," Ezra One said, beckoning.

"But we haven't figured out anything yet," Simon said, walking along beside Ezra One toward the security control zone.

"Yeah, we haven't figured anything out," Ishihara chimed in, banging her fist on some fingers reaching out for her from a cell.

"There's a company operator one step ahead of us. All we're going to do from here on out is follow bodies. You guys are only going to slow me down," Ezra One said, waiting for security personnel to open the gate and wave them through.

"So, we were worthless. What am I going to tell Marshal Rider?" Simon said, sadly.

"I wouldn't say that. You guys got stuck into this pretty far for a couple of civilians and held on when most people would have cut and run. Dealing with people like this is scary and no one is going to blame you for stepping back now. You took this all the way to Octavo's cell, way further than anyone else on Mars would have," Ezra One said, watching the huge stone doors part.

"Um, where is Pearl's transport?" Ishihara asked, pointing out to the empty transfer lot.

Simon ran out as quickly as the Aegis Armor would carry him. "There's something on the ground."

"'Be right back, P.' She left us here?" Ishihara said, throwing her hands into the air and looking around.

"Who do you know that Pearl trusts and could get into the cellblock?" Ezra One asked.

"My Aunt Ruth was a company operator, but…she's dead," Simon said, looking worriedly over at Ishihara.

"That old woman you live with?" Ezra One asked.

"Yeah," Ishihara said, blinking vacantly.

"Where is her body?" Ezra One asked.

Simon took a deep breath. "She's back at the workshop, and…"

"We left Dell there," Ishihara interrupted.

Ezra pulled out his mobile and scrolled through his contacts, pausing on Taylor.

"Calling us a ride?" Ishihara asked.

"Maybe you should, if you can. I've got a bad feeling about all this. Like, that's what I would normally do, have Silverstein tell me what to do next, but maybe that's what Cerise is counting on," Ezra One said, looking at his mobile, then up at Simon.

"I'll call Drake," Simon said nodding.

"Establishing link. Communications protocols active," Aegis intoned, using the onboard radio to contact the mining union frequency.

"Hey, Simon, what's going on?" Drake said, the sound of heavy machinery clanking in the background.

"I need a ride, something with an EVA Suit Lift and a little bit of personnel seating. Can you help us?" Simon asked.

"Us?" Drake asked, laughing.

"Yeah, us." Simon said smiling.

"When you say 'us,' does that include the fabulous derby personality, Camille Ishihara?" Drake replied, eliciting a clamor from the other miners nearby.

"It does," Simon said laughing.

"I think I can find a volunteer pilot or ten to help out with that," Drake said, laughing. "Where are you?"

"K-Block, just outside security control."

"Copy."

Simon disconnected the link, then nodded to Ezra One. "I've got someone coming."

"Yeah, we heard. Aegis had the communications playing over the speaker," Ishihara said, smiling.

"You heard all that?" Simon said, laughing nervously.

"Yeah, you want to tell me what that's all about?" Ishihara asked.

"Everyone likes derby, but with a certain mining union, you're probably a patron saint or minor celebrity. We wouldn't have pulled them out of that failed zone if Pearl and I hadn't been out looking for you. Drake's been bugging me about an autograph," Simon explained, eliciting an increasingly amused look from Ishihara.

"You asked a bunch of groupies to come get us?" Ezra One asked.

"Yeah, but don't worry, they owe me a chit."

Two Mining Company transports appeared less than twenty minutes later, flying dangerously fast as they cut between habitation spires and flight lanes overhead. They slowed only when Simon flashed the illuminators on his Aegis Armor to get their attention. Simon smiled as Drake stepped off, a crowd of his fellow union miners exiting both transports in celebratory fashion.

"Thanks for coming," Simon said, striding forward to take Drake's hand.

"I know you said you just needed one transport, but I had too many 'volunteers' for this official Mining Company operation," Drake said, jokingly.

The miners gathered around Ishihara waving log books and anything else that could take an inscription. Ishihara graciously signed their books and let them take pictures with their mobiles. Drake's celebratory mood drained quickly away as he looked around.

"I was kind of expecting to see your transport here, broken down, a sad fish-girl standing outside of it. I almost flew over because I didn't see it," Drake said.

"I think someone took her and the transport. A company operator," Simon said, keeping his voice low.

"Tell me what you need. We all love that fish girl. We'd be frozen corpses floating in a failed M-Zone if not for her," Drake said, nodding.

"We need to hurry, whatever we're going to do," Ezra One said, stepping from behind Simon and startling Drake.

"You're hanging with Drones now?" Drake asked, eying Ezra One.

"Ezra One's from off-world. We're trying to stop bad people from doing more of what almost got you and your union crew killed," Simon explained.

Drake nodded. "Where to, boss?"

"I need to go home, check on something," Simon said.

"LOAD UP!" Drake bellowed, turning back toward the transport.

The mining crew lifted Simon's Aegis Armor aboard and helped him out to take some rest while they traveled. Ezra One sat beside him, scrolling through data being posted to the public networks for any indication where Pearl might be. Ishihara plopped down beside Simon, putting her arm around him, eliciting a few envious looks from the crew on board.

"We'll find her. We'll find Pearl," Ishihara said, seeing how distraught Simon was.

"As the Deputy Marshal, aren't I supposed to be reassuring you?" Simon said, smiling sadly.

"No," Ishihara said, leaning in and kissing Simon.

Her face and hair brushed against his, her arms drawing him in. The mining crew clapped and cheered, banging tools on the front of their safety vests. Simon returned the embrace, holding her close. He was already feeling like his world was breaking, not knowing how his own Aunt Ruth was mixed up in everything. Ishihara seemed to pull it all back together with one loving gesture, her firm embrace gently pushing away doubt and distrust.

"Feel better?" Ishihara asked, smoothing Simon's lips with her thumb.

"Way."

"Can't this heap go any faster? These two are gonna make me hurl," Drake joked, banging a tool on the cockpit door.

"Almost there," the pilot said, laughing.

Both transports sat down outside the Vedter Machineworks, a startled group of scavengers fleeing the covered scrapyard out back. Simon stepped down the ramp, wearing only his assistive leg braces, pinning the Marshal's Star to his coveralls. He grabbed a pry-bar from a clamp outside the transport and began walking toward the open door leading to his workshop.

Ezra One came up beside him with Ishihara not far behind. "No, you guys stay outside," Simon said, waving them off.

"You sure?" Ezra One asked.

"Yeah, I got this," Simon said, nodding to Ishihara, who nodded right back.

Inside was what Simon feared he would find. Dell's vivisection was cruel, even when compared to what had been done to Octavo, and looked like it took much longer. The company operator had more tools and time at her disposal and she might have had good reason to hate Dell.

Simon walked back into the living area, to check on his Aunt's body. The body bag he'd left his aunt inside was cut open from the inside by the way the fabric curled outward. Her closet was empty, everything Ruth had valued taken from the room.

There was no sign of his aunt and it looked as though nothing else had been taken. The scavengers probably stepped inside and fled at the sight of what had been done to Dell. Small blessings.

Simon looked through Dell's clothing that someone had neatly folded beside what remained of him, strewn about Simon's work table. The clothing was folded the way his Aunt would fold his.

There was a mobile with authenticator chip missing and several data storage cards. Simon slid one into Dell's mobile and hit playback. It showed video of Dell assaulting Ishihara. Even the first few seconds was enough to make Simon angrier than he'd ever been before. He stopped the video playback and previewed the rest of the data storage cards before using a machine press to destroy them.

He lingered beside what remained of Dell for a moment. There's many reasons someone like Dell would keep video of what he'd done, but chief among those possibilities was that he'd been put up to it. They were going to use the video as leverage to hurt Ishihara. Her popularity had been building lately, quiet support for the derby and the girls alongside her public visibility.

"Aunt Ruth, what have you done?" Simon asked quietly aloud.

Simon grabbed a satchel of tools, the data module recovered from the android, and the makeshift explosives he'd planned to use in framing Dell. Slinging them over his shoulder he took a last look around his workshop, wondering if he'd ever see it again. He closed the door and locked it on his way out. He walked to where Ishihara stood, reaching out for her.

"Is it Aunt Ruth? Did she kill Octavo?" Ishihara said, steadying Simon.

"Yeah, and Dell. He's...oh, God, what are we going to do?" Simon said, leaning on Ishihara and trying to catch his breath.

"Let's find Pearl and then we'll figure it out," Ishihara said, walking arm in arm with Simon back to the waiting transport.

"I could smell it from here," Ezra One said, helping Simon aboard.

"What?"

"Death."

Simon nodded. "My aunt is alive. She's the company operator that killed Octavo."

"Is there any chance she's working with Cerise Laplace? Do you think she is part of whatever she is planning?" Ezra One asked, trying to sound sympathetic.

"If you see my aunt, take no chances," Simon said, grimly, strapping himself into a crew seat.

"We've got an SOS," the pilot said, looking back at Drake.

"Pearl's transport?" Drake asked.

"Yep, she sounds scared. She's keyed in medical with the SOS. Someone is hurt badly," the pilot replied.

"We have a location?" Ezra One asked, jumping up.

"It's coming from the private terminal at the port," the pilot reported.

"Go! Go! Go!" Drake ordered, closing the cargo hatch and strapping in.

The transport lurched upward, the pilot making a hasty departure. They jumped up into the flight lane, flying as fast as they dared past stalled automated transport vehicles, private transports, and other traffic. Ishihara helped Simon suit up, holding him by the forearms as she lowered him down into the Aegis.

"If someone's hurt Pearl…" Ishihara said, angrily nodding to Simon.

"I know," Simon said, gritting his teeth as the mantle and faceplate snapped shut enclosing him in the armor.

Minutes later, the transports broke out over the port district, the entire zone brightly lit and flush with heavy transport traffic. The pilot broke low, bringing the transport down outside the safe operating limits. People were getting blown off their feet below, the downward thrust making a mess of the street level traffic.

"Bring us up higher, you're going to kill someone!" Drake bellowed.

The pilot complied, cutting through old ore delivery systems that had been dormant for years. The second transport trailed behind, the other pilot hesitating slightly at the confined route. When they emerged from the conveyer tunnel, the private terminal wasn't far away. Ishihara stood beside the pilot in the cockpit, looking at the hundreds of landing zones nearby.

"There!" She pointed down at a lone transport at a remote private terminal.

The pilot adjusted course, dropping the throttle to speed up. The transport lurched suddenly as something struck the outside hull. Red lights began flashing in the interior, as the pilot began to pull up.

"Someone is shooting at us!" Drake shouted.

Ezra One ran a tether from his tactical harness to the safety catch inside the transport and hit the cargo hatch release. Deafening wind filled the interior as the pilot began to circle wide and to the right. Ezra One steadied his breathing and brought his rifle up, switching his goggles to long-range target acquisition.

There were android frames, stripped for tactical use and firing at them from the ground. His heart skipped a beat as the view through his scope caught Pearl kneeling in the landing zone beside her transport. Athos One was laying with his head on her knees, a pool of fresh blood beneath him on the tarmac.

"Damn it," Ezra One said, quickly firing at an android frame, locking his crosshairs on another, and firing again.

"Riding with you is always exciting!" Drake said, grabbing Ezra One by the jacket and trying hold him steady as he leaned out the cargo hatch on the tether.

"Can we land nearby without taking too much fire?" Simon bellowed in reply.

"I'm trying to land on a platform a little higher up, break line of sight with those...things," the pilot replied.

Ezra One continued to fire, but there were dozens of tactical android frames below with high capacity rifles. The transport ate up a lot of the incoming fire with a few rounds piercing the hull, ricocheting around inside. No one was hurt, but the damage made the landing rougher than the pilot had probably intended.

The tether holding Ezra One broke, sending him tumbling out onto the tarmac. He'd only just righted himself, and brushed the black from his chin as the first android frame appeared on the boarding ramp. Ezra fired, hitting the eerie thing right in the control box, but he could see the shadows of more coming up the terminal.

"Cover your ears!" Simon said, stepping out with his Aegis Armor and drawing his sidearm.

Ezra One looked back, eyes growing wide at the sight of the heavy caliber handgun Simon was pointing at the loading ramp. The report was loud, uncomfortably so without ear protection. Ezra One managed to get back behind the length of the barrel beside Simon before he fired, but it still made his ears ring. The round struck the ramp, detonating on impact.

As the first android frame stepped out onto the damaged ramp, it buckled, breaking with the weight of a second. The pair of them fell with the wrecked ramp into the darkness beneath the landing zone. A second later there was a dim crash somewhere far below.

"Nice shot," Ezra One said, heading for the walkway leading to the other landing zones.

Ishihara jumped down to the landing platform, turning to look expectantly at Drake.

"We'll wait here as long as we can," Drake said, looking nervously at the crowd of android frames changing direction in the terminal.

Ezra One led the way down to the platform where Pearl and Athos One were huddled beside her transport. Simon and Ishihara paused, sighing in relief that Pearl wasn't hurt, but Athos One was not so fortunate. He'd been shot, stabbed, and bludgeoned, his breath coming in ragged and wet.

Ezra One knelt down beside Athos One as Pearl held his head up on her knees, her hand smoothing out his ghostly white hair. "What did you do?" Ezra One asked.

"All I ever wanted was one beautiful girl to look down at me like she is now. I just wanted to save one girl and be a hero, like in all those faded paperbacks we used to keep in the jump ship. Remember those?" Athos One rasped, his eyes unable to focus on Ezra One.

"Avery One...did you ever tell her how you felt?" Ezra One asked.

"No, how could I?" Athos One replied, tears rolling down his bloody cheeks.

"With words, you dunce," Ezra One said, taking his friend's hand.

"You tell Taylor IA how you feel?" Athos One asked.

"No," Ezra One replied, watching Athos One take his last breath. "How could I?"

"He saved me, got me out of there," Pearl said, sadly.

"Who did this Pearl? Who?" Simon asked, putting a gauntlet-clad hand on her shoulder.

"Aunt Ruth and Cerise, they were going to steal an alien ship from Mister Silverstein and go to Mexico," Pearl replied, trembling, and trying to keep her composure.

"Show us where, Pearl. Show us," Ishihara said, reaching out for her hand.

Pearl gently laid Athos One's head down on tarmac before taking Ishihara's hand and standing up. She led them up into the terminal nearby. As soon as they stepped down into the hallway, they were treading in ankle deep water. They splashed along until they came to an empty private hangar. Aunt Ruth was floating face up in the water, her eyes wide open.

Simon picked her up out of the water, letting the suit do a biometric analysis. She'd been shot several times, exit wounds in her front and back. She'd been caught in some kind of cross-fire with at least one bullet hitting her in the face and coming out the back of her head.

"Where's the ship and where did all this water come from?" Ishihara said, looking over at the ruined android frames lying about in the water.

"The ship is the water. She dissolved as soon as Athos One started firing. I think he startled her," Pearl said, kneeling down and running a hand through the water.

"She?" Ishihara asked.

"Definitely. She's a sea creature like me, but she can swim in space, too," Pearl said, sadly.

"How do you know all this?" Simon asked, handing Ruth's body off to Ishihara.

"Can't you hear her?" Pearl asked, cocking her head to one side.

"No, not a bit," Simon said, smiling slightly.

"The ship has a limited degree of telepathy, but it only seems to initiate conversation with particular people. Special people," Ezra One said, his thoughts drifting back to the first time he rode in the ship with Taylor.

"Cerise is still out there, we need to find her," Ishihara said heading back toward the hallway.

"All this water is going to make her hard to track. Ishihara, take Aunt Ruth and Pearl back to the transport with the miners and lock yourselves inside. Simon and I will fan out, see if we can find her," Ezra One said, nodding to Simon.

Simon handed Ezra One a rig radio, after setting it to a particular frequency. "If I see her, I'll radio you. You do the same."

"Yep," Ezra One said.

Ezra One headed down toward the street level while Simon set about searching the other terminals. Ishihara walked quietly ahead, stopping with Pearl beside her transport. They took out personnel recovery bags and loaded both Athos One and Aunt Ruth into the hold. Pearl prayed to God, in the name of Jesus, for their souls while Ishihara wondered if her own soul would ever be able to rest.

"The miners are just up there. It looks like the other android frames couldn't plot a path over here or they shut down. You should be safe," Ishihara said, patting Pearl on the back.

"Where are you going?" Pearl asked.

"To get a drink," Ishihara said, pointing to a bar several levels down, almost at the street level.

"Okay, please hurry," Pearl said, jogging toward the landing platform above.

Ishihara grabbed her gym bag from the transport and pulled her athletic tape out. As she walked toward the bar, a place called "The Portside," she wrapped her knuckles. She walked with purpose, pausing to look in through the front window. It was like she thought.

Ishihara pushed the front door open and stepped inside scanning the dimly lit interior. Cerise looked up from her drink, smirking. "It's Camille, right? How did you know I'd be here?"

"If all my carefully laid plans got messed up, this is where I would go," Ishihara said.

"Did you tell your friends? How about your new friend, Ezra One?" Cerise said, downing the last of her drink.

Ishihara looked at the barkeeper laying on the floor. He was dead, Cerise having already taken her frustrations out on him. "No, they might try to stop me from killing you," Ishihara replied, stepping over the barkeep.

"Killing me? I'm thousands of years old. I've been augmented by advanced alien biotechnology that makes me stronger and faster than any human has right to be. You don't last through the millenniums without having had to fight for your life hundreds of times," Cerise said, cackling as she tossed her white jacket aside.

"You ever fought a girl from Mars?" Ishihara asked, circling around, her fists up defensively.

"No, but I'm going to enjoy this," Cerise said, leaping toward Ishihara skillfully aiming a kick at her midsection.

Ishihara turned into it, slowly turning the strike aside by bringing her elbow low. As she turned, she grabbed a heavy chair with her offhand and let the force of Cerise's strike spin her completely around. Cerise landed with catlike grace, a moment before Ishihara brought the chair down on her.

Cerise rose quickly, brushing the blow off and striking at Ishihara's eyes with her fingernails. Ishihara grabbed her by the wrists, then turned her face toward the floor, dropping her forehead into the top of Cerise's head.

Ishihara swung her like a club by the arms, clearing the glassware from the bar, before reversing her grip and slamming Cerise into the ground.

"Been a while?" Ishihara asked, looking down at Cerise's shocked expression.

Cerise nodded, gasping for air.

"Take a minute, catch your breath. I've got all night," Ishihara said, walking in a circle around where Cerise was lying.

Cerise screeched angrily, leaping from a prone position at Ishihara. One of her blows caught her across the brow, the other grazing her cheek. Ishihara grabbed Cerise around the midsection and backed up into the footrest around the bar for extra elevation. Leaping upward, she pulled her arms free so all her body weight could come down on Cerise.

The floorboards cracked along with Cerise's ribs. Ishihara pushed herself up, smiling down at Cerise as she continued to gasp for air. Ishihara went over to the bar and looked at the bruise rising up over her eye, shrugged, and poured herself a drink.

"We can work something out...I have money...just take me to Silverstein...turn me in," Cerise gasped.

Ishihara knelt down beside her, drink dangling from her hand. "Are you the one that put Simon in those leg braces?"

Cerise smiled. "That's what this is about? You think I crippled your man?"

"He thinks you did," Ishihara said, sipping her drink.

"I did that and a lot worse. I've undermined every attempt the people of Mars have taken to control their own destiny. The unions, mining companies, the teal, and every Drone and Metasapient living within and below the colony," Cerise said, sitting up, smiling through bloody teeth.

"Mmm-hmm. You ready for another round?" Ishihara said, downing the rest of her drink.

Cerise rose to her feet slowly, a feint for the several body blows she would deliver to Ishihara and the solid blow to the throat that would send Ishihara crashing backwards into a table. Cerise grabbed up a steak knife that had fallen from the table and lunged. Ishihara caught the blade in her forearm, smiling through bloody teeth as her broad offhand grabbed Cerise by the face.

"There you go, that's the bitch I came to fight with," Ishihara said, throwing Cerise against the wall.

Ishihara ran into Cerise as hard as she could, slamming her through the fragile plaster into the storage room beyond. Stepping through, she traded blows with Cerise, each hit stealing a little wind from each of them. Eventually, it was Cerise who dropped to the ground, blood pouring down into her face from a cut above her eyes.

Ishihara stooped down, putting one knee into Cerise's breastbone. "Where are the bombs? How do we stop all the mayhem you've got planned? Tell me and I'll just smash your head with a keg, nice and quick."

Cerise laughed, then coughed, blood rolling out from the corners of her mouth. "There are no bombs, and no mayhem. All of it, misdirection."

Ishihara rolled her painfully over with a knee, pulling Cerise's left arm around in a submission hold. "Doesn't hurt to be sure, though, right?" Ishihara said, grabbing two of Cerise's fingers and twisting.

"I've endured so much worse than this, more than you could possibly know," Cerise rasped from between gritted teeth.

Cerise pushed up, letting a blood-slick wrist slip between Ishihara's so she could grab the knife sticking out of her forearm. Cerise gave the knife a twist, making Ishihara jerk away reflexively. Ishihara fell backward, toppling heavy metal kegs that came raining down on her.

"Sometimes, you leave the knife in, not because it'll hurt your adversary badly, but because it might be useful later. Aunt Ruth and Athos One were those 'knives' through it all. How do you think Dell found you when you went to hide? How do you think it was that I was one step ahead all the time?"

Ishihara pushed kegs aside, groggy from taking a heavy blow to the head. "For what?"

"I didn't want to just steal Silverstein's ride, I wanted him to feel useless. I wanted to ruin Mars after losing everything. It had taken me so long to get the Cabal to accept me back and then Silverstein… he did what he always does."

Cerise lunged with the knife, but Ishihara wasn't as stunned as she'd been letting on, quickly lifting a keg like it was a kettlebell. The knife blade skittered and broke as Ishihara let go of the keg to deliver a quick jab to

Cerise's face. She ducked the blow coming in low to try and stab Ishihara with what remained of the knife.

"Nope," Ishihara said, wrapping Cerise up into a bear hug.

Throwing her up like a medicine ball, Ishihara bounced Cerise off the drop ceiling above. Tiles and extruded aluminum bracing came raining down with Cerise. Ishihara grabbed a half empty keg and wielding it by the handle, brought it around to smash Cerise.

Cerise narrowly rolled to one side, kicking out from beneath the debris. The kegs came down hard, throwing up decades of dust that had been trapped in the ceiling. Bloody and dirty, Ishihara came through the cloud, putting her shoulder into Cerise and knocking her through the wall on the opposite side of the door they'd come through originally.

The edge of the bar on the other side caught Cerise painfully in the back, fracturing a couple of vertebrae. Without hesitating, Ishihara brought her rock-hard fists around, pummeling her in the face until she dropped to the floor. Each blow knocked Cerise's head around almost like it wasn't connected, the force breaking cheekbones and her nose.

Ishihara fell back against the wall, breathless, almost plunging back through the hole they'd made a moment before. Cerise was very still, her chest barely moving as she struggled to breathe. Ishihara looked out the tinted windows of the bar. She could see the illuminators on Simon's Aegis Armor and a glint off what was probably the scope on Ezra's rifle.

"They'll be here any minute," Ishihara said, squatting down beside Cerise.

"Plenty...of time...to kill me," Cerise mumbled through broken teeth.

Ishihara smiled and closed her eyes. "Killing someone was what got me into this trouble in the first place. I can't bear the weight of a life I took on accident."

"Everything Dell did to you...I asked him to do it...and worse, but he...was too weak," Cerise said, smiling crookedly.

Ishihara shook her head. "You've been baiting me to kill you from the beginning. You're fresh out of endgame, contingency plans, and escape routes. You think death is the only way out."

"Isn't it?" Cerise said, looking up at Ishihara with the one eye that wasn't swollen shut.

"Not for me it isn't. Not anymore."

Ishihara stood up, raising a hand to Simon and Ezra One as they rushed through the door. The bar looked like a war zone. The tables were upended and broken glass lying about everywhere. Ishihara was bleeding from her side and forearm, fresh bruises rising up across her face and shoulders. She was covered in drywall dust, but smiling big all the same.

"I heard the commotion and radioed Simon. Are you alright?" Ezra One asked.

"Good ears. Yeah, I'm good now. You can take her," Ishihara said, grabbing Cerise up by her torn blouse and dropping her at their feet.

"Feel better?" Simon asked, putting restraints on Cerise.

"Way," Ishihara said, unwrapping the athletic tape from her hands.

"If you guys got this, I'll go get Pearl and your transport. We'll take everyone back to the Administrative Zone and let Silverstein sort this out," Ezra One said, slinging his rifle.

"Sounds good," Simon said, feeling his Aegis Armor getting hot.

Ishihara came out with a bottle of something strong and poured herself and Simon a drink. "I already had one, but I could use another."

As she poured the second drink, the zone lit up with every light and public monitor suddenly coming to life. Refineries and ore delivery tunnels that had been dormant for months or years suddenly began to operate again. There was a hiss overhead as malfunctioning compressors and life support systems suddenly began to function at peak efficiency.

Cool air descended to the street below, with the light, as the sound of brutal death metal began playing over every public announcement system. The civic announcement screen lit up with what appeared to be a digitally rendered titan, his steely body floating in some sort of incomprehensibly large digital realm. His eyes opened, spreading powerful blue light, holographic effigies of him appearing overhead, towering over everything.

"Mars, hear me. I am called C.O.N. My brother, who you knew as the Ares Governance System, has died. I have been brought in to take his place. I will reinstate all work contracts, open every mine, schedule every available transport, and empower every union and worker's alliance to full status."

The screens and holographic projections flickered, as thousands of contracts and union status agreements went out over the public networks.

"I am seizing every asset held by the old mining companies and returning them as an equal share to all citizens. I have instituted grievance and forgiveness protocols over the teal, and will free everyone willing to work and behave. To that end, I am going to empower a new circle of Marshals to provide enforcement of the Law."

The screens again flickered, holographic projections of C.O.N. wavered, as tremendous computing power was exerted to dissolve the old mining conglomerates and companies. Their assets flooded the accounts of every citizen. Repossession protocols across the colony vanished as debts and negative equity was forgiven.

"Did I just really hear all that?" Simon said blinking.

Ishihara nodded, holding her drink toward one of the large holographic projections of C.O.N.

Simon looked out wistfully at the Port of Mars, lights coming on that had done little but flicker for decades. "Where do we go from here?"

Ishihara put an arm around Simon, clinking glasses with him. "Somewhere better. Let's figure out where that is, grab Pearl, and go there."

END BOOK 7